Peachy
Scream

Also available by Anna Gerard

Georgia B&B Mysteries
Peach Clobbered

Black Cat Bookshop Mysteries
(writing as Ali Brandon)
Twice Told Tail

Plot Boiler

Literally Murder

Words With Fiends

A Novel Way to Die

Double Booked for Death

Tarot Cats Mysteries
(writing as Diane A. S. Stuckart)
Fool's Moon

Leonardo Da Vinci Mysteries
(writing as Diane A. S. Stuckart)
A Bolt from the Blue

Portrait of a Lady

The Queen's Gambit

3 1526 05520822 4

WITHDRAWN

Peachy Scream

A GEORGIA B&B MYSTERY

Anna Gerard

CROOKED LANE

NEW YORK

This is a work of fiction. All of the names, characters, organizations, places, and events portrayed in this novel are either products of the author's imagination or are used fictitiously. Any resemblance to real or actual events, locales, or persons, living or dead, is entirely coincidental.

Copyright © 2020 by Diane A. S. Stuckart

All rights reserved.

Published in the United States by Crooked Lane Books, an imprint of The Quick Brown Fox & Company LLC.

Crooked Lane Books and its logo are trademarks of The Quick Brown Fox & Company LLC.

Library of Congress Catalog-in-Publication data available upon request.

ISBN (hardcover): 978-1-64385-306-2
ISBN (ebook): 978-1-64385-327-7

Cover illustration by Brandon Dorman

Printed in the United States.

www.crookedlanebooks.com

Crooked Lane Books
34 West 27th St., 10th Floor
New York, NY 10001

First Edition: July 2020

10 9 8 7 6 5 4 3 2 1

To my fellow Booklover's Bench authors: Nancy J. Cohen, Debra H. Goldstein, Cheryl Hollon, Maggie Toussaint, and Lois Winston. Thanks for being my writing posse!

Chapter One

Finding a dead body in your formal garden has got to rate in the top ten Bad Things that can happen to a person. To be fair, war and plague and famine do have a lock on the first three spots. Poverty and chronic illness are pretty high up there, too. And, of course, it does pretty well suck being the person who croaked. But the whole finding-a-dead-man-in-the-backyard thing deserves at least slot number eight or nine on the countdown.

Especially when it turns out that the corpse in question actually was murdered.

My name is Nina Fleet. I pronounce it NINE-ah, like the number nine. At age forty-one, I'm owner, proprietress, and basic Jacqueline-of-all-trades at Fleet House, my fledgling bed and breakfast retreat here in Cymbeline, about an hour west of Savannah, Georgia. The town has a well-deserved reputation as a little gem of an antiquing and arts destination. That means we get lots of tourists and creative types rolling through, a few of whom stay in my humble abode.

Okay, not so humble. The place is a three-story Queen Anne home dating from the 1890s, built not long after Cymbeline was founded. It sits on a half-acre lot in Cymbeline's historic district and is separated from the street by a head-high wrought-iron fence. A sprawling magnolia that has to be a good century old holds sway over the far side of the front lawn, looking like something out of *Gone With the Wind*.

On the opposite side of the yard is the requisite peach tree, the variety known as Belle of Georgia Peach. My wraparound porch—partially screened in, so that at least one section provides refuge when the mosquitos swarm from dusk to dawn except during the winter—is the ideal place to lounge with a glass of lemonade (or adult beverage, for those of us who indulge). The backyard plays host to formal gardens and sprawling heritage roses, with a covered brick patio that is perfect for outdoor teas and barbeques. And in the very near future I hope to bring in some brides and grooms, since I'm working with a local wedding planner to add garden weddings to my business repertoire

The house is painted in what I've been told is its original palette of green and yellow, with scrumptious gingerbread trim accented in white. And don't forget the tower room atop the second story that gives a 360-degree view of the surrounding neighborhood. Bottom line, it's exactly the kind of house that comes to mind when someone talks about classic Queen Anne architecture. It had always been a single-family home until I bought the place earlier in the year and, following a series of interesting events, found myself arm-twisted into converting it into a B&B.

My partner in the venture is my black, gray, and white Australian shepherd with the trademark odd eyes (one blue, one brown) named Matilda, also known as Mattie. She's my right-hand (or should I say, right-paw) canine who serves as a combination loyal companion, trusty guard dog, and cute fluffy puppy in my website photos. I rescued her from the Atlanta animal shelter almost two years ago, right after my divorce was finalized, and I couldn't ask for a better best friend.

But, back to the dead guy.

I probably should sound a little more respectful, but I'd only known the victim a couple of days before he met his unfortunate end. And, to be quite honest, in that short time he'd proved himself to be a major horse's patootie.

Don't get me wrong. I'm outraged at the thought of a fellow human being murdered, the more so once I eventually found out the "why" of it. But I'm a bit embarrassed to admit that my determination to prove who had actually killed the man may have been less about justice for him and more about making sure that Fleet House didn't get a rep as a crime-site destination.

Still, I sometimes wake up in the middle of the night wondering how things would have turned out if I'd simply refused to open my front gate that Saturday morning.

But I didn't.

And it all started with that darned bus.

*   *   *

It was Saturday morning, the first weekend of August. I'd just said goodbye to a group of Atlanta-area writers who'd rented the place for a weeklong summer retreat. They were the kind of guests I liked: neat, friendly, and quiet. Well, except during the final night's Margarita Happy Hour out on the patio, but even then the raucousness was mostly limited to loud laughter and dirty plays on words.

The writers had left first thing after breakfast, leaving me a narrow window of time to clean the rooms and get things ready for the next visitors. For the moment, I was my sole housekeeping employee, meaning that all the work was falling to me. Until the prior weekend, I'd had an agreement with Cymbeline High School's "Young Entrepreneur" summer program. I would get a few hours of free labor from a couple of the participating teens when I needed the help. In return, the kids earned credit hours in the program. Plus, I let them keep any room tips, which usually had them walking out with an extra fifty in their pockets. But with school about to start in a couple of weeks, the program had ended for the summer.

Normally, I could have found some neighborhood kids to fill the labor gap until the school year started up again. The trouble was that all available hands were on deck in downtown Cymbeline, as the following weekend would kick off the town's seventh annual Shakespeare on Cymbeline Square (or SOCS, as it appeared in various promotion).

The three-day event lured aficionados of the Bard from all over Georgia, as well as neighboring states. Of course, the town's name of Cymbeline (being one of Shakespeare's plays) was one reason the festival received so much publicity. And then there were various "punny" Shakespeare-related names of local businesses that tourists got a kick out of (Ides of March Dry Cleaning and Brutus Burgers being but a couple of examples).

According to the FAQs on the festival website, SOCS had started as a hokey Renaissance Faire designed to boost tourism during the slower hot month of August. But as the organizers and attendees grew more sophisticated, the festival slowly morphed into more than carnival rides, giant turkey legs, and wenches in bursting bodices. Now, under the direction of retired college professor Denis Joy, it had become an almost scholarly event, complete with authentic craftspeople and musicians representing the sixteenth century. The highlight of the festival, however, was the nightly performance of one of the Bard's plays by an amateur Shakespearean troupe.

And, lucky me, my bed and breakfast was the one the actors had chosen for their stay during this year's festival!

To be sure, I'd been a bit confused back in mid-June when a woman had called saying she was the secretary of GASP, and that she was looking to rent out my B&B for a couple of weeks during festival time.

"Professor Tessa Benedict," she'd identified herself in self-important tones. And then she'd explained the acronym. Turns out GASP was not some Bondian supervillain organization, but stood for the Georgia Amateur Shakespeare Players. They were based out of Atlanta and were the troupe that would be performing *Hamlet* at this year's festival.

"There are seven of us in the road troupe," she told me, "plus our director, so that's eight people total. We have two married couples, and the rest are gentlemen. Unfortunately, our original

B&B had to cancel our stay because of some emergency remodeling they have to do, so I do hope you can accommodate us."

She had probably already contacted the other dozen or so other competing B&Bs in town, which likely were already booked since the prior year for the festival. But her bad luck was going to be a windfall on my part.

"As long as the gentlemen don't mind doubling up, we have room," I had assured her. "But I've only been open a couple of weeks. May I ask how you learned about me?"

"Our director gave me your contact information. He insisted that we really must stay at your place. Besides which, you do have a Shakespeare garden on the property, do you not?"

I did. For those not in the know—which had included me, until my evil troll of a gardener, Hendricks, had explained—a Shakespeare garden is a formal series of herb and flower beds containing only plants that are mentioned in the Bard's works. Mine was situated in the backyard just beyond the brick patio, slightly raised above the level of the sloping yard. It was circular, with a splashy three-tiered concrete fountain in the center, though the outer pathways around it had been squared off on all sides. Thus, a drone's-eye view of the garden would show a large circle set inside a slightly larger square. Graveled paths divided that circle into four pie pieces of closely planted beds. To the rear of the garden proper, a line of thick, head-high Indian hawthorns that Hendricks had sculpted into a broad green wall separated garden from the rest of the backyard. A narrow opening in that living wall's center led to a couple of steps that made the slight elevation change to the rest of the yard easier to manage.

While I knew the Cymbeline Chamber of Commerce had my B&B on their notable gardens list, this would be the first time the Shakespeare garden would have been a specific draw for any guests. Thus, I was more than a bit pleased to assure the professor that I had the garden in question and to take her credit-card information.

Now, it was well after three PM, my standard check-in time for new guests. I had finished cleaning the rooms almost two hours ago, and I'd already prepped the kitchen and brought in fresh-cut roses to decorate the public areas. My peach tree was just now yielding fruit, and so I'd also harvested a dozen plump, ripe Georgia peaches. They'd go in a big bowl in the dining room for my guests to indulge in.

With those chores out of the way, I still had plenty of time to change from cut-off jeans and a logoed Fleet House T-shirt into brown capris topped by a crisp white linen top. I bundled my shoulder-length brown hair into a neat innkeeperly bun and then, for good measure, enhanced my equally brown eyes with some cinnamon-colored shadow. And, since my guests still hadn't arrived yet, I took the opportunity to lounge on the front porch with a book I'd been trying to finish for a good two weeks.

I heard the bus before I saw it.

From inside the front door, Mattie gave a howl of welcome (though I realized later it probably was a cry of warning). Setting aside my paperback, I headed down the porch steps.

By now, exhaust fumes were wafting through my wrought-iron gate, unloading a small country's-worth of carbon footprint into my front yard. As honeysuckle covered a good portion of the fencing, I couldn't see much more than the white top of the bus. Still, I could tell it was not one of the ubiquitous sleek gray touring buses that regularly prowled our picturesque brick avenues on the weekends. For one thing, it was about half the size of those behemoths. But it wasn't until I reached the gate that I got the whole picture.

As noted, this bus was neither sleek nor gray. Instead, from the roof down, it was blue . . . genuine 1960s flower-power blue. The bus company's name, Wild Hare Tours, was prominently splashed across the vehicle's side in an equally electric shade of yellow. Beneath the name, in much smaller letters, was the company website of the same name. A cartoon of what doubtless was the corporate logo—a frenzied white rabbit dressed in jogging shorts—loped atop the lettering and lent a goofy sort of charm to it. I noted, however, that the bright paint did not quite camouflage the original black lettering that still faintly proclaimed the vehicle as the former property of some local school district.

A very bad feeling rose inside of me.

Back in June when I'd first opened for business, I'd spent a mostly contentious few days in the company of an unemployed actor named Harry Westcott, who did a bachelor version of the tiny house thing out of one of those half-sized school buses. Except for our mutual interest in solving the murder of a local real-estate developer, he and I had not gotten along . . . mostly because Harry claimed that *he* was the rightful owner of Fleet House. And, like the Terminator, he'd warned me as he left town for an acting job down in Baja California that he'd be ba-a-a-ack.

But as far as I knew, the guy was still out West filming. Besides, this fume-spewing heap obviously did not transport the awaited Shakespeare troupe. I mean, I couldn't picture the officious-sounding Professor Benedict riding three hours from Atlanta in such a beater. Though given the hippy-dippy vibe of the bus, I definitely could picture a Jerry Garcia type behind the wheel.

Pushing away thoughts of past unpleasantness, I opened the gate and stepped out, professional innkeeper smile on my face. I heard the unmistakable pop, hiss, and squeal of bus doors opening. A moment later, the driver was standing on the sidewalk while the doors closed behind him again with an exhausted little gasp.

I gave a little gasp of my own when I found myself facing, not a Grateful Dead refugee, but a thirty-something Renaissance man.

For the bus driver was dressed like an extra from that HBO series about young Henry Tudor. His courtier's short, red-and-black velvet doublet was topped by a starched white ruff the approximate diameter of a turkey platter. He swept off an anachronistic pair of designer sunglasses, revealing bright-blue eyes beneath dark brows, and made an elegant bow in my direction.

I didn't bother to curtsy back. Because, alas, I knew him well.

"You," I choked out in dismay. "What happened to the cable TV series in Baja?"

"Internet series," Harold A. Westcott III, aka Harry, loftily corrected me as he put the sunglasses back on. He named one of the major online networks and continued, "We just wrapped the first eight episodes, and *John Cover, Undercover* is officially on their mid-fall lineup. But in the meantime, I have obligations here in Cymbeline."

The bad feeling returned with a vengeance worthy of Hamlet himself. "Don't tell me," I managed, shaking my head in denial. "The Shakespeare festival?"

The actor gave me a cool smile and nodded.

"I guess Tessa didn't mention it, but I spent some time in Atlanta, and I'm currently the director of the Georgia Amateur Shakespeare Players. We're here, and we have reservations at your fine B&B . . . oh, and we have a play to put on for the good folks of Cymbeline. Now, perhaps you'll show us to our rooms."

Chapter Two

While I watched in stunned silence, Harry turned and whipped open the bus door again. The troupe began trooping out, dragging rolling bags and laptop cases, and struggling with a couple of hanging bags each. Chattering loudly, they pretty much ignored me as they marched through the gate I'd just opened and headed up the flagstone walk toward the house's front door.

Of course, it made sense now, though I'd not known of Harry's Atlanta connection until this minute. When Professor Benedict had called to make reservations, she had said that their director had quite specifically told her to contact me. Obviously, Harry had seen another sneaky opportunity to get back inside my house, confident that I'd not dare kick him out as long as the troupe was in residence.

Which would give him ample time to unleash whatever his latest scheme to steal my house from me was.

Yep, as I'd mentioned, Harry and I share history. Some of it's friendly, some of it a bit scary, none of it romantic . . . but most of it irritating as heck. He's the grandnephew of my home's former owner, Mrs. Daisy Lathrop, and he'd been under the impression that he was going to inherit her house when the old woman died. But it turned out that his childless great-aunt never updated her will. And so when the place went up for sale soon after her passing, I'd been in the right place at the right time to buy it.

Call it an impulse purchase. A year after a regrettably public divorce from my golf pro husband—yes, he's *the* Cameron Fleet, tour and media darling—I'd had a nice chunk of cash in the bank but still found myself aimlessly drifting through the next chapter of my life. On a long-weekend antiquing jaunt here in Cymbeline, I'd randomly parked in front of the house while checking my GPS for directions and found myself smitten. With nothing to hold me in Atlanta—Cam and I never had any kids, and the rest of my family lives in my home state of Texas—I'd called the number on the "For Sale" sign. By day's end my cash offer had been accepted.

I'd only had a couple of weeks to enjoy my new home when Harry got wind of what happened. Soon after, he had begun a campaign of e-mails, voice mails, and mean letters from some random attorney. It had culminated in his actually showing up on my doorstep and then weaseling his way into staying in my newly opened bed and breakfast. We'd called a temporary truce during the whole solving-the-murder thing, mostly because Harry had been a suspect in the formal investigation, and I had reason to believe he was innocent.

Once the true killer had been caught, Harry had cut short his stay when the TV series opportunity popped up. I'd watched his exhaust-belching bus —same bus as was currently parked at my curb, but not yet wearing its current paint job—rattle down the road on its way to Baja and prayed that I had seen the last of him.

Apparently, my prayers hadn't been fervent enough.

I snapped out of my momentary paralysis and rounded on him. He'd pulled his own set of rolling bags from behind the driver's seat and was busy closing the bus door behind him.

"Don't bother," I told him, folding my arms over my chest. "You and your troupe are going to be back on board just as soon as I run up to the porch and turn those people around. No way am I letting you stay here again."

"Seriously?" Harry slanted me a look over the top of his sunglasses. "You do realize that the troupe—which includes me—has prepaid for a two-week stay. That's a pretty nice chunk of change to be turning down," he said, and reminded me of the amount in question.

I gulped a little—it was, as he'd said, a lot of money—but still shook my head. "No problem, I'll give you a refund. Now, do you want to tell your folks you're leaving, or are you going to leave the dirty work up to me?"

Harry shrugged. "I'll tell them. But keep in mind that there's not a free room to be had in Cymbeline until after next week, not with all the out-of-town vendors and visitors coming for the festival. And if the troupe doesn't have a place to stay, then this year's event will be minus its Shakespeare play. That probably will mean a fifty percent drop in attendance, and a lot of revenue lost for the town."

"Not my problem," I said with an answering lift of my shoulders, even as it occurred to me that it was.

For the festival was a heck of a big deal to the community. Like many other small towns, Cymbeline had gone into a major decline starting in the 1960s. With jobs scarce, the younger generation began fleeing their hometown for employment in Savannah or Atlanta, or even farther afield. But more than a dozen years ago, Cymbeline had forcibly reinvented itself as a tourist destination. The result was an influx of jobs to the area, along with a return of those now middle-aged former residents. Events like SOCS helped keep the tourists—and the money—coming.

Moreover, despite my short tenure in Cymbeline, I had a pretty fair idea about how small towns worked. Harry might haul his ruffled self back onto his bus and drive off with his players, but I could guarantee he'd make sure that everyone he passed on his way to the city limits would know why the troupe didn't have a place to stay. And then, when this year's Shakespeare festival went bust, I'd be the one the whole town blamed.

Harry knew it, too, for he edged closer.

"Look, I'll sweeten the deal," he urged in a conspiratorial tone. "I'll talk to Denis Joy about adding your B&B to the sponsorship list. He's head of the festival committee, and he can put your logo on the festival website. Plus we'll see about getting you some signage at the outdoor stage. You can't pay for that kind of advertising."

Of course, you could. That was, if you had planned far enough ahead. When I had asked the festival committee a few weeks earlier about doing some promo, I'd learned that the primo ad space had been locked in for months. But I'd seen the rate sheet, and what Harry was offering wasn't inconsequential . . . assuming, of course, that he had the pull to get it done. Besides, I'd long since signed a contract with Peaches and Java, the local coffee shop-slash-bakery, to handle breakfasts for a party of eight for the next ten days.

"OK, fine, all of you can stay," I agreed in an ungracious tone, and then paused in case an offstage soundtrack sounded an ominous note to tell me that I'd just made a very bad mistake.

Harry, meanwhile, nodded slightly and put an elegant hand over his heart. He turned a smile on me that was not a triumphant, toothpaste-commercial-worthy display of perfect dental work but seemingly a genuine expression of gratitude.

"Hey, it'll be fun," he assured me.

At that, I felt an unexpected tingling sensation in areas that had not tingled in some time. If I hadn't mentioned it before, Harry was definitely leading-man material, at least in the looks department. Neatly chiseled features that were neither too sensitive nor too craggy; just a hint of manly stubble; black hair that had been razored into deliberate boyish disarray. I'd learned from his online bio that, at thirty-nine, he was only a couple of years younger than me. That meant no uncomfortable age difference that would cause folks to gossip, should he and I ever . . .

Ruthlessly, I quashed my momentary reaction and the thoughts that had followed. No way would I consider "ever-ing" with Harry. Certainly not until I had notarized assurance from him that he'd dropped his crazy claim against me that I wasn't the legitimate owner of his great-aunt's house. I'd not heard anything from him since he'd gone to Mexico, but that didn't mean he wasn't still plotting. As he'd told me when he had left, now that he had a decent-paying acting job, he could afford an attorney again.

"Uh, Nina," Harry spoke up, his voice shaking me from my reverie, "you want to let those folks in?"

"Right, yes, let's go," I agreed, and started back up the walk to the front porch.

"There was a nasty wreck on I-75 right outside of Macon," he explained as he followed after me, indicating the route they would have taken from Atlanta. "Traffic was backed up for an extra hour. We were running late, so I didn't take time for a pit stop. You might want to show everyone the, er, facilities first."

"Got it."

By now we'd reached the porch where my new guests were assembled. I summoned a bright smile. "Welcome to Fleet House. Let's go inside, and I'll let everyone freshen up first before I show you to your rooms."

I opened the screen door. Calling a quick, *Stay girl*, to Mattie, I threw open the front door and ushered everyone into the main hall that ran shotgun-style down the middle of the house. I glanced back to see that Mattie, who'd been sitting obediently as instructed, was giving a little whine and excited thump of her bobbed tail as she spied Harry. He, in turn, checked to make sure that no one was looking before giving her a quick scratch behind her ears.

Traitor, I thought in resignation, and then returned my attention to my guests.

The passage was dark and narrow, with picture rails running high along the walls on both sides. I'd inherited remnants of Harry's great-aunt's original picture gallery consisting of oils, hand-tinted photographs, and even a daguerreotype of a teen-aged

Confederate soldier. Usually, most people spent a little time gaping at this little time capsule of history, but not today

"Powder room is right here," I said, pointing just beyond the main staircase.

A tall, silver-haired man who appeared to be in his late fifties promptly pushed past the others and disappeared into the small bathroom, slamming the door behind him. The remaining half-dozen guests abandoned their luggage there in the hall and rushed to line up outside the half-bath, muttering among themselves. I followed after them.

At the head of the line was a bluff, gray-bearded fellow whom I guessed to be about the same age as the man who'd commandeered the toilet. From the look of his blue jeans, boots, and plaid shirt, he did most of his clothes shopping at the Big and Tall Man's Clothing and Tractor Supply store. His smile was genial, and his brown eyes glinted with good humor as he stuck a large hand in my direction.

"Marvin Lasky, ma'am," he declared as we swiftly shook. "We're sure lookin' forward to staying in this nice house of yours."

"Nina Fleet. And I'm very pleased to . . ."

Before I could finish my introduction, however, he leaned forward and gave the powder-room door a beefy-fingered rap.

"Folks is waiting to pee," he called to the occupant within. "Get a move on, Len, before someone has an accident out here."

"Don't be so crude, Marvin," the woman in line behind him softly reproved, though she was doing a genteel version of the potty dance herself as she awaited her own turn.

She caught my glance and gave me an apologetic shrug. "He's right, though. It was a long drive."

Since I'd not yet done my guest check-in, I didn't officially know her name. But she didn't sound like the officious Professor Benedict with whom I'd spoken on the phone, so I figured she was bathroom-hogging Len's wife, Susie Marsh. The bloated diamond on her left hand confirmed my suspicions. I pegged her for being in her early thirties, though it was hard to judge for certain, given her liberal application of high-end cosmetics. That would make her a couple of decades younger than her husband and thus qualified her as a bona fide trophy wife.

I pointed toward the carved staircase.

"Upstairs, first door on the left, if you don't want to wait," I cheerfully told her, giving directions to the main second-floor bath.

Not needing further encouragement, she scampered toward the stairway as fast as her three-hundred-dollar sandals would take her. She was followed by a middle-aged woman whose graying waist-length hair had been twisted into a single long braid and who wore what appeared to be hand-spun Mother Earth garb circa 1970.

Has to be Professor Benedict, I decided, but definitely not what I'd pictured. A little too granola-looking for the self-important attitude of the woman who had made the reservation. Though, of course, disembodied phone voices could be deceiving.

That left still lined up behind Marvin a scholarly-looking, hippie-type gentleman pushing retirement age who was probably Mister Professor Benedict; a square-faced African American guy about Harry's age who could have played college football had he been a foot taller, and a hipster college student-type absorbed in his smartphone.

"I hate to interrupt," Harry abruptly decreed, coming up behind me, "but I could use a hand getting the bus parked. We'll do the rest of the introductions in a minute."

I bared my teeth in an agreeable smile.

"Sure. Gentlemen, wait right here once everyone is, er, finished, and then I'll check you in and show you to your rooms."

While Harry and I headed out the door toward the street, I threw him a look. "Why are you decked out like a courtier? *Hamlet* doesn't debut until next weekend."

"It's part of the whole tour package."

We'd reached the front gate now, and he gestured at his recently repainted bus.

"I actually had this in the works before the last time I was in town," he explained. "I figured the best way to make extra cash between acting jobs is to run a tour company."

"Aha," I said, giving myself a figurative slap upside the head. "Hare . . . Harry. I get it now!"

"I thought it rather clever myself," he replied with a modest smile. "If you check out my website, you'll see I do tours all over the state. So far there's a Capitol City tour of Atlanta, a Haunted Savannah tour, and an antiquing tour that includes Cymbeline. I dress the part and do colorful commentary throughout. I figure in the fall I'll be booked solid. This trip with the troupe is my trial run, so to speak."

"So, don't tell me. This"—I gestured at his Henry VIII attire—"is your Shakespeare tour outfit?"

He nodded. "Yes to the costume, but no to the tour. I'm just the troupe's ride back and forth to Atlanta. The company is paying for gas and expenses. But I figured we'd see plenty of traffic, so I wanted the public to get a good look when they drove past me. Now, be a dear and get the driveway gate so I can pull my conveyance off the street."

While he hopped back into the bus and cranked it up again, I played the requested "dear" and dragged open the pair of wrought-iron gates that kept random tourists from using my driveway. Technically, he wasn't supposed to park a vehicle of that size in my neighborhood for more than twenty-four hours; however, I suspected that the local code enforcement was going to have better things to do this coming week than look for scofflaws on private property.

After considerable coughing and choking—on my part, as well as the bus's—we situated the fume-spewing heap in the driveway in such a way that there was still room for my green Mini Cooper to escape the garage. If the troupe needed to travel en masse during their stay, I told Harry, they could Uber themselves around town.

We headed back inside via the kitchen, which opened into the hall where the GASPers, as I'd privately dubbed them, awaited us at the foot of the main staircase. I saw in amusement that Marvin and Mattie had already made their mutual acquaintance, with the former giving the latter a belly rub.

I hurried over to the small secretary desk near the front door, where I kept my clipboard with my current guest list. Grabbing it and a pen, I side-stepped the luggage and returned to where everyone was waiting.

"Welcome again. Now, let's sign everyone in, and then we'll get you settled in your rooms."

I made quick work of confirming names and collecting signatures from everyone, which included handing out a short printed list of the house rules. That done, I continued, "You'll find your individual bedroom key on the dresser in your room. Now, let me show you where you'll be living for the next ten days," I finished, and led a procession up the main stairway to the paneled hallway above.

Chapter Three

Letting strangers make themselves at home in my home still felt a bit odd, but I was getting used to it. It helped that my own room was on the first floor, beyond the parlor. The bedroom was actually the house's former billiards salon and boasted a small attached full bath, making for a nice owner's suite. Even better, it had its own exit onto the side porch, off of which was an area away from the guests for Mattie to attend to her doggie needs.

With the rented rooms and baths all on the second floor, and with most of my guests spending their days wandering the historic square and neighborhoods, it was easy to maintain my personal space even when the B&B was full. Especially since I'd mounted on my bedroom door a tasteful burnished metal plaque I'd found at Weary Bones Antiques that said "Private." And so far these guests—except for one notable exception whose initials were Harry Westcott—seemed like decent enough sorts.

While we'd maneuvered the bus into the drive a few minutes earlier, with me hanging out the bifold door as lookout, Harry had given me a rundown of his troupe. I'd already met Marvin Lasky.

Despite his farmhand wardrobe, the man had recently sold his small electronics development company, Peachtree Communications, for few million. Thus he had plenty of spare time to play around with his Shakespeare hobby.

As for the blonde trophy wife with the uncertain smile, I'd been correct in assuming she was Susie Marsh. Susie, of course, was married to Len Marsh, he of the distinguished silver hair and long bathroom stay. Len was VP of the U.S. division of some multinational electronics company headquartered in Atlanta. While he probably didn't have Marvin's same mad money, per Harry he still pulled in the big bucks—which Susie, in turn, spent. But when it came to the troupe, Harry confided, Len and not his wife was the high-maintenance one.

The Earth Mother who had followed Susie upstairs was indeed Professor Tessa Benedict, married to Bill. In their early sixties, both were professors at the Atlanta University of the Arts and were founding members of GASP. The Benedicts were diametric opposites of the Marshes—at least, stylistically.

The Birkenstock-wearing Bill sported the same ratty ponytail he likely had worn ever since the Grateful Dead cut their first album, even though his hairline had receded to mid-scalp. While he'd eschewed the tie-dye, his wardrobe was still vintage sixties—blue jeans, wrinkled paisley button-down shirt (untucked), and a brown suede vest worn shiny in spots.

Tessa's straight-from-the-commune outfit consisted of a flowing skirt pieced together from squares of cotton saris topped by a peasant blouse that exposed a bit too much of her Earth Mother assets. I'd already mentioned the long gray braid, which I secretly envied. In fact, I had to give her props for not succumbing to the typical societal pressures that insisted women over sixty should chop off their hair and settle for a granny perm or man-cut. Despite their peace and love vibe, however, both of the Benedicts had that grim pedagogical gleam in their eyes, the one that brought back painful memories of pop quizzes and weekend homework.

Now, I pointed the two married couples to the larger two bedrooms, each of which had a queen-size bed. A full bath had been built between them, Jack-and-Jill style.

"You'll have to share the facilities," I told them apologetically, though it should have come as no surprise, since I'd given Tessa the rundown on the room setup when she'd called. "But there's the other full bath at the end of the hall and the powder room downstairs if things get too crowded."

I gestured the Marshes into the first room that, because of its color palette ranging from lilac to plum, I privately called the "Prince Chamber." You know, *Purple Rain*, and all that. I'd actually toned down the original decor somewhat, removing the plum-colored carpeting that covered vintage pale-wood planking and replacing the lavender curtains with crisp white. But the wallpaper with its cascades of purple flowers still hit you in the eye when you walked in.

"Oof," Len muttered as he took a look around him.

Susie, however, clapped her manicured hands. "Ooo, purple, I love it!"

While they settled in, I opened the door of the next room. This one had more of a French provincial feel with its original toile wallpaper, the pastoral pattern in shades of pale blue and brown. The Benedicts gave it an approving nod.

"This vintage wallpaper is quite in fashion," Tessa observed as she carried her hanging bag to the bed.

Bill nodded and followed after.

I turned to the remaining guests.

"All right, gentlemen, any preferences on how you'd like to split yourselves up between the other two rooms?"

"Me and Radney can bunk together," Marvin promptly spoke up. "That is, assuming one of them rooms has two beds. I mean, I like the guy, but . . . "

Radney was Radney Heller, the black guy built like a fire plug. From what Harry had said, the man was some sort of research and development bigwig at the same company where Len was VP. Despite his short stature—only a couple of inches taller than my own five foot five—he was an imposing figure with his beefy biceps and shaved head. At Marvin's comment, however, his stoic expression cracked into a rueful smile that made him suddenly approachable.

"Yeah, and those beds better be on opposite walls, or my man Marv is going to be sleeping in the hall with the dog."

"No worries. We've got twin beds in this one," I assured them both and opened the door to show them the room I'd dubbed "Country Living."

The wallpaper here was a pinkish-gray pattern consisting of cabbage roses and stripes, with the coverlets on each bed a darker pink trimmed with off-white Battenburg lace that matched the off-white lace curtains. Even the antique, hurricane-style bedside lamps with hanging crystals continued the theme, with hand-painted pink roses on their off-white glass shades.

Both men winced visibly—okay, so maybe I needed to consider going a bit more gender-neutral in at least one of the rooms—but they accepted their fate politely.

"It's real nice, ma'am," Marvin observed with a shrug as he took it all in before tossing his hanging bag onto one of the twin beds. Radney managed a bemused smile and followed suit.

Now, only one other guest besides Harry still remained. Chris Boyd.

Harry had told me that Chris was the newest and youngest member of GASP . . . and, apparently, their token hipster. It was a label hung upon a certain type of youth, the kind who tended to be progressive, vegan, and into Instagram. Last I'd heard, hipsters were fast going the way of the emo kids before them, but I'd seen enough of them wandering around Cymbeline to believe the trend wasn't quite dead yet.

Mostly, it hadn't stopped Marvin from referring to the youth as "Emo Boy" when he'd thought no one was listening.

True to type, the androgynous Chris wore his dyed black hair slicked back and mostly hidden under a black knit cap. His pale features were halfway obscured by a pair of black plastic-framed glasses that might or might not have been an affectation. His clothing was a trendily ironic updating of grunge. Skinny black jeans, Converse sneakers, and an oversized white T-shirt topped by an undersized red-and-yellow checked flannel shirt —the kind Marvin might have worn twenty years and fifty pounds ago. I had yet to hear him speak, mostly because he'd been wearing a set of wireless earbuds and had his nose buried in his phone since he'd left the bus.

"So, are you and Chris going to share a room, then?" I asked Harry.

The actor gave me a disbelieving look.

"You're forgetting that I'm the play's director, on top of being the tour operator," he replied. "I can't share quarters with a member of the cast, and I can't move in on a guest. It wouldn't look right."

"So where do you suggest you stay, then?"

"Well, I can think of one other place."

In this day and age, a comment like that would have earned most men a roasting on Twitter, if not worse. I knew what Harry meant, however, and it wasn't like it sounded.

On his last visit, he'd showed me the tower room, which I'd assumed was simply a decorative architectural feature atop the second story, not actual living space. Turns out he'd lived in it for a few summers when he was a kid visiting his great-aunt. In return for his revealing the hidden door that led up to it, I'd let him clean up the room—which had not been touched in a good decade—and allowed him to stay there for a few days.

"We'll see about that," I told him. "For now, let's get Chris settled."

Harry nodded and gave the youth a not-so-subtle nudge to get his attention.

"Heads up, kid," he said as Chris shot him an annoyed look. "Ms. Fleet wants to show you to your room."

This entailed walking a few more steps down the hall and opening the final door. I did both, and then gestured the youth to take a look.

Small as it was, this room was the sparest in decor. The wallpaper had a more modern vibe, its design of tiny cranes amid bamboo in shades of sand and the palest of pinks evoking an Asian feel. I'd added a wall scroll with red kanji symbols representing love, wisdom, and health. The window I'd covered in a simple linen shade that resembled a miniature shoji screen.

But the biggest change was the bed. I'd recently swapped the room's original cherry four-poster for a pair of twin beds, the better to accommodate more guests. They sported simple linen pillows and were arranged against the wall in an L-shape like daybeds to make the most of the minimal square footage. A sleek wooden lap desk perched on the foot of one, serving in lieu of a nightstand.

"It's a bit small," I apologized as I showed him inside, "but you get it to yourself."

Chris pulled one ear bud from his ear—I'd begun to think the accessory was surgically attached—and looked around.

"It's deck," he said succinctly.

From his nod of seeming approval, I took the expression to mean something positive. Without looking at me, he returned the ear bud to its place, dumped his canvas backpack on one bed, and sprawled his thin length across the other bed. Faint squawks seeped past the knit cap, the sound emanating with surprising ferocity from the tiny earbuds.

I pulled the door shut and turned to Harry.

"Let's get the rest of the luggage up here, and then we'll figure out your room."

Chapter Four

We schlepped the rolling bags and suitcases from downstairs hall to upstairs hall with relative speed. After a couple months of doing this, I'd developed a pretty good set of arm muscles, not to mention definite tightening of the old glutes. We matched up the bags with each guest; then, leaving them to unpack, I turned to Harry.

"If you really want the tower room, it's yours for the duration. But I warn you, it looks a little different from the last time."

"I don't care what it looks like, as long as you had an AC unit installed," he replied with a shrug.

Anyone not knowing the secret would never have found the room, as the door leading to it was cleverly hidden within the hallway paneling. Like the downstairs hall, this passage was lined with dark wood, though instead of wainscot, the paneling was installed from floor to ceiling. Matching half-round wooden trim added a decorative touch, forming what resembled a series of tall, narrow picture frames aligned side by side.

But a closer examination of one panel would reveal that a four-inch section of the trim was slightly offset from the rest of the molding. In fact, I was able to turn it almost like a knob. Which was exactly what it was, and what I now did.

A portion of the paneling popped open like a narrow door, letting loose a blast of hot air and exposing what at first appeared to be a closet. I reached in and tugged a length of string dangling there. An LED lightbulb that I'd recently installed on the inner wall blazed to life, revealing a broad ladder solidly mounted above and below, though its pitch was far too narrow for it to be climbed without using both hands and feet. Peering up, I could see the shadowed section of railed landing above.

"After you," I told Harry.

Had I known the room was going to be used, I already would have opened the windows to let out the residual heat and turned the new window AC unit I'd installed to full blast until the place cooled to bearable temperatures. Which, during a blazing hot Georgia summer, took a while. Once the temperature equalized, the room was quite livable. But for the moment we'd have to sweat.

By now, Harry had reached the landing and flipped on the lights. As he did, he gave a grunt of surprise. I grinned a little as I joined him there.

The circular room was perhaps twelve feet in diameter and ringed by eight single-hung windows that gave a bird's-eye view of the surrounding neighborhood. On his last stay, Harry had set up the place like a tiny studio apartment, complete with a bed and sitting area. But since his departure, I'd commandeered the tower for my own use . . . well, mine and a few of my new friends.

The only remaining furniture was the narrow bed and a battered wooden chest of drawers. Those items had been pushed to the far wall near a tiny vintage sink that, thanks to a local handyman, now ran hot and cold water. The wooden floor, freshly sanded and varnished, gleamed in the afternoon sun that streamed in the westernmost windows.

Harry gave the newly cleared space a quizzical look as he wiped sweat from his forehead; then, catching sight of an open wooden box holding rolled lengths of colorful squishy rubber, he nodded and smiled.

"You turned it into a yoga studio," he said, tone approving. "Is someone teaching a formal class up here?"

"A woman named Wendy Tucker from the fitness center came a couple of evenings a week," I told him. "She teaches hot yoga— you know, the kind where you sweat your butt off for an hour and a half doing all the poses. I provide the space, and the students pay her per lesson. It worked out great, since I didn't even have to turn on the AC. Of course, I get to take the class for free. And it's lots of fun."

"We decided to go on hiatus for August since so many people are involved with the festival and end of summer obligations," I went on, "but once school starts we'll pick back up again. If nothing else, I figured holding the classes was a nice plug for the B&B."

While I was explaining all this, I turned on the window AC unit and opened a couple of windows to get a cross breeze.

"It cools down pretty quickly," I told him. "I assume you're okay staying up here with just a bed and chest of drawers?"

Though, of course, given that he used to live in his bus, even a stuffy bare tower room was the height of luxury.

"This will be fine," he told me. "Now, if you don't mind, I'd like to change into something more comfortable. Tights and hot weather aren't the best combination."

I stifled a snicker and nodded. To be truthful, I was so used to Harry in various costumes that I'd almost forgotten he was still wearing his Elizabethan regalia.

I was halfway back down the ladder stairway, when he abruptly leaned over the railing and hailed me. "Oh, Nina, I almost forgot."

He paused, and I glanced up, waiting to be showered with well-deserved thanks. After all, I'd let him and his troupe stay despite what counted as blatant deception on his part.

Instead, he said, "On the way in, I promised our guests they'd get afternoon tea. See what you can rustle up, will you?"

*   *   *

Since, technically, I always put out afternoon refreshments for my guests—fresh-brewed coffee, iced tea, lemonade, along with cookies, cake, and fruit—I had already "rustled" things up when the troupe came downstairs to the dining room about thirty minutes later.

"Brewed, not instant?" Len Marsh inquired with a nod at the gallon jug of tea perched on its stand.

"Cold brewed," I assured him, feeling a bit smug. "But if you like sweet tea, you'll need to add your own sugar."

Of course, that set off a discussion of the relative merits of sweet tea (the unofficial drink of the South) versus plain tea. A sidebar debate then ensued regarding cold brew versus sun tea, since that summer staple apparently had been found to harbor bacteria and was now on the bad list. I exchanged knowing glances with Mattie. The GASPers were an argumentative lot, it seemed.

Once the troupe had filled their plates and glasses, I left them to their own devices for a quick cleanup in the kitchen. When I went to check on refills a few minutes later, I found Harry and everyone else except for Radney seated at the dining-room table. Bound sheaves of paper that I assumed must be scripts sat in front of each actor, while Harry, as the director, had an oversized white binder beside his plate. Tessa had an open laptop in front of her, which I assumed was for taking script notes.

Marvin acknowledged me with a smiling nod before returning to the notes he'd been making on a legal tablet. Chris, of course, was staring at his phone, earbuds firmly in place as he used both thumbs with blinding dexterity to text something to someone. Tessa and Susie were murmuring back and forth to each other, not seeming to notice that Bill was seated between them.

As for Len Marsh, he seemed absorbed in the small square of peach cobbler that he was eating along with his coffee. Not that I blamed him, since the cobbler was the famous (at least, in Cymbeline) version handmade by Daniel Tanaka, who with his wife Gemma owned Peaches and Java.

Harry held court at the head of the table, a knife and the remains of one of my peaches on a plate next to his elbow. He was now dressed in modern attire, meaning artfully distressed black jeans and a turquoise linen shirt, the color of which made his blue eyes look even bluer.

Reminding myself that the vibrancy of his eye color was none of my concern, I brushed up a scattering of crumbs from the sideboard and made sure the coffee pot still had a few cups left in it. But when I turned to go, Harry held up a restraining hand.

"You don't have to leave," he told me grandly. "Being a civilian, you might find it interesting to see what a troupe like ours does to get ready for a performance. I don't think anyone would mind, would they?"

Said troupe members shook their heads and mumbled their agreement to my staying. Meanwhile, I gave Harry a considering look. I'd not yet decided if he had something up his thespian sleeve regarding his claim to my house. Maybe the smart thing would be to take him up on his offer and, at the same time, keep an eye on him.

"Sure, sounds like fun." Indicating one of the spare dining-room chairs positioned up against the wall, I added, "I'll just sit over here and listen quietly."

He nodded and then returned his attention to the troupe.

"All right, people, we'll do a read-through now during tea, then break for supper. I'll be available tonight for any preliminary coaching, and then we'll have our first rehearsal right after breakfast tomorrow morning. So, any questions before we begin?"

35

He was answered by the sound of a throat clearing loudly. As one, we turned in the direction of where Len Marsh sat.

Since we'd had only the slightest of introductions, I hadn't had much of a chance to size up the executive beyond the obvious. So far, however, he definitely was giving off the vibes of the stereotypical rich guy who figures his bucks somehow make him worthier than the rest of us. Though what Len didn't know (unless Harry had stooped to gossiping with him) was that, up until my divorce, I'd been one of those same rich folks.

Well, if only by extension.

It had been my tournament golfer husband who had parlayed a talent for strolling about the greens and swinging a club into a seven-figure salary. And I had to admit that it had been nice to breathe that rarified air after years spent barely eking by on his income as a club professional along with my own modest corporate salary. But by the time Cam and I split up—mostly because I finally figured out that playing golf wasn't all he was doing out on the various tournament courses—I'd had my fill of the so-called upper crust.

But back to Len. While the rest of the group had opted for vacation comfort in their wardrobes, he was dressed in business casual—sharply pressed khakis and an expensive polo shirt embroidered with a tiny version of his corporation's logo. I had to admit that the look did work for him. He was still a handsome man, if a bit past his prime, with strong, even features that gave him an air usually described as "distinguished." The steel-gray eyes and matching silver hair—surprisingly lush for a man his age—complemented a face that would have looked at home on the inside pages of any Fortune 100 annual report.

Now, however, his features had assumed a martyred expression that gave him the look of a Brooks Brothers saint. Worse, his gaze was turned in my direction.

"Actually, my question is for our innkeeper . . . Ms. Fleet, was it? I trust that this bed-and-breakfast is in compliance with the Americans with Disabilities Act. I require special accommodation for my handicap," he said and gestured toward his right leg, currently tucked under the table

I heard a faint snort from Marvin's direction.

"The only handicap old Len there has is his personality," he muttered, drawing a snicker from Chris, seated beside him.

Len drew himself up and started to sputter, while Susie hurried to smooth the waters. "Now, y'all know full well—you, too, Marvin—that Len is still recovering from his injury. He still has to take those pain pills for his knee."

She glanced my way, her pale eyes wide with remembered dismay.

"I almost died when I got the call from the police," she confided. "Poor Len was clipped by a car one night last month while he was out riding his bike by the college campus. The fool driver didn't have his lights on, and the only reason Len wasn't killed was because he managed to leap off his bike and out of the way in time. He hurt his knee landing wrong-ways on the sidewalk."

"Wow," I replied, a bit inadequately, while Len made a show of gingerly sliding his injured leg to one side and stretching it out. "Did anyone get the car's tag number for the police?"

"No, Len was the only witness, and he wasn't exactly in the position to be taking notes. But they got paint scrapings off his road bike, so if they ever find a suspect they'll be able to check that evidence against the person's car."

Len, meanwhile, cleared his throat again.

"I appreciate everyone's sympathy"—he paused and gave Marvin a baleful look that said quite the opposite—"but I'm more concerned about how I will manage my stay here. While the room you assigned to my wife and me was quite, um, adequate, I really require first-floor accommodations."

Fortunately, I'd done some research on this very subject soon after I opened and could address it with some confidence. On top of being a historic residence, I had five or fewer rooms for rent and lived in the house myself, all of which exempted my place from being ADA compliant.

I explained as much to Marsh, adding, "I know it's not ideal, but maybe we could set up a sleeping area for you downstairs in the parlor?"

I fully expected him to respond in the negative, but to my surprise he graciously nodded.

"That might be an option. And I noticed that your porch extends around most of the house. I assume I will be allowed to smoke out there, rather than having to walk all the distance to your designated smoking area several times a day."

Meaning that he'd read the welcome pamphlet in the room, as that was where the smoking area was mentioned, a graveled area in the far corner of the backyard hidden by a short wooden fence.

I caught Susie's pleading look, which I'm sure was accompanied by a telepathic message. Something along the lines of, *We all know he's going to be a jerk about it, but I'm the one who's going to have to listen to it.*

Feeling unwilling sympathy for the woman—chances were she really was earning that trophy wife salary—I gritted my teeth and nodded. "As long as you keep a reasonable distance from the doors and use an ashtray, I can make an exception under the circumstances."

Seemingly satisfied, Len returned his attention to his script. Susie flashed me a grateful smile, while Marvin snorted again. Harry, meanwhile, merely looked impatient.

"If that takes care of the questions, let's get started." Then he paused and frowned. "We're missing one person. Where's Radney?"

"Radney's right here," came a grim voice from the hall doorway.

Radney Heller stalked into the dining room, a sheaf of papers clutched in one hand and the other balled into a fist. His dark features were set in anger, and he moved with jerky steps as if holding himself in check. Grimacing, he thrust the bundle toward the group in an accusatory fashion. I could see now that the printed pages appeared stained with some thick amber-colored liquid.

Marvin was the first to speak up.

"What's the matter, Rad-Man?" he asked in a conciliatory tone. "Something leak in your shaving kit?"

"An avoidable accident," Tessa smugly spoke up before Radney could reply. "I always pack my toiletries in one of those zip plastic bags before putting them in my suitcase. That way, if something spills, nothing gets ruined."

"Oh, I do that, too."

This came from Susie, who was giving Tessa an approving nod. Warming to her subject, the younger woman went on: "Of course, that's only when traveling by ground. When Len and I fly, I have to use those silly three-ounce travel bottles. You know, the ones the government says you have to . . ."

"Thanks for your packing tips, Susie," Radney cut her short with exaggerated politeness. "You, too, Tessa. But plastic bags aren't worth a thing if someone sneaks into your luggage and deliberately loosens the cap on your body wash for you."

Chapter Five

If Radney had been going for dramatic effect, he failed epically—at least, in my book. When it came to sabotage, messing with someone's toiletries didn't rise much above a juvenile prank. Still, being the dutiful innkeeper, I leaped from my chair to grab a folded tea towel off the sideboard.

He gave me a stiff nod as he took the cloth. "Thanks, ma'am, but what would really help is for the person who did this to man up and admit to it. These were my script notes."

"Wait, Radney," Harry interjected with a frown, sliding his chair back just a bit. "Are you really accusing someone in our group of sabotaging your toiletries? Who had the opportunity, and . . ."

"And why would someone even bother?" Len smoothly finished for him.

Radney gave the latter a hard look, but his reply was for everyone.

"There was time enough when we were loading the luggage in the bus before we left Atlanta," he said. "And after we got here, and everyone was waiting on the bathrooms, the luggage was just sitting there by the front door. Anyone could have messed with it. As for why . . ."

"Assuming it was deliberate, all they did was soap up a few pages," Susie cut him short, though her tone was consoling.

"That's right, *Rad-Man*," Len added, and I was certain I wasn't the only one to hear the sarcastic emphasis he put on Marvin's nickname for the man. "Besides, you're a clever enough fellow. I'm sure you can re-create anything that was lost."

Radney appeared to be on the verge of replying in a fashion unbecoming a thespian. Then, from the corner of my eye, I caught Susie's little head shake in his direction in what seemed to be a signal between them.

No one else seemed to have noticed it, and I swiftly turned my attention away from her. Could it be that Susie had a thing for one of her husband's coworkers—and perhaps vice versa?

Radney, meanwhile, swallowed and then let out a breath as he wrapped up the papers in my tea towel.

"Okay, everyone's right, it probably was just one of those things. And like Len said, it's fresh enough in my head that I can re-create it. Let me get rid of this mess, and I'll be right back so we can get started on the read-through."

I escorted him to the kitchen, where he disposed of his papers in the trash and then began washing the soap from his hands. Meanwhile, I took the towel to the laundry room and tossed it in the basket of "to-be-washed." By the time I returned, he was drying his hands on a couple of paper towels, which he then proceeded to use to dab the sweat off his bald head.

"Sorry, ma'am . . . Nina," he corrected himself when I smiled and shook my head at his formality. "I didn't mean to make a scene. But you get Len pulling his Mr. Bigshot routine . . ."

"Yeah, I see how he can be a bit obnoxious," I replied in a deliberate understatement. "But at least you've got Harry to rein him in while you're here for the festival."

"Here, maybe. But in the real world . . ."

Radney bared his teeth in a gesture that was less a smile than a grimace.

"Harry probably told you that Len and I work for the same company."

When I nodded, he continued, "I might be head of R&D, but Len's in charge of approving funds for my department. I'm pretty good at playing office politics, but that's not always enough when it comes to dealing with Len. You don't bow and scrape enough for him, he won't hesitate to put the kibosh on your project, even though it could cost the company big time—and set you back when it comes to promotions."

I nodded again. Back when I'd worked in the corporate world, I'd run into my share of minor despots like Mr. Len Marsh. "I hear you. But you don't really think he'd stoop to messing with your toiletries, do you?"

"I wouldn't put it past him to be that petty. And this isn't the first incident. About a week ago . . ."

"Hey, Rad-Man," Marvin's voice boomed through the closed swinging door between dining room and kitchen, interrupting whatever it was Radney meant to say. "You wanna get a move on? We can't start rehearsals without you."

"Yeah, yeah, on the way," Radney called back as the used paper towels joined his ruined pages in the trash. To me he said, "I think you're right. For the next ten days I'll let our boy Len be Harry's problem."

He headed back through the connecting door, and I followed. Radney had piqued my curiosity in mentioning that there had been a previous incident, but not so much so that I felt the need to make him explain before he rejoined the others. Besides, I had enough on my plate keeping an eye on one Harold A. Westcott III. I didn't need to get involved in the internal skirmishes of an amateur theater group.

As Radney took the remaining empty seat at the table, Marvin clapped his beefy hands together and briskly rubbed them in anticipation of action.

"All right, Spielberg, let's get this show on the road." Then, when Harry gave Marvin a lifted brow, the latter amended his demand with a meek, "Sorry, boss, it's your show . . . I'll shut up now."

I suppressed a grin. Obviously, Len was not the only troupe member who needed to be held in check.

Seemingly satisfied that the pecking order had been restored, Harry opened his binder.

"Very well, people, you received your assignments a month ago," he began, "and I know as a group you manage a few informal rehearsals without me. Plus, most of you have performed Hamlet a time or two in the past, so we're not coming to this cold. Now, let's review the casting so that there are no questions."

He flipped to the next page and went on, "Keep in mind that, because we're a small group, almost everyone has more than one role, and I've combined a couple of redundant characters into a single part. And, as you know, for the purposes of the festival this is a truncated version of the play, meaning we only run for about an hour and a half. We've cut all the action that doesn't take place at the castle, and pared down our scenes to the essentials."

I nodded at that last, impressed. While hardly an expert, I'd seen *Hamlet* performed often enough to know that it was one of the Bard's longest works, clocking in at anywhere from two to four hours depending on the director and the medium.

He glanced over at Len. "All right, Marsh, you have the title role. But with all this talk about disability, you've got me worried that your knee won't be up to the sword fight. Maybe we should recast?"

"No, no, I'll be fine," the man broke in, and vigorously shook his white head. With a look at me, he added, "I mean, since our hostess has agreed to accommodate my condition, I'm sure I'll be well enough by then."

Harry nodded. "Susie, you're playing Ophelia. Bill and Tessa, you'll be playing King Claudius and Queen Gertrude, respectively. Bill, you're also the ghost of Hamlet's father. Marvin, you will handle the roles of Polonius and Horatio. Radney, you will take on Laertes . . ."

"And a fine son, you are," Marvin broke in, grinning and clapping his stage offspring on the arm.

". . . and also Marcellus," Harry continued with a quelling look at Marvin. "Chris, we've combined Rosencrantz and Guildenstern into a single character, which you will play. You will also

45

be the gravedigger and will be onstage for any non-speaking role where we need a courtier or other lackey.

"Whatever," Chris muttered. "But I still don't see why I don't get to play Hamlet. I'm the only one young enough for the role. Len oughta be playing Hamlet's grandpa."

"Age has little to do with it."

This came from Tessa, who was staring sternly over her reading glasses at Chris, the professorial gleam in her eye unmistakable. Sure enough, she launched into a lecture.

"As a student of the Shakespearean era, dear boy, you must recall that Burbage was the first to play the role. He first portrayed Hamlet while in his early thirties and performed it for almost ten years. Even my esteemed husband has played Hamlet before, with no one complaining about his lack of youth."

"That's true," Bill interjected with a humble smile. "I do know the part backward and forward."

Tessa gave him an encouraging nod and continued, "As for the character's actual age, a literal reading of the play puts it at anywhere between twenty and thirty, though many scholars such as myself argue that the play was written to show a compression of time, and—"

She was interrupted again, this time by a sharp tapping, which was Harry using his pen, gavel-like, upon his binder.

"Thank you, Tessa."

Turning to Chris, he went on, "Len has the acting chops, Chris, and you don't. The role of Hamlet is a difficult part with numerous soliloquies, and it requires a confident public speaker to carry it off. Now, would anyone else like to question my casting decisions? Good. Finally, we have arranged with the Cymbeline High drama department for their students to handle the play-within-the-play, plus they will serve as stage extras where needed. And with everyone now on the same script page, let us begin."

I took that opportunity to make my own exit stage right. If the rest of the rehearsal was going to go that same way, then I wasn't missing much. Besides, I had things to do now, like drag a cot into the parlor and make up a nice soft bed for good old Len.

As I was setting up the room for him a short time later, it occurred to me that I hadn't asked if Susie would be joining him downstairs, or if she preferred to sleep alone in the purple room. I suspected it would be the latter, but I'd double-check with her when the troupe took their break.

When I was finished with my housemaid routine, I returned to the kitchen to check out supplies for the next morning's breakfast—all the non-baked items I supplied myself—only to find someone waiting there for me. And it wasn't Mattie, who usually made it to the kitchen this time of day for her pre-supper snack.

"Hey, Number Nine," Marvin hailed me. "You've got a pretty slick setup here. I wasn't expecting something off one of them cooking shows."

"I wish I could take the credit," I admitted, "but I can't. This was all here when I moved in."

And Marvin had good reason to be impressed. The kitchen was a brash combination of late nineteenth-century architecture and twenty-first-century technology. The counter-to-ceiling, glass-fronted cabinets painted a crisp white were original to the home, as was the whitewashed floor with its scattering of rag rugs. And the farm-style stone sink that was big enough to bathe in was also original.

With a final approving look around him, Marvin held out the now-empty platter that previously had held a selection of cookies. "Looks like we kind of polished them all off," he said with a grin. "You make 'em yourself?"

"With my own two hands," I assured him. Which was the truth. I'd sliced those rolls of refrigerated cookie dough and put them on a baking sheet all by myself. "Is there anything else I can get for you?"

"Just needed more ice," he said and refilled his half-empty tea glass with ice from the refrigerator's in-door dispenser.

He seemed quite at home in a kitchen. This despite the reputedly large number of zeroes attached to his bank account balance. And, overall, I was liking him best of all the GASPers. I didn't even mind what could have been an annoying habit of his, hanging nicknames on everyone.

He had come up with my particular moniker when Harry and I were bringing up the luggage and he'd overheard me giving the official proper pronunciation of my name speech to Radney. As nicknames went, I rather liked being dubbed Number Nine. It made me sound like a jumpsuit-wearing lady spy from some sixties-era TV show.

As the final cube clinked into his glass, Marvin turned back to me. His expression was serious now as he sighed and slowly shook his head.

"God, give me patience, and give it to me now. All I can say is, the next couple of weeks ain't gonna be a picnic for any of us."

"Len?" I guessed in a sympathetic tone, earning a grunt by way of reply. "Yeah, he's a peach, all right . . . though I must say I was surprised he was understanding about the whole room situation."

"You let him smoke, so he's happy. And I doubt that bum knee of his is as bad as he makes out." Then, changing the subject, he mused, "I wonder how much he slipped our friend Spielberg there to snag the lead."

"You think he bribed Harry into letting him play Hamlet?"

Though, to be sure, it was the offering the bribe part that surprised me a little, not the fact that Harry might take one.

Marvin took a swallow of tea and then shrugged. "I wouldn't put it past him. Being a sneaky little so-and-so is second nature to the man. Sure, he'll greet you like you're his long-lost brother, but while he's shaking your hand, the other one is busy sticking a knife in your back."

Apparently, Radney wasn't the only one with a beef against Len Marsh. Curious, I ventured, "Sounds like you know Len pretty well. I mean, outside the GASP group."

"Yeah, I know him. The two of us cofounded Peachtree Communications twenty years ago."

Recognizing this as the name of the company he'd just sold, I gave Marvin the patented Harry Wescott brow raise. Since I lacked the finely tuned facial muscle control that Harry had, that meant both brows went sky-high.

"You and Len were partners? So why did he leave and go work for another electronics company?"

"Let's just say he done me wrong, and leave it at that."

I nodded, pretty sure that Marvin wasn't referring to romance. Still, something was odd about the situation. The so-called wrong seemed to have worked out just fine for Marvin in the end, since he'd been the one to cash in when the business was sold.

Or had he? Had the actual proceeds been far less than rumor claimed? Or had Len pulled a Harry and filed some lawsuit against Marvin after the fact? Not that it was any of my business.

"So if you hate Len so much," I said instead, "why stay in the GASP troupe with him? And why voluntarily maroon yourself with him out here in Cymbeline for almost two weeks?"

Marvin looked at me like I was plumb crazy.

"Number Nine, are you plumb crazy? How many times do you think a fellow like me gets a chance to act on stage in one of the Bard's most famous plays? This is my lifelong dream, and I'm not letting that jerk get in the way of it."

"Aha, suffering for your art," I replied with a wise nod. "That's what all the greats did. Olivier, Gielgud . . . "

"Belushi, Farley," he finished for me, his tone now ironic. "Yeah, I get the picture. Time to pull up my big-boy pants and just worry about having a good time while we're here."

"Something like that. I mean, the guy can't be all bad if he's a sucker for Shakespeare like you."

Marvin merely shook his head.

"Well, I've played hooky long enough," he replied instead, seeming content to let the subject of Len drop. "Break's over, so I'd better get back to the parlor before Spielberg sends a posse out after me."

"Okay. But just be sure when y'all are practicing the sword-fighting scene with Len that no one puts actual poison on anyone's sword. It would be a real showstopper if he died for real."

I smiled at my clever reference to the way Laertes sneakily offed Hamlet in the play. Marvin, however, didn't seem to see the humor in my joke.

Sourly shaking his head, he muttered, "The line might start with me, but it darned sure stretches a long way back. Our boy Len ain't the most popular of folks."

So I was learning. First, Radney and now Marvin had admitted having a grudge against the guy. But they didn't speak for the whole troupe . . . or did they?

I gave the man a quizzical look, not certain if he was kidding or not about the whole killing thing. And then he added, "Let me put it to you this way, Number Nine. If Len Marsh dropped dead right this minute, there's not a person in our little group who'd shed a single tear over him. And that includes his wife."

Chapter Six

After that unsettling little bit of commentary on Marvin's part, I was more than glad to leave the GASPers to Harry for the rest of the afternoon. Since it was too hot to take Mattie for a walk, she and I retreated to my room, where my personal office was also set up. Might as well get some B&B business done, I told myself.

I'd just finished aligning the housekeeping schedule—having Harry in the tower room and Len in the parlor was throwing off my numbers a bit—when Mattie lifted her head and gave a sharp woof. Her bark was promptly followed by a rap on my door.

"Coming!" I called, and saved my document.

So much for the "Private" sign on the door. Although I did try to make myself accessible to guests in the evening, at least on their first night's stay. It probably was Len come to complain that the parlor bed I'd set up for him wasn't quite up to his standards. If so, I'd have to give him two options—go with the makeshift downstairs accommodations or grit his teeth and manage the stairs.

But when I opened the door, instead of the Brooks Brothers saint, I found my least favorite actor-slash-director lounging against the jamb.

I favored Harry with a bland expression. "Yes, may I help you?"

"Actually, I'm here to help you. We're about to call in a delivery order to the Dancing Tiger, and I was wondering if you wanted me to order you some supper. My treat, of course."

The Dancing Tiger being the nearby Chinese restaurant that, in my opinion, had more than earned its average four and a half stars on Yelp. Which was why I had the menu numbers of my favorite dishes memorized

I blinked. Yet again, Harry was being solicitous, which was not a normal state of affairs for him. So what did he want?

"What do you want, Harry?" I demanded, clutching the knob in case I needed to slam the door in his face. "What's worth a number 23 and a side order of spring rolls?"

He gave me a pained look. "I don't want anything. I'm simply trying to show my appreciation for your hospitality and for accommodating my star performer and his, er, temporary infirmity. I would hope you'd accept my offer in the spirit it was intended."

"Oh."

I glanced down at Mattie, who'd joined me at the door. Her head was cocked in questioning doggie fashion, gaze fixed firmly on the actor. Then, with a small woof and a flick of her ears—the canine equivalent of a shrug—she turned and trotted back to the desk, flopping down there in a furry puddle of black-and-gray-and-white fur.

"Fine," I replied, trying not to sound churlish. And then, because I knew I did, I added, "Thanks. Chinese does sound good. White rice not fried, and don't forget the order of spring rolls. They're for Mattie."

"Noted. I'll add you both to the list. As soon as the food arrives, I'll send someone to fetch you. We're still commandeering your dining room, so no need to clear anything away. We'll eat there and then continue with our read-through."

"Perfect," I agreed and waited for him to turn away so I could decently close the door on him.

But when he made no move to go, I swallowed a sigh and asked, "Anything else I can do for you?"

"Actually, I was hoping we might talk. I've observed a bit of frostiness on your part ever since the troupe arrived."

"It's not the troupe that's the problem."

"Fine, ever since *I* arrived. You're not still holding a grudge about that whole lawsuit thing, are you?"

I slanted him a wry look and shot back, "Let's just say that I keep waiting for the other shoe to drop. For all I know, your whole reason for bringing the GASP people here was to get back inside the house. You figure that if you lived here for ten days, you'd have a case for tenancy."

"Would that work?" He gave a considering nod. "Thanks. Let me run that past my lawyer and see what he says. Now, off to call in that food order."

He spun about and headed down the hall, leaving me to stare after him and mutter bad words that made Mattie's ears twitch alarmingly. I hadn't meant to give him what obviously he'd taken as advice. But if I recalled correctly, there was more to the tenancy thing than simply overstaying one's paid-for vacay.

"Don't worry, girl, we still have the upper hand," I assured Mattie as I firmly closed the door.

But, just in case, after supper I'd send an e-mail to my cousin Kit, who was an attorney back in Dallas and undoubtedly would have some suggestions on how to handle the situation.

It was almost an hour later when Mattie woofed again, and I heard another knock. Gesturing the pup to follow, I opened the door to find Susie Marsh standing there, an uncertain smile on her lips.

"Harry sent me to tell you the food is here."

"Great, because I'm starved," I told her with a reassuring smile back. "Mattie is looking forward to her spring rolls. I let her have them every so often as a special treat."

"Aw, that's sweet," Susie replied and gave the Aussie a tentative pat on her fluffy head before we started down the hall. "I've been wanting a dog—you know, for company when Len travels—but he keeps saying he's allergic."

Right. Not that I wasn't sympathetic to allergies, but I hadn't heard any sneezing from the guy since he arrived. And I'd learned over the years that, half the time when people claimed an animal allergy, it was simply code for *dogs are smelly, barky, shed, need walking, and I don't want to deal with it.* But that was probably better than Len letting his wife get a pet and then making her get rid of it the moment he decided the pup was too much trouble.

"So, how did you get interested in joining the Shakespeare troupe?" I asked instead. "Was it one of those bucket-list things like with Marvin?"

This time, her smile was untroubled.

"Actually, I was a theater major in college. I'd even gotten a little acting work here and there, though it wasn't enough to pay my tuition. When I met Len ten years ago, I was waitressing to make extra cash," she said, mentioning the restaurant chain known for its owl logo and scantily clad servers. "Of course, he didn't want his wife-to-be appearing in tampon ads and hawking used cars on the local channels, so I quit everything as soon as we got married."

Sounds like Len, I thought with an inner snort. Aloud, I merely said, "That's too bad. But if that was his attitude, how did both of you end up in the troupe?"

"We were at this Halloween charity event in Atlanta called Peachy Scream, and GASP was performing little vignettes of the supernatural elements in Shakespeare's plays. You know, the witches' scene from *Macbeth*, the ghost of Hamlet's father."

"Sounds like fun."

"It was," she agreed. "Not that I expected Len to enjoy it, but by the time the performance was over, he was hooked. It must have been all the peach daiquiris they were serving or something. He tracked down Tessa, and before you knew it, he and I were part of the troupe. Of course, a big donation really helped secure our spots, but we both are pretty good, if I do say so myself. And since we don't have kids—well, any that are both ours—it gives us something to do in our free time."

"Free time?" I echoed, wondering how a VP of a multinational corporation had time to indulge a theater hobby.

Susie gave another of her tentative smiles. "Well, most of the free time is mine, but Len's got lots of vacation accrued. That's how we're able to take off all these days for the festival."

By then we'd reached the dining room, from which the enticing aroma of steamed rice combined with garlic, ginger, and soy were wafting. I heard an ominous growl from Mattie padding alongside me that came, not from her throat, but her tummy. We'd eaten from the Dancing Tiger enough times before that she knew what was to come.

"Ah, there you are," Harry grandly declared from behind a veritable wall of takeout bags as Susie and I entered the room. "Your order has your name on it, so feel free to dig in."

While everyone sorted through the bags, I passed around a stack of everyday plates and, for the non-traditionalists, a few sacrilegious knives and forks. Of course, Harry proved adept at wielding the wooden chopsticks supplied with the takeout, though the others seemed grateful for the westernizing of their meal.

But utensils were not the only unusual accoutrement on display. In front of Harry's plate sat a lifelike skull. I wasn't surprised he had one—meaning one in addition to the skull surrounding his devious brain. On his last stay, he'd mentioned owning his own personal "Yorick" as part of his Shakespearean regalia. Likely he intended for his little friend to set the mood for the troupe at that night's table reading.

Once everyone had indulged, the troupe obligingly helped pile the dirty dishes and utensils together. As usual, Mattie trailed after me into the kitchen, obviously hoping there would be more for her than just the spring rolls. But I was a bit surprised when Tessa followed me too.

"We shouldn't really let this go to waste," she declared in her trademark lecturer's voice, indicating several half-full cartons of side dishes she was juggling. "There's enough left for another meal."

"I'll get you some storage containers."

I set the plates and bowls in the sink; then, pulling three large, glass-topped Pyrex containers from a lower cabinet, I added, "Feel free to stick everything in the refrigerator once you're done. I keep the shelf in the middle empty for guests to use."

While she handled the leftovers, I filled one side of the double sink with hot soapy water for a quick washup, expecting Tessa to return to the dining room. She surprised me again. Once she had stowed everything in the refrigerator, she picked up a folded dish towel from the countertop and began drying the rinsed plates I was putting into the dish drainer.

"I never use our dishwasher, either," she confided with an approving nod as she rubbed the crockery dry. "Not eco-friendly."

"Hey, we do our best here," I replied a bit inadequately, as I normally was a fan of tossing everything into the dishwasher and hitting a button. If I wanted a five-star rating from the professor, it seemed I would have to wait and run the dishwasher at night after everyone was in bed.

"I appreciate the help," I went on, hoping she was just being polite by offering a hand, "but it's really not necessary. You're a guest. Besides, I don't want to keep you from rehearsal."

"Don't worry, they won't miss me. They'll be yakking about nothing for another fifteen minutes unless Harry shuts them up," she replied with a dismissive flick of her gray braid over her shoulder.

I nodded and handed her a dish to dry. Since it was just the two of us, maybe I could take advantage and do a little fact-finding about a certain sneaky actor.

"So, how do you like having Harry as director of the Georgia Amateur Shakespeare Players?" I asked with an innocent glance at her while I continued scrubbing crockery. "It didn't seem, well, like everyone was on the same page with him as far as casting."

Her stern demeanor promptly brightened.

"Oh, no, you have it all wrong," she gushed, suddenly sounding like a breathless groupie. "Everyone loves Harry . . . er, Mr. Westcott. It's almost like having Ron Howard or James Cameron heading our troupe. We trust him implicitly when it comes to directing."

Which sentiment was not quite what I was hoping for. Apparently, as far as Tessa was concerned Harry was no less than the second coming of Kubrick. But, just to be sure, I tried again from another angle, hoping she might expose a few chinks in the Westcott armor.

"How long has Harry been with you? Was everyone here already part of the troupe when he joined it?"

She nodded.

"Our actual troupe is much larger, but all of us except for Chris have been the GASP core group for the past four or five years. Harry—Mr. Westcott—walked into one of our rehearsals a couple of seasons ago while he was in Atlanta and asked to join the troupe. Of course, we were all pretty starstruck, working along-side someone with his professional resume. And then, when our director quit over creative differences back in the spring, he self-lessly agreed to take over directing the play for this year's festival here in Cymbeline! What a fortunate turn of events!"

I considered that last fact for a moment. If Tessa's timeline was accurate, Harry would have taken on the director's role before he and I had ever met. That meant I couldn't accuse him of diabolical machinations there. I decided to let the situation ride. Maybe tomorrow after breakfast I could buttonhole another of the troupe and see if my questioning led to anything more concrete. And so I summoned an enthusiastic smile.

"Yes, you certainly were lucky," I agreed and handed her the final plate. "Though I guess Cymbeline was the real winner. It would be hard to put on a proper Shakespeare festival without a play."

"Why, I can't even imagine it. Though I am disappointed with the casting of Len as Hamlet. I truly do think that Bill would be the better choice. With luck, maybe Len will reinjure his knee and be forced to withdraw from the role."

With that, Tessa put away that last clean dish. Pretending I hadn't just heard her wish an injury on a fellow player, I wiped down the counters while she returned to the dining room. Once

I'd hung up the damp towels, I gave a final peek through the connecting door to make sure my guests were resettled. The table reading had commenced, and everyone appeared to be behaving themselves. Which meant that my innkeeper duties were pretty well completed for the evening.

"C'mon," I told Mattie, "Let's hang out together, just us girls."

After a final disappointed look in the direction of the fridge, the pup obligingly followed me back to our room.

Mattie and I spent the rest of the evening doing a little online surfing and then lounging in bed catching up with a couple of our favorite TV shows. Around eleven, I got up to make a final check of the house.

Apparently, Harry had finally let the troupe go for the night, for the dining room was empty. I flipped on the overhead light to make sure the room was somewhat in order for breakfast in the morning. Scripts remained in front of a couple of chairs, along with someone's closed laptop, but otherwise all was in place. Harry's skull still held court in front of his spot, favoring me with a leer as I turned out the light again.

Moving along the main hall, I could see light shining under the closed door of the parlor where Len Marsh had settled without issue into his makeshift accommodations. I tiptoed closer to that door and gave a quick sniff, relieved that no telltale cigarette smoke wafted from within. At least this first night he was following house rules.

I rechecked all the door locks and turned off all but a couple of small bulbs burning in the hallways. Everything upstairs seemed quiet too. I'd halfway expected to find Harry roaming around, maybe in the kitchen brewing a cup of his nasty rooibos tea, but it seemed even he was tucked in for the night.

So far, so good. Other than some contentious conversation earlier, the GASP troupe was proving to be model guests. As long as they didn't resort to swordplay in the halls, maybe their stay would be uneventful, even with one Harry Westcott present.

Chapter Seven

I slept uneventfully enough myself and was up a little past six. This gave me time to let Mattie out for her morning potty break and leg stretch while I poured out her food. That done, I showered and then dressed in my semiofficial summer uniform of jeans rolled up to capri length and a short-sleeved linen T-shirt (today's color being olive) before the Tanakas's daughter, Jasmine, arrived by bicycle at seven with the morning's catered breakfast from Peaches and Java.

"Good morning . . . come on in," I greeted the teen, holding open the front screen door for her.

She responded with a yawn and a sleepy smile as she struggled inside carrying four large cake boxes from which drifted all manner of enticing aromas. "Mornin', Miz Nina. Uh, what's with that weird-looking bus in your driveway?"

"That was the ride for the Shakespeare troupe that's staying here," I told her, taking the top two boxes and leading her toward the dining room. "You know, the ones who'll be performing at the festival."

I didn't bother to explain about Harry. I'd let Gemma know about that as soon as I could break free in the next day or so and visit her at lunchtime.

She shrugged in typical teenage dismissal of adult foibles. Her lion's mane of golden brown ringlets beneath a teal Peaches and Java ballcap bounced about her shoulders. Soon to be a high school junior, Jasmine was a stunning mix of her African American mother's and her Hawaiian/Japanese American father's DNA. With her dark golden complexion and almond-shaped amber eyes, along with that riot of curls, she could have been cover model for any teen magazine out there.

Fortunately, her parents were both sticklers for scholarship—Daniel with an MBA from the University of Hawaii, and Gemma with her RN from one of Georgia's top nursing colleges and a dozen years working in the local hospital's ER. And so, in addition to helping with the family business, Jasmine was on the fast track to a scholarship to one of the region's major universities.

We settled the boxes on the dining-room sideboard, and I gave Jasmine her usual tip. Then, leaving the girl to make her own way out, I headed to the kitchen, where I already had my serving plates warming.

I started the coffee brewing and the hot water for tea boiling while I arranged the usual tray of mini cereal boxes and fruit, along with a few individual servings of Greek yogurt and a pitcher of orange juice that would supplement the bakery offerings. I also pulled a carafe of peach nectar and a bottle of champagne from the fridge.

This was what I'd settled on as my B&B signature specialty, a peach mimosa toast at the first breakfast with every new group of guests. So far, the concoction had been a hit with everyone who tried it. I pulled nine crystal flutes out of the cabinet and gave them a quick swipe inside and out before arranging them on the tray with the champagne.

As soon as I'd finished my prep in the kitchen, I would unbox Daniel's fare—for this week, mini-quiches, open-faced egg white and avocado sandwiches, breakfast burritos with homemade salsa, and a selection of pastries including his famous peach cobbler. Still toasty in their double layer of tightly sealed foil, they'd go on the pre-warmed serving plates or else on one of my small warming trays

I had just set up the serving cart ready to wheel everything into the dining room when I heard a murmur of voices beyond the closed dining-room door. I glanced at my watch and grimaced. Only 7:20 AM. Someone was early to the breakfast party.

But before I could register a flicker of exasperation, another sound pierced the silence . . . this one a blood-curdling shriek of, "*Oh, no-o-o-o!*"

Forgetting my pique, I abandoned the cart and rushed through the swinging door into the dining room, nearly smacking into Radney in the process. I tossed the man a quick apology and glanced about for any signs of mayhem that would have elicited such a scream. But as far as I could tell, there were no dead bodies beneath the dining table, and no smoking guns on the sideboard.

Instead, all I saw was Tessa, wearing a surprisingly stylish knee-length, white seersucker sundress and sitting at the table in front of an open laptop. Her expression was one of abject horror.

By now, the Marshes had walked into the room, Len in his usual khakis and company polo, and once again conspicuously limping. Susie looked ready for a fancy brunch in her pink capris and coordinating pink flowered top, her lipstick the same rosy hue as her outfit. Both appeared as confused as I felt but joined the professor at the dining table, taking the same seats where they had sat the night before.

"Tessa, is something wrong?" I said, feeling a bit foolish asking the question, since something obviously was amiss. Then, when she made no response, I turned to Radney. "Any idea what happened?"

He shrugged. "Not a clue. We walked in together, and Tessa sat down at her laptop while I walked over here to see if there was any coffee yet. And that's when I heard her scream."

"Scream? Who screamed?"

This from Marvin, who ambled in wearing an oversized red-and-black Atlanta Falcons jersey over torn jeans.

Radney replied, "Something's up with Tessa."

As the woman seemed fixated on her computer, it occurred to me that maybe she'd received some bad news in an e-mail. But before I could ask that question, Bill had joined his wife at the table.

"What's the matter, dear?" he ventured. "Can I help?"

"No one can help!" she wailed. "My laptop has a virus-s-s-s!"

While Tessa frantically punched keys on her laptop, Harry and Chris entered the dining room. Harry was wearing an Elizabethan-esque flowing white shirt over tight jeans (and looking surprisingly manly despite the floofy blouse). Chris wore an oversized plaid shirt—this one yellow and black—and jean shorts cut off at the knees. Both winced along with the rest of us as Tessa shrieked again, threatening permanent damage to our collective eardrums.

And then Harry took charge.

"Tessa, settle down and let's see what's going on here," he said in an authoritative tone, marching over to the table and taking the seat beside her. "What makes you think your laptop is infected, and why do you think someone here is responsible?"

With an offended sniff, the woman angled her laptop so he and the rest of us could see the screen.

"Because it worked fine last night," she answered in a calmer voice, "but when I turned it on just now, all I got was this blue screen that said *Your Laptop is Infected*."

Sure enough, large white letters against a bright-blue screen said exactly that, along with several lines of text that included phrases like *fatal exception* and *critical error*, followed by a line of frowny face emojis.

"The Blue Screen of Death," Marvin intoned, using the phrase that struck fear into the hearts of inexperienced computer users everywhere.

Tessa gave everyone an *I told you so* look.

"I told you so," she exclaimed. "Someone came down here last night and deliberately sabotaged my laptop!"

While the rest of us gave silent thanks that it wasn't our laptop that was so infected, Harry shook his head.

"Let's not jump to conclusions, Tessa. People get computer viruses all the time. All it takes is clicking on the wrong link somewhere online. I know it's upsetting, but it's probably just one of those things."

"Sure, just like it was *one of those things*"—she gave the words air quotes—"that Radney's body wash spilled in his luggage."

I suddenly recalled my private conversation with Radney in the kitchen the night before. Before Marvin had interrupted, the R&D engineer had started to say something about the body wash incident not being the first "accident" that had happened recently among the troupe. Could this seeming computer sabotage be another?

Harry, meanwhile, turned to Marvin. "Fine, you've told us what the problem is. You're an engineer, so can you fix it?"

Marvin raised his hands in a gesture of surrender. "Hey, I'm hardware, not software. We need an IT guy."

We all looked at Radney, who shook his head.

"Mechanical," he said succinctly. "You got a CAD problem"—*computer aided design*, I knew he meant—"I can help. Otherwise, like Marv said, you gotta call IT."

A glance at Len elicited a similar response.

"Manufacturing and sales," he said with a shrug. Then, nodding in Chris's direction, he added, "Why don't you ask the kid? People his age all know computers backward and forward."

"That's true," Susie, who'd been silently watching the drama, suddenly exclaimed. "My little niece in California is eight years old, and she can program every device in my sister's house."

Harry nodded. "What about it, Chris? Do you think you can help?"

While everyone else had been absorbed in Tessa's drama, the youth had been eyeing the boxes sitting on the sideboard. At Harry's question, he returned his attention to the group.

"Yeah, sure, whatev," was his sighing reply as Harry vacated his chair and then gestured Chris to sit down beside Tessa.

The youth plopped into the empty seat, turning the laptop to face him as he reached for Tessa's mouse. He clicked and typed furiously for perhaps thirty seconds, then set down the mouse and shoved back in his chair.

"Seriously? This prank is so 2010. I can't believe anyone was fooled by that."

"Prank?" I echoed, leaning closer in an attempt to see the laptop screen.

Meanwhile, Tessa had grabbed the mouse and spun the computer around for a look. She did a few clicks of her own and gasped.

"You fixed it. The blue screen is gone, and my shortcuts are there!"

"Well, duh." Chris rolled his eyes behind the oversized glasses. "You never did have a virus. Someone hid your shortcuts and changed your wallpaper to that fake blue screen. Now can we eat? I'm hungry."

He hopped out of the chair and headed for the sideboard again, with me on his heels. Gesturing him to wait a minute, I began unloading the mini-quiches onto a tiered plate. The rest of the troupe erupted in commentary.

"Kid is right," Marvin said. "It's just a dumb joke. I remember someone did that to our HR gal on April Fool's Day a few years back. About got fired for it too."

"But how could someone put that fake error message on Tessa's computer? Wouldn't you have to be an IT person?" This from Susie, who'd apparently forgotten her contention that such things were well within the realm of even eight-year-olds.

Radney shook his head. "Not at all. I bet if you go online right now and Google *computer pranks*, you can find instructions on how to do it. All someone would need was a thumb drive with a PDF of a fake blue screen, and access to Tessa's computer."

"But you'd need to know my password," the professor protested, pulling the laptop closer to her.

Len snorted as he lined up behind Chris waiting for me to finish putting out breakfast.

"You use a touch-screen password," he reminded Tessa. "All anyone would have to do is watch you enter it a couple of times and they've got it."

"Or look for smudges on the screen," Marvin added, joining the line. "Them fingerprints show up pretty easy, especially if you're eating greasy egg rolls while you're using your laptop."

"Especially if your password is a big old T," Susie agreed as she queued up behind Marvin. Then, realizing that she'd spilled the digital beans, the woman slapped both hands over her lipsticked mouth in exaggerated dismay.

"Oh, Tessa, I'm so sorry. I didn't mean to give it away."

"Well, if even you could figure it out," the older woman replied with a sniff, "then I guess it wasn't any big secret. I'll change my password after breakfast."

She shoved her chair back and stomped over to the breakfast line, followed by Harry. By now, I'd unpacked all the pastry boxes and hastily arranged the food on plates and platters.

"Help yourself, everyone," I said. "I'll be right back with the cart with the drinks and rest of the food. And don't forget, we've got mimosas on the menu this morning."

But as I returned with my wheeled cart, over the clink of serving utensils on china, I heard a mild "Excuse me."

It was Bill. He was still seated at the table while everyone else was busy filling their plates. When his polite attempt at gaining attention failed, he summoned a surprisingly strident voice that probably served him well in the classroom.

"*Excuse me!*"

Marvin chuckled. "Simmer down, Woodstock. You got something to say, we're all ears here."

Bill didn't appear to appreciate the nickname, for he gave the other man a sour look before continuing. "We seem to have forgotten the most important thing here. We've established that anyone could have pulled this prank, but we still don't know who did it."

That observation stopped everyone except Chris, who took the opportunity to slide a second breakfast burrito on his plate. Then denials and accusations began to fly.

"Not me," Radney insisted, shaking his bald head. "You can ask Marvin. Once my head hits the pillow, it's lights out until the alarm goes off."

"Yeah, pretty much like he said," that man agreed. "I hit the hay maybe five minutes after we finished last night, and I was asleep in bed all night."

Then, with a nod in his former partner's direction, he added, "But it sure is convenient that old Len here managed to swing himself a private room downstairs. Heck, he could have tinkered with the laptop and then pocketed all of Number Nine's fancy silverware, and no one would be the wiser."

"I beg your pardon," Len countered, tanned cheeks flushing. "I spent last night with my bad knee propped on pillows trying to get some rest. The effort it would take to wander around in the dark without causing myself further injury wouldn't be worth any sort of practical joke payoff."

"I believe you, honey," Susie piped up. "Now, all y'all quit picking on Len. He's still injured."

"Oh, please." This from Tessa, who was loading up on the breakfast burritos herself. "He only limps when he thinks someone's watching. And for all we know, you could be the prankster, Susie. After all, you were alone in a room last night too."

"Yeah, well, so was Chris," Susie shot back.

The youth gave them both a baleful look. "Nice. I was the one who fixed Tessa's laptop, remember?"

"If it helps with the timeline," I spoke up as I arranged the yogurt cups, "I did a final lockup of the house around 11 PM. I checked this room along with the other public areas, and I remember seeing a closed laptop sitting here on the table."

"We shut things down around ten," Marvin confirmed. "So there would've been time between then and when you saw the computer for someone to mess with it. But my vote's that Tessa did it herself. You know, looking to get herself some atten—".

The shrill blast from what sounded like a referee's whistle calling a time-out split the air, cutting his comment short.

"That will be enough," Harry coolly proclaimed, rising from his seat and dropping a silver coach's whistle into the breast pocket of his poufy shirt. "My guess is that whoever desecrated Yorick is our culprit."

He turned the skull back around to face us. I saw in surprise that Yorick now sported what presumably was one of Len's cigarettes clamped between his teeth.

I stifled a giggle, earning a stern look from Harry, who continued, "I don't care who messed with Tessa's computer, or why, but this is the last prank I want to see. Something like this happens again, and I will replace every single one of you with kids from the Cymbeline High drama club. Understood?"

Chapter Eight

Apparently satisfied that he'd gotten his point across, Harry consulted what was either a Rolex wristwatch or—more likely—a Chinese knockoff of same.

"It is now 7:40. Everyone has twenty minutes to eat, and fifteen minutes after that to attend to any personal needs. At exactly 8:15, I want to see everyone and their scripts outside in the Shakespeare garden. If we're lucky, our hostess will give us a quick tour of everything growing there to put you in the Elizabethan mood. And after that we'll spend the rest of the morning out on the patio *REHEARSING. OUR. PLAY!*"

"Uh, Spiel—, er, Harry?" Marvin ventured, raising a beefy hand as the echo of Harry's last words died down. "The temperature's supposed to hit in the high nineties before lunch. You sure you don't want to rehearse inside?"

Harry gave the man the patented Harry Westcott brow raise. "Tell me, Mr. Lasky, where will we be performing during the festival?"

"Uh, outside?"

"Exactly."

He gestured at Marvin's black-and-red jersey with its stylized falcon logo. "You don't see your football team holding practice in a nice air-conditioned gym, do you? They drill outside in the heat to acclimate themselves so they're not keeling over during an actual game. We're merely taking a page from their playbook."

Which made sense. Even though the performances were scheduled for the evening, the nighttime temperatures wouldn't drop all that much. Adding in the costumes and the stage lights, it would make for hot conditions for the actors.

At Marvin's nod, Harry checked his watch again. "It is now 7:42. I suggest that everyone fill your plates and start eating."

While everyone finished up at the sideboard, I played bartender. I hurriedly stirred the peach nectar into the pitcher of orange juice, then filled the champagne flutes halfway with the mixture and drizzled in a touch of grenadine. I'd gotten pretty proficient at opening champagne bottles, but Radney gallantly jumped up to do the honors while I sliced a fresh peach and plopped a narrow wedge in each glass. That done, I filled the flutes the rest of the way with champagne.

"Oh, doesn't that look pretty!" Susie exclaimed. Setting down her plate in front of her chair, she added, "Here, let me help you hand out the drinks."

I gave her a grateful nod. Carrying the mimosas two at a time, we sidestepped the rest of the troupe as they began settling back in their respective seats. There was a brief moment of confusion when I came back with my second round and noticed that Chris had apparently absconded with someone else's mimosa. Now, flute in hand, he appeared ready to take a swig.

"Sorry," I told him with an apologetic smile, swooping over in that direction. "If you want to drink, I need to see your driver's license first to make sure you're over twenty-one."

I thought for a minute the youth would comply, for he stuck his hand in his shorts pocket as if going for his wallet. But then, he shook his head.

"Fine, never mind," he muttered, and handed his glass to Len beside him. I had deliberately left one flute of the juice and nectar mix unadulterated and now handed Chris a virgin version of mimosa minus the champagne.

Once everyone was settled, I returned to the bar cart for a mimosa of my own—hey, no reason the innkeeper can't indulge—and lifted my champagne glass in a toasting gesture.

"If I can have your attention everyone, I'd like to give you an official welcome to Fleet House," I told my guests with a smile. "We'll be here together for almost two weeks, and I'm looking forward to making friends with you all. May your stay here be a memorable one."

While everyone did the obligatory *Hear, hears* and clinking of glasses, I set down my flute and went back to the sideboard to do a bit of rearranging so that the platters still looked full. It was a trick I'd learned from Gemma. *Nothing looks worse than picked-over food,* she'd warned me.

As I arranged, I could hear the comments on my signature drink, mostly positive. Only Len muttered, *Tastes a bit sour to me,* though he took another large sip from his glass despite that. Buffet touch-up done, I served a plate for myself. Then, reclaiming my mimosa, I took the only empty chair, which happened to be alongside Harry.

I wasn't trying to crash the troupe's meal. As ye olde official innkeeper, it was my job to hang out at the breakfast table with my guests, at least on their first full day. It gave them the opportunity to ask me questions about the house and grounds, or about the town and places to see. But this morning no one had time to ask about anything. All energy was being expended on shoveling down Daniel's awesome baking.

Except for Harry, of course. He'd moseyed up to the sideboard after everyone else and filled his plate sparingly with the high-protein and low(-ish) fat offerings, then poured a cup of hot water for tea (his own). The last was currently steeping before him as he casually forked up small bites of quiche. At exactly 8:00 AM per my watch, he picked up his knife and lightly tapped it against his crystal water glass.

"Ladies and gentlemen, time is up. Please take your personal breaks and then meet in the garden in fifteen minutes."

The announcement was met by muttering, but the troupe gamely rose from their chairs, Tessa with laptop protectively tucked beneath her arm.

"Don't worry," I assured them. "I'll keep the leftovers warm in case Captain Queeg here gives you a mid-morning break. And there's still peach mimosa mix and champagne on the drink cart. Feel free to grab a refill now, if you want."

That offer drew a few smiles from some of the GASPers, who crowded about the bar cart to take hasty advantage of it. Except

Anna Gerard

for Len. Half a glass of mimosa still in hand, he made a beeline for the door. From the way he reached with his free hand for the cigarette pack in his shirt's breast pocket, I assumed he was headed for the smoking area behind the garden.

With mimosas replenished, the others followed more slowly. I'd make the rounds of the bedrooms later to pick up the empty glassware. For the moment, however, I waited until I everyone had left the dining room before turning back to Harry.

"You do realize that a leisurely breakfast is part of the B&B experience?"

He nodded and raised a final forkful of quiche in mock acknowledgment before taking an exaggerated bite.

"Yes, yes, I do," he replied through a mouthful of fluffy eggs and cheese. "Which is why I'm taking my time finishing up here. My compliments to the chef, by the way."

"That would be Daniel Tanaka, as I'm sure you know. And your troupe wolfed down Daniel's awesome cooking so fast I doubt they even tasted it."

He shrugged and spooned up a bite of cobbler. "Call it a teachable moment. Maybe tomorrow we won't have to spend half the morning playing detective trying to figure out who's playing tricks."

"So you're not worried that someone is trying to undermine the troupe?"

Harry snorted. "Believe me, these little antics are nothing compared to what goes on behind the scenes on a movie set. Someone's trying to unnerve the rest of the cast so that they start flubbing lines and missing cues."

78

"And the prankster looks like the star of the show, as a result," I said, finishing his thought. "But would you really replace them all with the Cymbeline High drama club?"

"Not a chance."

He grinned, momentarily reminding me of the Harry I knew and tolerated.

He continued, "For one thing, those kids are in summer vacation mode, so they'll be harder to keep in line. For another, all the GASP players own their own costumes. I don't want to scramble last minute for a proper sixteenth-century wardrobe to outfit a whole new cast."

Which made sense. But another question had been nagging at me.

"What about whipping *this* cast into shape in time for next weekend?" I asked him. "That's a pretty short timetable. Shouldn't you have been rehearsing for weeks already?"

Harry downed the rest of his mimosa and then shook his head.

"If we were putting on a brand-new play, yes . . . but you're forgetting this is a Shakespeare troupe. Everyone is familiar with the material, and most of them have performed in past productions of *Hamlet* over the years. Plus they've had their cast assignments since last month. A hard few days of rehearsals here at the B&B, and a dress rehearsal Thursday night on the actual outdoor stage, and we'll be set."

He said it with such confidence that I figured he must know what he was doing.

"You're the director," I brightly replied, and then pushed back from the table. "And since I'm the innkeeper, I'd better get the dishes out of the way so I can head to the garden for my lecture series."

While Harry dunked a fresh teabag, I made quick work of the cleanup and dealt with the leftovers. By the time I headed out to the garden, Mattie trotting after me, Harry's designated fifteen minutes were up. All of the troupe except the Marshes had gathered in the chairs set up under the back patio, enjoying a final bit of shade and moderate temperature before the summer heat began cranking up.

I didn't envy them practicing outdoors, but Harry had a point. I'd glimpsed some of their costuming when the troupe had first arrived. Unless they were acclimated to the heat, the sun combined with layers of satin and velvet would pretty well guarantee at least one player keeling over.

"Hello, again," I greeted everyone, feeling suddenly nervous though I'd given this talk to guests before. But the troupe all gave me encouraging smiles, with Radney adding a reassuring nod. Even Chris looked up from his phone a moment, so I took a deep breath and plunged on.

"This, as you have guessed, is my Shakespeare garden," I continued and gestured at the circular garden beyond the patio. I gave them a quick description of the layout and went on: "The first thing I always like to point out is the tiered fountain in the middle. If you look closely at the column holding the largest of the three basins, you'll find that it's engraved with one of the most famous quotations from *Romeo and Juliet*."

"*That which we call a rose, by any other name would smell as sweet,*" Bill unexpectedly finished for me in dramatic fashion.

I nodded. "Exactly. The garden was installed more than thirty years ago by Fleet House's original owner, Mrs. Daisy Lathrop. You might be interested to know that she was also your director's great-aunt."

This drew surprised murmurs from everyone, as I expected, but it was Harry's reaction I waited for.

Fortunately, he merely gave a slight nod of acknowledgment, apparently content to keep our on-again, off-again feud private for now.

"Shakespeare gardens first became popular in the early nineteen hundreds," I continued, warming to the topic. "They now are found pretty much all over the country, mostly at libraries and universities and public parks. Depending on the designer, the garden may be devoted to the flora mentioned in a single play, or it might be planted with flowers from various of his sonnets."

"My garden is somewhat different. You'll notice that paved walkways divide the circle into four equal and distinct sections, like pie pieces. Each of those quarters is its own smaller garden devoted to its own Shakespearean play."

The troupe nodded again.

"The mini-garden closest to us and to the right features plantings mentioned in *Macbeth*," I went on. "*Romeo and Juliet* is the theme of the garden directly across from it. Flowers and shrubs from *Hamlet* fill the quarter to the rear of *Macbeth*. And, of course, we have *Cymbeline* as the theme of the fourth section. Now you might be wondering . . ."

"Where's Len?" Susie interrupted me as she rushed out onto the patio, high-heeled sandals clicking on brick. "I went upstairs to freshen up, and when I came back down and checked the parlor, he wasn't there."

"Susie, how rude," Tessa scolded her, and added a wagging finger for good measure. "You're interrupting Nina's most interesting talk about her garden."

Susie's pink-lipsticked mouth twisted like she was holding back a retort. But, always the lady, she promptly gave me an apologetic nod. "Sorry, Nina. Len told me he was feeling a bit peaked earlier, so I was concerned when I couldn't find him."

"He's probably in the can again," Marvin opined with a snort.

I shook my head. "I don't think so. He went off for a smoke right after breakfast. He's probably still back behind the fence."

"Len!" Marvin bellowed in the direction of the smoking area before Susie could reply to that. "Get a move on. Folks is waitin' on you."

As we waited for a reply, it occurred to me that I didn't smell any cigarette smoke wafting from that direction. But before I had time to wonder about that, from beyond the row of dividing hedges Mattie let out a bloodcurdling howl.

"What the . . .?" Radney exclaimed, leaping from his seat, while Harry and Marvin rose too. Even Chris looked momentarily startled behind his oversized glasses.

I too had jumped at the unexpected sound. Mattie never barked or howled just to hear herself make noise. When she did, it meant business. As in a zombie apocalypse in process, or a wild rabbit loose in the yard. Though it was more likely she had seen Len in the smoking area and—as Marvin had put it—was encouraging him to get a move on.

"Hang on, everyone," I said. "I'm going to check on Mattie. If Len is still back there, he probably walked up on her and startled her."

"More likely the poor dog gotta look at his ugly mug and got scared it was Bigfoot," Marvin retorted, drawing an amused snort from Radney.

Mattie came bounding through the hedge opening just as I circled the fountain. But when the executive didn't make an appearance, I frowned.

"Wait at the patio," I told the Aussie, gesturing her in that direction. "I'm going to get Mr. Marsh." But rather than trotting back to the porch like a good girl, she whipped around and dashed back through the hedge wall again. I followed after her.

The smoking area was about fifty feet away, and it was obviously empty. Unless Len had decided to take a full lie-down nap on the bench there. But as I started down the steps and across the yard, I heard a sharp bark from the Aussie behind me.

I swung around . . . and that's when I saw a pair of long, khaki-covered legs protruding from the hawthorn hedge.

Chapter Nine

"Harry, come quick!" I shouted automatically even as I wondered why I was calling for him rather than Susie or one of the others.

Though, of course, a moment later not only Harry but the rest of the troupe came rushing through the hedge opening, almost falling over one another in their haste. By then, I was already kneeling beside Len's prone form—at least the part of him that wasn't hidden by the hawthorn into which he'd apparently fallen. He wasn't moving, and I couldn't tell just from his legs if he was simply unconscious, or . . ."

"Keep Susie back!"

This from Harry as he knelt beside me, though the warning came too late. Catching sight of her husband sprawled in the hedge, the woman screamed and crumpled into the arms of Marvin, who fortunately had been on her heels. Radney, meanwhile, had shoved past the others to join me and Harry.

"C'mon, let's get him out of there," Radney exclaimed. "Harry, if you can get his legs, I'll ease him out of the bushes so we can lay him there on the grass."

Don't let him be dead, don't let him be dead, the mantra spun through my mind as I watched them settle the still figure on the lawn. Len's eyes were shut, and several bloody scratches—no doubt from when he'd pitched into the shrubs—stood out in contrast to the grayish pallor of his face. But other than that I saw no signs of trauma to him, at least from my angle.

In silent panic, I tried to see if he was breathing or not, while Radney leaned over him, listening at his chest as Harry checked the man's neck for a pulse.

Fearing the answer, I asked, "Is he . . .?"

Radney and Harry exchanged glances. Then Harry did the solemn headshake thing you always see on TV that means, *He's a goner.*

I clamped both hands over my mouth to hold back a cry. *OMG! Someone finally did murder Len!*

But barely had that thought flashed through my mind than I shoved it aside. Just the shock, I told myself in dismay. That would be the only reason such an idea would pop into my head. The fact that half the troupe had been voicing their dislike of the man from the minute they arrived at the B&B didn't mean someone had taken things to the extreme.

Or did it?

I heard Susie shriek again and then burst into noisy sobs as she clung to Marvin's arm. So much for Marvin's contention that she wouldn't shed a tear over her husband. I took a deep breath to center myself.

You're the innkeeper. Hold it together.

"Ahem," Bill spoke up from where he and Tessa and Chris huddled to one side. "Shouldn't someone be calling 911?"

Right. I slapped at my jeans pocket, only to realize that I'd left my phone inside. But Harry stood and whipped out his cell.

"On it," he said, moving a short distance from the body as he started punching numbers.

While Harry gave the dispatcher the necessary information, Chris took a hesitant step forward. "Can't someone do CPR or something?" he asked in a shaky voice that squeaked to almost sonic levels.

Radney grimaced and slowly got to his feet again. "Sorry, kid. I think he's beyond help now."

"No!"

Leaving Bill and Tessa to cling to each other, the youth hurried over to where Len lay. To my surprise, he dropped to his knees in the same spot where Harry had been and began to exert frantic chest compressions on the still figure, pausing every few moments to listen for a heartbeat, or a breath. But of course, it made no difference. As Radney had pointed out, Len was already past saving.

"Chris, let him go," I choked out after a minute of this, unable to watch the youth's futile efforts any longer. But when I moved to stop him, Radney put out a restraining hand.

"Doesn't hurt for him to try," he said in a low voice. "He'll run out of gas in a couple more minutes. But in the meantime he can tell himself he's helping."

Which was more than the rest of us were doing, I realized, feeling suddenly ashamed. I couldn't bring Len back, but I could at least show the rest of the troupe that I could take charge. Time for the mental-emergency to-do list.

I shot a questioning glance at Harry, who had just ended his call. "Is an ambulance on the way?"

"Already dispatched," he replied, sticking his phone back in his pocket and heading back to join us.

Check.

Turning to Marvin, who was still clutching the newly minted widow as she sobbed, I clipped out, "Take Susie inside . . . not the parlor, the dining room. There's some cognac in the sideboard. Give her a little, if she'll drink it, to help calm her down."

Marvin nodded. "Gotcha, Number Nine," he replied and began steering the crying woman back in the direction of the house.

Check.

To Bill and Tessa, I said, "You two, open the driveway gate for the emergency vehicles. Stay out there until they arrive, and show them the way back here."

Bill grabbed his wife's hand. "On it," he said, echoing Harry's words of a few minutes earlier.

Check.

While the pair hurried off, I turned back to Chris. As Radney had predicted, the youth had finally exhausted himself with his failed attempts at reviving Len and had sunk back onto his heels. His eyes behind the oversized glasses were wide and brimming with tears. While I doubted he'd had any great affection for the departed Len, coming face-to-face with death like that doubtless was a shock.

I know it was a shock to me.

"Chris," I urged gently, "why don't you and Radney take Mattie inside now? I don't want her getting in the way when the EMTs show up. Seriously, that would really help me out."

He didn't reply but took the hand that Radney offered to help him stand. With a nod in my direction, Radney whistled for Mattie, who obligingly followed the former as he urged the youth up the steps and into the garden, headed for the house. Which left me alone behind the hawthorns with Harry—and, of course, Len.

In the past minutes I'd tried to avoid looking at the unmoving figure lying a few feet away. Gingerly, I glanced his way now. His gray pallor had bleached to white, and his stillness was profound. From my decidedly unmedical perspective, the only thing the paramedics would be able do for him was load him up and transport him to the local funeral home.

"So, what do you think?" Harry asked.

I shot Captain Obvious a disbelieving look. "I think Len is dead."

"I know that. I meant what do you think killed him? Stroke? Heart attack?"

Knife in the back?

Unfortunately, it wouldn't have been the first time I'd seen a man dispatched with a blade. But there had been no sign of blood as Radney and Harry had moved the man about. Once again, I was letting my imagination get the better of me in assuming that something nefarious was afoot.

"He's the right demographic," I agreed instead. "Late fifties, stressful job, smoker. And then he'd been taking those pain pills for his knee. Maybe it was one of those health-related things that was bound to happen."

But why right here and right now? Why at my B&B?

Because I couldn't actually say that out loud without sounding heartless, instead I went on, "This is pretty a tough break for the Shakespeare festival. I guess you'll have to cancel, since you can't go on without your Hamlet."

Harry gave me his patented raised brow, his tone more than a little judge-y as he replied: "That's pretty heartless. You ask me, Len's the one who had the tough break. We can worry about the festival later. Right now, what's important is being there for Susie and helping her get through this."

And then, just as I was feeling as low as the worms that would eventually be making Len's acquaintance, Harry reverted to his usual self.

"Who am I kidding? We're in a jam now. The play *is* the festival, and we have to go on somehow."

"But you said that everyone in the troupe knows all the various roles," I reminded him. "Can't someone else take the lead?"

"Bill knows the part, but no way am I going to put a pony-tailed, geriatric Hamlet on any stage of mine. And I already explained that Chris doesn't have the acting chops to handle the role"

"Then what about Radney?"

Harry shook his head. "I'm all for color-blind casting, but take a look at the arms on that guy. No audience is going to believe his Hamlet sat around sulking for months after someone offed his dad. Besides, he doesn't know the part."

Which left only one other cast member, since Susie would surely be in no shape to take on any role. Before I could test Harry's views on gender-blind casting—frankly, I would have been psyched to see Tessa give the role a shot—another voice drifted from the garden beyond.

"Emergency guys are here!" Marvin bellowed from the back door.

Leaving Harry to stand guard over Len—not that I expected him to get up and go anywhere—I rushed back to the house, cutting through the kitchen and exiting into the driveway.

The paramedics were already unloading their gurney there. They looked like the same crew that had been to the place a couple of months before for another similar disaster. Fortunately, none of them made any comment about return engagements. Instead, the lead tech—a tattooed Latina with short spiked black hair—asked, "Ma'am, where's the patient?"

Cutting through the Shakespeare garden wasn't going to be an option. I could tell that the gap in the hawthorn hedge would be far too narrow for the EMTs to negotiate with a gurney and their accompanying equipment. And so instead I led them down the driveway.

Between the patio and the garage was a broad strip of grass that served as an alternate path to the main lawn that lay behind the formal garden. To be sure, the riot of heirloom rose bushes growing along the garage wall was a hazard in itself, with errant blossom-and-thorn-laden canes ready to snag unwary passersby. But the crew managed without difficulty, rounding the far end of the hawthorns where Harry and Len waited.

The next few minutes consisted of the paramedics hooking Len up to their various equipment and reading vitals off monitors. One of the crew, a baby-faced guy who looked like he was straight out of high school, remained with me and Harry, taking down Len's information as best we could supply it. But as I answered questions, I kept glancing over at the controlled chaos a few feet from us. Though the paramedics moved with swift efficiency, it was obvious that they were simply going through the prescribed motions. Finally, the lead EMT signaled the others to stop.

"He's gone. Time to call for a doc to pronounce," she said and reached for her two-way radio.

The rest of the crew nodded, while Baby Face explained to me that, technically, they weren't allowed to declare a dead person dead. That job fell to the coroner, whom the dispatch operator usually contacted along with the sheriff at the same time the EMTs were sent out to what likely was a fatality. That, or they had to call one of the ER doctors at the hospital to get an official okay over the phone.

"Oh, wait," he exclaimed, interrupting his own explanation. "Hey, Rodriguez, never mind. Reverend Bishop is here."

"Actually, it is the Reverend Doctor Bishop, at your service," a mild, melodious voice corrected him. "You were fortunate to catch me on the way to my Sunday morning service."

I turned to see a tall, thin man wearing a black suit and clerical collar walking down the garden steps to join us. He was of African American heritage with a brick-red complexion and a neatly trimmed afro and beard, both of which had once been a deep rusty color but now were liberally streaked with gray. Yet, even given the latter, he could have been anywhere from forty years of age to two decades older than that, as his face—at least, the part not hidden by whiskers—was remarkably wrinkle-free.

He paused in front of me and with a gentle smile plucked a business card from his suit coat pocket. "You must be the new owner of this lovely home," he said, handing the card to me. "I am the Reverend Doctor Thaddeus Bishop, pastor of the Heavenly Host Baptist Church here in Cymbeline. You may call me Dr. Bishop."

He extended a long, elegant hand in my direction—a hand that had recently seen the services of a manicurist. I cringed a little inwardly at the state of my own ragged cuticles. With my inn-keeping duties, it was hard to maintain perfect nails. I tucked the card into the pocket of my T-shirt and shook hands.

"Nina Fleet, owner of Fleet House Bed and Breakfast," I introduced myself, confused at his presence as he obviously wasn't a doctor. Plus it had taken me a moment to realize that Bishop was his surname and not one of his honorifics. "Are you here to give Mr. Marsh last rites?"

"Not exactly. In addition to my pastoral duties, I am also the county coroner."

"And that's not his only side hustle," Harry said from behind me. "The Rev is also the local funeral director. Kind of convenient, if you think about it."

The man's gentle smile tightened almost imperceptibly as he caught sight of the actor.

"Ah, Harold Westcott. It has been a while since our paths last crossed, but rest assured that I do not hold a grudge. May I offer my belated condolences on the passing of your great-aunt?"

At Harry's noncommittal nod, he added, "As for your attempt at levity under these sad circumstances, let us just say that I am called to attend the citizens of Cymbeline at all stages of their life journeys."

Turning to me, he went on, "Was the gentleman here alone, or was he accompanied by family or friends?"

"Both. He's here with his wife, and they are part of the Shakespeare troupe staying here for the festival next week."

"Ah, then we will want to question them about his recent health and habits."

"Uh, Dr. Bishop," the lead EMT interrupted, "can you pronounce this, er, gentleman so we can load him up? I don't think we should let him lie in the sun too long."

The pastor gave a regal nod, "A valid point. Excuse me, Ms. Fleet."

He sidestepped me and went over to where Len lay. He pulled a pair of blue latex gloves from his pocket and pulled them on, then knelt beside the dead man. He tilted Len's head side to side—checking to see if he'd been coshed over the head, I assumed, something we'd neglected to do—then leaned forward for a closer look at the bloody scratches on his cheeks.

"Was he found like this, on his back?"

"Sort of," Harry answered for us. Indicating the broken branches of the hawthorn he went on: "He was halfway lying in the hedges. Two of us pulled him out."

"I suppose that explains the injuries to his face. But you moved the body?"

The mild tone turned slightly accusatory on that last, so I hurried to clarify. "We didn't know Len was a "body" at that point. We thought he was still alive. One of the troupe tried giving him CPR."

The pastor sighed. "I see."

To Rodriguez, he went on, "I believe we can safely agree that this gentleman is deceased. I would also suggest that the circumstances of his passing are unexplained, given the fact he appears to have been in the prime of life. For that reason, I will call for an autopsy. Of course, it might have been your garden-variety heart attack or stroke, but we should also consider drugs, allergic reactions, even insect stings or snakebite."

That last suggestion had both me and Harry reflexively checking our feet as we took a few swift steps backward. Not that there weren't poisonous snakes in Georgia, but I had yet to see a serpent of any stripe in my yard. Probably Mattie kept them at bay.

Bees were another story, however, as they visited the garden regularly. They also found my single peach tree irresistible when it bloomed, their buzzing within the branches loud enough to hear halfway across the yard. But the local beekeeper, who had half-a-dozen hives set up on his second-story roofless balcony a few blocks from me, had assured me that bees were rarely the stinging risk that most non-beekeepers assumed. Unless, of course, someone was acutely allergic.

Dr. Bishop, meanwhile, continued, "Let me take a few pictures first, and then you are free to remove the decedent."

While the Reverend stripped off his gloves and whipped out a recent model smartphone, I gestured Harry aside. I wanted to know why the local funeral director had gone all forensic on us.

Or, at least, that's what it looked like. For he was now bent over taking pictures of Len's body from various angles. That done, he started in on views of the surrounding grounds while the EMT crew waited impatiently.

Had he seen something that made him decide that more than a heart attack had happened here?

"What's with the photos?" I asked Harry sotto voce. "Shouldn't the sheriff's deputies be doing that? Or is that side hustle number three?"

Not that I truly expected him to know.

But to my surprise the actor whispered back: "In Georgia, part of the coroner's duties is investigating any unexplained death. They make sure evidence gets collected, and they get to decide if they want the medical examiner to conduct an autopsy. And they don't even have to be a doctor or a cop . . . they just have to be over twenty-five years old and have a clean criminal record to be elected. Ask me how I know this."

I hesitated, sure I'd regret asking but unable to suppress my curiosity. "Fine," I whispered in return, "how do you know this?"

"Because I worked at the Reverend's funeral parlor part-time when I was in high school. He's still ticked at me because he thinks I swiped his official Georgia coroner's coffee mug."

Hence the grudge. Unless a teenaged Harry had done something worse, like pose dead bodies in rude positions or something. But before I could delve further into this unexpected glimpse of the actor's past, another voice spoke up.

"You conducting an investigation Dr. Bishop?"

The question came from a stocky, uniformed woman about my age. Blond hair in a tight French braid and eyes hidden behind mirrored sunglasses, she cut a stern figure as she stood at the hedgerow opening staring down at us.

Sheriff Connie Lamb—also known as the law in these here parts, as they say in those old Western movies. Unfortunately, I'd had dealings with her within days of opening my B&B a couple of months earlier. While I'd admired her tough efficiency in handling a high-profile murder, I hadn't been in any hurry to cross paths with her in a professional capacity again.

Behind the sheriff stood a young, red-haired deputy wearing wire-rimmed sunglasses—Mullins was his name—whom I also recognized from that previous investigation. The pair gave me and Harry cursory nods, their attention fixed on the pastor for the moment.

"Ah, Sheriff Lamb," that man replied, halting his photography. "I was anticipating your arrival. Yes, I believe an investigation as well as an autopsy is called for."

Chapter Ten

D r. Bishop ran down the same laundry list of possible causes for Len's unexpected passing as he'd mentioned to Rodriguez, adding, "I saw no signs of outward trauma other than the scratches, so chances are we will find nothing amiss. But I would prefer to be safe rather than sorry. Perhaps while I finish here you would like to question Ms. Fleet and the decedent's family and friends about the circumstances?"

"We'll handle it, Reverend, and keep you in the loop."

"Excellent. As I told the crew earlier, I was on my way to my morning service when I got the call. If I hurry with the paperwork"—he paused for a glance at this watch—"I might still make it on time."

The sheriff nodded to Mullins, who hurried over to the pastor and listened as he and Rodriguez conferred over some forms the Reverend had pulled out. Sheriff Lamb, meanwhile, strode down the steps to where Harry and I waited.

"Ms. Fleet," she greeted me, whipping out a notepad and pen. "I wasn't expecting to do this again with you."

"Me neither."

The sheriff was referring to the fact that, earlier this summer, I'd been first on the scene to find a man who lay dying in an alley on the town square. The subsequent police investigation had us crossing paths several times until what turned out to be a murder had been solved.

But, just so I don't hog the glory, Harry had been involved, too—originally because I'd thought he was the one sprawled behind a dumpster with a carving knife in his chest. And later, because Harry had been convinced *he* was the intended victim, not the murdered man.

The sheriff glanced Harry's way now, and the actor breezily greeted her. "Hi, Connie. Long time no speak."

I knew from before that the pair had gone to high school in Cymbeline together, which was why he apparently felt he could greet her with such familiarity. The sheriff, however, wasn't having any of that.

"Hello, Mr. Westcott. While I'm on the clock, it's Sheriff Lamb," she coolly reproved him. "Now I understand Ms. Fleet's presence here, since this is her B&B. But why do you happen to be here as well?"

"I'm the troupe director for the Georgia Amateur Shakespeare Players," was his lofty reply. "We're staying here while we finish rehearsals for the Shakespeare festival next weekend. Though things are a bit up in the air right now about that, as you might guess. Len"—he gestured toward the dead man—"was our Hamlet."

"Tough break," she observed, scribbling a note. "Now, let's go over everything that happened this morning leading up to finding the body, starting with the gentleman's full name."

Between me and Harry, we gave the sheriff a rehash of what we'd told Dr. Bishop a few minutes earlier. Despite that odd flash of suspicion that had swept over me at the beginning, I had no real reason to think there was anything nefarious about Len's death. Thus I refrained from mentioning that he wasn't the most popular member of the troupe. You know, the old *no speaking ill of the dead* rule that had been drilled into most of us since childhood.

Once we'd covered the high points, Lamb asked, "And did Mr. Marsh give any indication of feeling unwell at any time since he arrived here?"

I shook my head. "Not that I recall. Though he did have a previous knee injury that was giving him trouble. In fact, I had to turn my parlor into a guest room for him, as he was having difficulty managing the stairs."

She frowned. "Do you happen to know if Mr. Marsh was taking any medication for the pain?"

"I think Susie—that's his wife—said something about pills. Right, Harry?"

The actor nodded. "No clue what he was taking, but I'm sure Susie can show you any bottles."

"And Ms. Fleet, did you serve anything unusual for breakfast—something that could have caused an allergic reaction, like strawberries or peanut butter?"

"It was all the usual breakfasts foods I always serve my guests. Quiches and breakfast burritos and pastries and so on. The only thing slightly unusual were the peach mimosas."

Then, when the sheriff gave me a quizzical look, I explained, "They're basically the same thing as your garden-variety mimosa, except you substitute half the orange juice with peach juice before adding the champagne. Oh, and you drizzle a bit of grenadine on top."

By then, Dr. Bishop had finished up with the EMTs. The sheriff excused herself momentarily, and the pair exchanged a few private words while Harry and I pretended we were simply hanging out in the garden on a summer's morning.

Finally, with a regal wave in my direction—Harry, apparently, still being in the older man's bad book despite the protestations about grudges—the Reverend took his leave. Then it was time for the paramedics to head out. While half of them collected their scattered gear, the remaining EMTs slid Len onto their lowered gurney. Raising it up again, they blanketed and strapped the man in for the journey to wherever it was in Cymbeline they kept decedents, to use Dr. Bishop's favorite word,

"I'm not sure why I'm so upset," I admitted, dabbing my sleeve against my damp eyes while we watched the crew wheel Len away. "I mean, it's awful that Len is dead, but it's not like I knew him that well. I'd only met him yesterday."

"Hey, you're human," Lamb assured me, sounding pretty darned human herself at that moment. "Plus it's a shock any time you stumble across a body, especially for a civilian. And no matter what the old-time cops might tell you, it never gets easier. Believe me, there's nothing scarier than coming face-to-face with mortality, even if it isn't your own."

Then, getting back to business, she closed her notebook.

"I think I've got everything we need out here. If you don't mind showing me inside, I want to chat with Mr. Marsh's wife to find out what medications her husband was taking so I can pass on that info to the coroner to give to the ME. Unfortunately, we can't release his body until after the autopsy is done. But from the look of things, chances are it was a pretty straightforward cardiac event. Hopefully we'll have a cause of death determined pretty quickly."

As Deputy Mullins headed off to his own cruiser, I escorted the sheriff inside. Harry followed after. I could hear what I assumed were Susie's faint wails drifting from the direction of the dining room. Either Marvin hadn't found the cognac, or it hadn't taken effect yet.

We paused outside the closed dining-room door, and I turned to the sheriff. "Why don't I go in first and warn her that you need to ask a few questions?"

At her curt nod, I gave a quick rap at the door and then slipped inside.

I found Susie slumped in her usual chair, still crying while pressing one of my mid-century tea towels against her mouth as a makeshift handkerchief. Marvin sat in the chair next to her, silently patting her free hand and looking distinctly uncomfortable. A snifter of cognac a couple of fingers full sat untouched before her.

I grimaced as I envisioned the elbow grease it would take to remove pink lipstick from vintage linen, but that wasn't the issue at the moment. Gently, I said, "Susie, the sheriff is here. She needs to ask you a few questions about Len's medications."

She made a snuffling sound that I took for assent, so I leaned back out the door and gestured Sheriff Lamb inside.

I saw her give the skull a quizzical look, but all she said was: "My condolences, Mrs. Marsh. I know this is a terrible time, but I really need to ask you a couple of questions for the coroner. Are you up to that?"

Susie nodded. Then, as Marvin rose to leave, she grabbed his hand and pulled him back into the chair. "No, wait," she choked out. "Can't Marvin stay with me?"

The sheriff nodded her approval, so I left the three of them and rejoined Harry in the hallway. While earlier his expression had been mildly disconcerted, he now wore a look of calculation that, in my brief acquaintanceship with him, usually boded no good.

I gave him a stern look of my own. "What are you planning?"

"I'm planning on saving the day," was his airy reply. "I've come up with the perfect solution to our Len dilemma. The show *will* go on."

"So what's the brilliant solution?"

"Let's just say I know someone who knows Hamlet's part intimately and has the looks and stage presence to pull it off."

Something told me that I knew just who this "someone" was. But since the B&B bill was already paid, it mattered naught to me, as the Bard might say, who took that role. My concern at this point was doing what I could to help the authorities make a swift determination as to why Len Marsh had died on my watch.

"So, do you think Susie will want to stay here with the rest of you until they release Len's . . . er, Len? Or does she maybe have some family who can come get her?"

"Good question. I'll talk to her once Connie leaves and find out for sure. The only relatives I've heard her mention are in California, so the troupe is probably the nearest thing she has to a family. Unless she's close to any of Len's folks, but from some of the comments I've heard her make in the past, I kind of suspect not."

I nodded. The whole "young trophy wife hated by the older husband's family and friends" was a cliché for a good reason.

"Keep me posted," I told him. "I'm assuming rehearsals are cancelled for the rest of the day. If I can help you with anything, let me know."

"I appreciate that," he replied, sounding as if he actually did. "Maybe you wouldn't mind running upstairs and seeing how everyone else is doing."

I nodded, since I also needed to retrieve Mattie from wherever Radney and Chris had taken her. Leaving Harry outside the dining-room door, I headed upstairs. Bypassing the room where Susie was staying—packing up Len's things from the parlor was probably going to fall to me—I rapped at Tessa and Bill's open door and poked my head inside.

"How are you two holding up"

They'd been sitting on the bed near each other, backs to the door and heads tilted toward each other, whispering together like a couple of teens. At my question, they both whipped about with oddly guilty expressions.

"Oh, hello, Nina," Tessa said. "Bill and I were just discussing the, ahem, situation. This was quite unexpected. I fear we haven't quite taken it in yet."

"I think we're all in shock," I agreed, a bit surprised to see no obvious show of grief from them. While Marvin might have been wrong about Susie, maybe he'd been right that the troupe wouldn't care if Len permanently exited stage right.

Then Bill frowned. "I wonder how this will impact the festival. The show must go on, as they say. Perhaps I should remind Harry that I know Hamlet's lines up and down, and would be happy to fill in for our deceased cast member."

"I'm sure Harry has a backup plan," I replied, resisting the temptation to repeat Harry's comment about a geriatric Hamlet. "He's going to talk with Susie as soon as the sheriff leaves. She won't be able to take Len's body back to Atlanta until after the autopsy, so I'm not sure yet if she'll stay here at the B&B until then."

The pair nodded their understanding.

"It would make better sense for her to stay here," Tessa opined. "It would do her no good to go home to an empty house. At least here she'll have something to distract her."

"And she'll have us for moral support," Bill added, surprising me in light of the lack of concern he'd just shown for Len. Though maybe it was easier to care about a pretty young widow than it was that widow's late spouse.

I left the pair and headed to the next room, which was the one Radney and Marvin shared. The door was closed, so I gave a polite knock. Radney answered a moment later, cell phone to one ear. He gestured me inside, giving me the "wait one" raised finger as he finished his call, his end of the conversation consisting mostly of a few "uh-huhs" and an "I'll let you know" before he hung up.

"Sorry, Nina. I took the liberty of calling the office and telling Len's executive assistant what happened. I didn't want Susie to have to do that."

"That's kind of you. I'm sure she'll appreciate your thoughtfulness."

"Yeah, well, talk about that being the least I could do."

He dropped onto one of the twin beds, swiping his free hand over his bald head as he sat there and gave me a helpless look.

"I'm kind of surprised how hard this is. I didn't much like the guy, but I've worked with him for years at the day job. And then there's all that time spent with troupe. I mean, an hour ago we were all sitting at the same table, talking, and now . . ."

I nodded as he trailed off. Radney, at least, recognized that a man had just died. They might not have been friends, but there was that decent acknowledgment of a fellow being's passing that had been lacking with Bill and Tessa.

I repeated to Radney what little I knew so far. He nodded, and then asked, "What about the festival? We're not canceling the play, are we?"

And just when he'd risen to the top of my good guy list.

I tried not to roll my eyes. Was there something about actors, amateur and pro alike, that made them so single-minded? Though, in fairness to the GASPers, the festival was a pretty big deal to the town. Looking at it from that angle, it spoke well for the players that they seemed willing to soldier on.

"I think Harry has a backup plan for the performance. I'm sure he'll summon everyone later with an update." Then, changing the subject, I asked, "So, what did you and Chris do with Mattie?"

"Last I saw, the kid took your pup to his room . . . you know, for comfort or something."

"Yeah, she's pretty good about making a person feel better. I'll go talk to him next."

I left him scrolling through his phone, presumably for the numbers of more people to notify, and headed for Chris's room. Of all the GASPers, he was the one I worried most about right now . . . besides Susie, of course. I'd admired how he'd been the only member of the group who had tried to help Len. But chances were he'd never seen anyone dead before—at least, not unless they were already neatly laid out in an expensive casket surrounded by flower arrangements. But an up close and personal view of the body of a man he knew had to have been traumatic.

"Chris," I called through the closed door as I gave a quick rap. "It's Nina. Do you have Mattie in there with you?"

The only response was a muffled bark from the Aussie. Concerned, I twisted the knob and peered inside.

As on the day before, he was stretched out on one of the two twin beds, earbuds in and head propped on pillows as he stared at his phone. The oversized glasses lay on the bed beside him, his bare face looking even younger and more vulnerable. Mattie sat at his feet, chin on paws, as she turned an inquiring look from me back to the youth.

Ignoring the whole shoes on the clean bedspread thing, I asked, "Chris, are you all right? Chris? *Chris*?"

That last word was almost a shout. Apparently, it was loud enough to pierce the volume coming from his earbuds. He turned in my direction and plucked one out, then sighed. "Yeah?"

So much for vulnerable. After his valiant efforts on Len's behalf earlier, I'd expected to find him prostrate with grief. Or at least suitably sad. Instead, he had the resigned look of someone who was being disturbed in the middle of a crucial round of Candy Crush or whatever the game du jour was.

Frowning a little, I said, "Sorry to intrude, but I was looking for Mattie."

"You told us to keep her inside while the paramedics were here, so I figured this was the best place. Sorry if that wasn't okay."

"No, that was just fine. And the paramedics are gone." Then, when he continued to stare, I went on, "The sheriff is talking to Susie right now."

This comment sparked a look of interest. Plucking out the other earbud, the youth fixed me with a wide-eyed look. "Sheriff? Why is he here? They don't think someone killed Len, do they?"

I stared right back. Why would Chris, of all people, jump to such a conclusion? Sure, I'd wondered the exact same thing, but for all of fifteen seconds.

"She," I reflexively corrected the pronoun. "And not as far as I know. Sheriff Lamb needs information about any medication Len was taking. Since it was an unexpected death"—I refrained from giving the words finger quotes—"the coroner has called for an autopsy, just in case."

He shrugged, the stare gone. "I suppose that makes sense. Still, you know how it goes. Old people die all the time."

Old? Len was in his mid-fifties, which made him not much more than a dozen years older than me. Which in Chris's world probably put me into the decrepit category too.

But before I could educate the kid about the realities of aging, he brightened and added, "Maybe now Harry will let *me* play Hamlet."

Another contender.

I sighed and patted my leg to summon Mattie, who promptly slipped off the bed and joined me. As I turned to the door, I remarked, "I'm sure Harry has a plan in mind. I'll let him know you're up here when he's ready to call a troupe meeting."

But Chris had already stuck the earbuds back in his ears, effectively tuning me out. Shaking my head, I left the room. While Mattie padded with me down the hall, I mulled over the conversation I'd just had with the youth.

Back in the garden, Chris had seemed understandably upset by what had happened. Just as quickly, he had resumed his *too cool for school* 'tude, only to then wonder, like me, if Len's death was something other than an accident.

I shook my head. Probably, like me, he watched too many cop shows on TV.

"Not my circus, not my monkeys," I reminded myself.

Instead, it was time to revert to my role as innkeeper. I would check in with Harry and see what Susie's plans were. Then, assuming I wasn't needed elsewhere, later today I would take on the sad task of packing Len's things that remained in the parlor.

Chapter Eleven

The morning had dragged on interminably once Sheriff Lamb had finished talking with Susie. I ran into Marvin in the upstairs hallway right after a pizza lunch that I'd called in for the troupe, my treat. I was bringing up extra towels. He was leaving Susie's room, stealthily closing the door after him. Catching sight of me, he gave what appeared to be a guilty start.

"I was just checking in on Susie again," he said, though the flush in his cheeks seem to indicate that something more might have been transpiring besides friendly comforting. "She's still pretty upset, so I thought another swig of that fancy cognac might help her. I left the bottle in there with her. I hope that's okay."

"Sure. And it probably wouldn't hurt for us to take turns making sure she's all right," I replied, charitably ignoring the fact that his breath now held a distinct whiff of said fancy cognac.

He nodded as we started down the stairs together.

"I guess Spielberg, er, Harry already told you that she's staying here for the duration?"

"Yes, I talked to Harry about it before lunch. It's probably good that she does stay at the B&B. Any arrangements that need to be made I'm sure she can handle by phone or Internet. And in the meantime, she's got all of us for support."

Marvin snorted.

"Well, she ain't getting it from anyone else. Right now she's worried that Len's people are going to swoop in and take the house and all the cash. She said they had a pre-nup, but all them Marshes are just like him . . . a bunch of hyenas. That's why she hasn't notified the family yet. *Let 'em read it in the obits*, is what she told me."

I winced. On the one hand, I could understand that attitude if the in-law dynamics were as toxic as Marvin indicated. On the other . . . well, it was pretty brutal not to let family members know that one of theirs was dead.

Circus. Monkeys. The reminder drifted through my mind, enabling me to refrain from commenting.

Once downstairs, I left Marvin on the shaded front porch with a glass of iced tea from the big jug in my refrigerator. Earlier, Radney, Tessa, and Bill had called for an Uber and gone down to the square for a look around.

"Harry gave us the day off," Tessa had explained. "There's not much else for us to do except sit around and mope."

Which made sense. That left Chris still closeted in his room, with Harry, I assumed, upstairs in the tower room. With everyone out of the way, I'd put up what was left of the pizza and do the dishes. Later, I'd tackle packing Len's things.

Cleanup didn't take long, though I spent a few extra minutes inventorying my champagnes flutes that had held the breakfast mimosas. Sure enough, one was missing. I was positive I remembered seeing Len carry off his glass after breakfast, but I didn't recall noticing it on the patio or in the garden. Unless he'd set it down in the hallway on his way out, it had to be somewhere in the backyard.

Suddenly feeling compelled to find the missing glass, I tossed aside my dish towel and headed for the backyard.

Mattie followed me out into the summer heat. Somewhat to my surprise, we found Harry there, lounging on one of the patio benches. As usual, it felt at least ten degrees cooler in the shade, and even cooler with the slight breeze, meaning it wasn't crazy for him to be taking in the afternoon there.

He too had a glass of iced tea in hand. Yorick sat beside him . . . if a skull could be said to sit. I was glad to see that the cigarette was gone.

"Sharing a little quality time with your friend?" I asked with a smile.

Harry shrugged. "Yorick tends to keep his thoughts to himself. The only way I'll get any intelligent conversation is if you care to join us."

Feeling oddly complimented by this, my smile broadened. That was, until I recalled what I was doing out there.

"Actually, I'm on a scavenger hunt. You didn't see one of my champagne glasses out here, did you? I think Len carried his outside with him, and with everything that's happened, it's kind of disappeared."

"I'll help you look. Why don't we start in the Shakespeare garden? I'll take the east side, and you can take the west."

I nodded my agreement. Harry gave his bony buddy a pat on his smooth head, leaving the skull where it sat. Mattie gave it a curious sniff. Then, apparently deciding she preferred his silent company to ours, she flopped down on the bricks beside the bench. Her one blue eye and one brown eye watched us with lazy interest as we began our search.

The obvious place to look was any level surface in the garden—a stone, a short wall—that might have made a makeshift shelf. After a few minutes of fruitless searching, however, I brushed away the sweat dripping into my eyes and shook my head.

"I don't see anything. Maybe he still was holding it when he collapsed, so that would mean out there in the yard somewhere."

We took the two steps down through the garden gap to the backyard proper. The gash in the hedges where Len had landed stuck out like the proverbial sore thumb. Moreover, now I could see ruts in the grass near the drive where the gurney had been wheeled in and out. Hendricks would *not* like any of that at all.

"Hendricks is *not* going to like this," Harry echoed my concern. Then, when I looked at him in surprise, he clarified, "That old geezer was doing Aunt Lathrop's gardening back when *I* was a kid. I can't believe he conned you into keeping him on."

"Since I garden about as well as I cook, I figured it was worth the aggravation to keep the grounds up to your great-aunt's standards."

He looked a little surprised at that last, but nodded.

"Thanks for that. Hendricks can fill in the ruts with sand, and in a couple of months no one will see the damage. The hawthorn will be harder, but he'll figure something out."

"Speaking of which, we should probably try looking in the hedges first," I suggested. "I didn't smell cigarette smoke this morning, so Len probably never made it as far as the smoking area."

Harry nodded and knelt to one side of the broken hedges, leaving me to the other. Gingerly, because I hadn't forgotten Dr. Bishop's comment about snakebite, I parted branches and fished about within the leaves, looking for a glint of glass. I rousted a couple of mosquitoes and a shiny black beetle with my efforts, but saw nothing resembling the missing glass.

"Any luck?" I called to Harry a minute later.

"Nothing yet. And be careful. The glass might have broken when he dropped it. You don't want to slice your hand open."

I crawled a bit deeper into the bushes, aware that I was doing more damage but certain Hendricks wouldn't know the difference between the earlier breakage and the new. By morning, all the broken branches and stems would sport equally brown leaves and drying blooms. And if the old man complained about it too much, I'd simply give him a lecture on . . .

A glint of orangey light above where I was crawling caught my attention and cut short my mental scolding.

"I found it!" I cried as I spied the intact champagne flute suspended like a Christmas ornament between two hawthorn branches. Even more improbably, a good half-inch of peach mimosa remained in the flute's narrow bowl. "Give me hand, would you?"

While Harry gripped my free arm for balance, I carefully extracted the glass from the tangle and then stood. "Just needs a good washing," I said in satisfaction. But as I started to dump out the remaining liquid from the glass, I noticed something else.

"Harry, come back here, would you?" I said, as the actor had already started up the steps toward the garden again. "Does this look odd to you?"

I raised the champagne flute once more, this time indicating a small line of dried residue on the glassware's inner surface. Harry took the glass from me, squinted at it, then shrugged.

"Looks like some junk fell into it . . . probably pollen," he replied and handed back the flute. "That or it's just dried peach nectar."

"I don't think it's pollen," I countered, taking another look. "And in all the times I've made my peach mimosas, I've never seen this happen before. It almost looks like some sort of dried powder."

The actor gave me a considering look. "What are you trying to say, Nina?"

"I —I'm not sure."

To be more accurate, I had a good idea of what I wanted to say but, unlike Chris, I didn't yet dare voice it aloud. I distinctly remembered looking at every single flute before I'd mixed the mimosas. Whatever else was in the glass now had to have been introduced after I'd served it to Len.

The question was, what was "it"? And how had it gotten into Len's glass?

Before I could take my internal theorizing any further, Harry spoke up again.

"All right, here's another possibility. What if Len was washing down one of his pain pills with your mimosa at the exact moment he had his heart attack, or whatever? Maybe he spit his meds back into his glass before he collapsed, and the pill dissolved in what was left of the mimosa while the glass was baking out here."

Relief that swept through me.

"Harry, you're brilliant!" I told him, and meaning it . . . at least, in this particular instance. "Your explanation makes perfect sense. If that residue isn't pollen, then that's probably what it is, one of Len's pills."

And not something else. Not something more sinister slipped into his glass by some unknown person.

"Good. So now you can wash that glass with a clear conscience."

"Are you kidding? It's still evidence. I've got to turn it over to someone."

Harry's features tightened in disapproval.

"Seriously? Take it from an actor, Nina. You don't want to go around drumming up drama if you're not getting paid for it. Wash the glass, and be sure you send a nice flower arrangement to Len's memorial service."

"Seriously?" I echoed, shooting him a disbelieving look. "Don't you think I—we—owe it to Len to make sure the cause of his death is thoroughly investigated? I couldn't sleep nights know I'd destroyed what could be crucial evidence."

"Or what could be pollen."

Then his expression thawed slightly. "I'll give you that much. If I kicked off unexpectedly, I'd want someone like you in my corner to make sure everything was on the up-and-up. So maybe we can bag that glass and drop it off to Connie in the morning."

I shook my head and reached into my T-shirt pocket for the business card that the Reverend Doctor Bishop had given me that morning.

"Actually, I should bring it to Dr. Bishop, since he's the coroner. Besides, I have a feeling he'll be a little more open to checking it out. I'm sure he can get the residue tested."

Harry gave a wry chuckle. "If his setup is anything like when I worked there, he can probably do it right there, without waiting weeks for a toxicology test. His basement is like a mad scientist's lair. Scary as all get-out."

"So that means you'll go there with me tomorrow?" I asked in a hopeful voice.

He shook his head.

"Not a chance. We're starting up rehearsals first thing in the morning. Plus I'll have to start damage control with Professor Joy and the SOCS committee tomorrow, as they'll probably have heard about Len by then. We don't want panic in the streets with folks worrying that the festival won't have its play."

Then, as visions of Cymbeline's populous rioting on the square demanding more Shakespeare flashed through my mind, he added, "Besides, I'm only agreeing with you to humor you. I'm pretty sure you're going to find out whatever is in there is pollen or moth wings or something equally unexciting.

"I hope so," I replied.

Heck, whatever was in the drink could be eye of newt or toe of frog for all I cared, just as long as Len's autopsy came back as death by natural causes.

Chapter Twelve

You have reached the voice mail of the Reverend Doctor Thaddeus Bishop, pastor of the Heavenly Host Baptist Church and owner of the Heavenly Path Funeral Home and Crematorium. If you are in the midst of a spiritual crisis, press one. If you wish to secure our funeral services for you or your loved one's final journey, press two. If you have other business to conduct, you may press three.

The dulcet tones in the recorded message were that of the good Reverend. I went with choice number three and listened.

Thank you for contacting the Reverend Doctor Thaddeus Bishop, the same velvety voice continued. *If you are calling on a Sunday, please be aware that I do not conduct any business not of a spiritual nature on the Lord's Day. If you are a telemarketer or are attempting a telephone scam, you might as well hang up now, as the ongoing burden of my duties does not allow time for such nonsense. If, however, you have a legitimate need to converse with me, please leave your name and phone number and the nature of your business after the tone. May the Lord bless you.*

I smiled a little at the blunt wording, wishing I dared put a similar warning to scammers on my own business line. But for now I waited for the beep and then began recording.

"Hello, Dr. Bishop. This is Nina Fleet. We met at my B&B this morning when you came here to—"

I hesitated, not sure how to put it tactfully. *To declare a man dead* was a bit too straightforward. *To perform your coroner's duties* was a bit too formal.

"—to assist with Mr. Marsh," I settled on. "I wanted to let you know that earlier this afternoon I found the champagne flute he'd been drinking from before he died, and there appears to be some unusual residue on the glass. I thought it might be important to your investigation. I'd like to bring the glass by tomorrow sometime before lunch, if that's all right."

I repeated my name and left my cell-phone number, then hung up. Mattie, who was sprawled belly-down on my bed, lifted her head and gave me a quizzical look

"Everything's taken care of, girl."

Still, I couldn't help glancing over to my dresser, where the glass in question currently sat in one of those resealable plastic bags. The bag, in turn, I'd slipped into an empty potato-chip canister. The packaging served the dual purpose of protecting the glass from damage and disguising it from prying eyes. Not that it had been difficult to get Harry's promise to keep my errand on the down low.

Don't worry, I refuse to stir up the troupe more than they already are, had been his exact words. *And please don't say anything to Susie about the glass. She's already enough of a basket case as it is.*

Deliberately, I turned my attention back to Mattie.

"It's after six," I told the pup. "Come on, let's get some supper. And guess what? We've got the place to ourselves for the next couple of hours."

Around five, Radney and the Benedicts had made a triumphant return from their venture to the town square with a fistful of fliers from various local restaurants offering pre-festival specials. While Susie, via Marvin, had declared herself not up to leaving her room, the remaining troupe members had been eager for distraction after the day's tragedy.

Harry, I was pleased to see, had encouraged the expedition. He'd even deigned to join it—this despite the fact that he was a professed vegetarian and the final choice of eatery had been Brutus Burgers (which, contrary to its name, was probably Cymbeline's best casual steakhouse).

Since it would be dark by the time they'd be finished with their meal—and, thus, somewhat cooler—they had elected to brave the remaining late afternoon heat and walk the three blocks back to the square rather than try to squeeze into a single Uber. Before they left, Marvin had tried to persuade me to join them.

"C'mon, Number Nine. You deserve a night out too," he'd cajoled, finding me in the kitchen making up a couple more batches of cold brewed tea for the next day. "I'll buy."

"Thanks. It's tempting," I had replied, "but I wouldn't feel right leaving Susie all alone here."

"Suit yourself," he said with a shrug. Then, with a sly little grin, he'd added, "I guess you don't scare easy, do you?"

I set down the gallon jug I'd just filled with tea leaves and cool water and gave him a questioning look. "Not really. Why?"

He grinned. "Knowing Len, he'll probably be a jerk even in the afterlife. I can just picture him pulling a 'ghost of Hamlet's dad' on us. You know, wailing around out in the garden after dark."

"Thanks, Marv," had been my wry reply. "If Len does show up, I'll be sure to remind him where your room is so he can do his wailing there."

But, probably as he'd intended, Marvin's joke had stuck in my head. Though it was still full daylight out, the house's main hallway at this time of day was shadowy even with the lights on. I told myself I was being foolish, but I couldn't help shivering as I glanced toward the back door that led out to the garden. While I wasn't superstitious in that way, I had to admit I was glad of Mattie's stoic company as we headed to the kitchen.

I scooped Mattie's food and gave her fresh water; then, as she crunched away, I pulled out the fixings for some chicken salad on lettuce for me. As I chopped and diced, I deliberately made some extra for Susie. Not that she'd yet shown any interest in eating. Radney had brought her a slice of veggie pizza at lunchtime, which had gone untouched. And mid-afternoon, I'd gone up to her room with bottled drinks and healthy snacks in case she needed a little something.

"Thanks, Nina, but I just can't think about food right now," had been her tearful response when I'd left the tray inside her darkened room. "I'm going to take one of my pills and nap for a while."

121

With that in mind, I refrigerated her portion of the salad for later. Then, opening the radio app on my phone to a New Age channel and pouring myself a glass of boxed white wine, I pulled up one of the barstools for a casual meal at the kitchen island. By now Mattie had finished her own supper and lay at my feet as I ate. Her motivation, I knew, was not so much affection as the fervent doggie hope that I'd spill a bit of chicken salad onto the linoleum floor.

"Don't worry, girl," I told her, slipping off one shoe to give her a little massage on the rump with my toes. "I'll save the last bite for you."

As I chewed and listened to the music, I realized that this was the first chance I'd had to catch my breath since morning. Which also meant I had a few minutes to think about the ramifications of what had happened today. For now it was dawning on me that I, too, likely needed to do a bit of damage control on behalf of my business.

By now, news of Len's death likely had spread around town, helped by the ubiquitous online neighborhood network platform that was growing in popularity in even as small a burg as Cymbeline. Of course, Harry had already said that he would be the one to assure the Shakespeare festival committee that all was well despite the unfortunate loss of one of the troupe's members.

My situation was different. A man had died on my property, hopefully of natural causes. But no matter the cause, potential guests might well shy away from Fleet House because of that.

"Darn you, Len Marsh," I muttered, and then immediately felt guilty. I would recover from this figurative bump in my life road, but obviously Len . . . and to a lesser degree, Susie . . . would not.

I stifled a groan. I needed advice from my friend and fellow business owner Gemma. After I paid my visit to Dr. Bishop tomorrow, I'd drop by Peaches and Java to see what she suggested.

Feeling better now I had a plan of action, I gave Mattie her promised bite and then let her out into her side yard to take care of business. While she did her sniffing and wandering, I went back to the kitchen for a quick cleanup. A coffee-cake muffin was left over from that morning's breakfast, so I grabbed it along with a refill on my wine. I'd enjoy my dessert on the front porch, at least until the mosquitoes came out.

But as I left the kitchen again and started for the front door, I saw something new. A sliver of light shone beneath the closed door of the parlor . . . the same room where Len had spent his last night. Moreover, I could hear what sounded like a murmur of voices from behind that closed door.

I shivered again.

Darn you, Marvin, and your ghost of Hamlet's father!

Rationally, I knew that at least one of the troupe had to have returned early, though what they were doing in the parlor, I couldn't guess. Setting down my muffin and wine on the hallway table, I quietly moved toward that closed door, ears straining as I tried to figure out who was talking—and to whom. For a few seconds, it was quiet again. Then the conversation resumed, this time louder and sharper.

"I don't care, Ralph. The minute the market opens tomorrow, sell that stock and roll it into my personal account before anyone knows he's dead."

The unmistakable sound of Susie's voice drifted from beneath the parlor's closed doors. I halted there, hand on knob, and unashamedly listened for more. But apparently I'd caught the tail end of the discussion with this unknown Ralph—*Banker? Broker? Personal assistant?*—because I heard a final, *You do that*, and then silence again.

I frowned. Susie obviously was over her nap . . . and, it seemed, over her grieving. So much for the prostrate Widow Marsh that Marvin had spent the afternoon comforting. In fact, this was a whole new Susie Marsh. Or was it?

Feeling an unexpected flash of righteous indignation on Len's behalf, I threw open the door and stepped inside.

Chapter Thirteen

"Oh!"
"Oh!"

Susie Marsh's startled reaction was genuine . . . mine, not so much. Still, I made a show of gasping and throwing up my hands.

As for Susie, she had spun about from leaning over an old-style briefcase that was open on the cot. Catching sight of me, she stared with eyes and mouth wide, the morning's pink lipstick long since worn off. Then she quickly twisted about to shut the briefcase's lid. When she turned back toward me again, both hands were pressed over her ample breasts as she gave a choked laugh.

"Oh, my goodness, Nina, you scared the heck out of me. I thought you'd gone out with the others."

"You scared me, too," I replied, somewhat truthfully. "I thought you were still asleep upstairs. I wasn't going to leave you alone in the house, and I thought I'd pack up Len's things so you didn't have to do it yourself. But it looks like you beat me to it."

Susie nodded and glanced around the parlor where Len's belongings still were neatly strewn about.

"I—I was just getting started. I knew Len wouldn't want any-one but me going through his things. I mean, he'd have been embarrassed to know someone else was packing his unmentionables."

"Actually, that's one of the innkeeper's unofficial duties, gath-ering up whatever a guest leaves behind," I told her. "I'd be glad to finish if you want to go back upstairs and lie down again."

"Oh, heck no! I couldn't stand another minute in that horrible room."

Then, realizing what she'd said, she clarified, "No offense, Nina, it's really quite lovely, but you know what I mean. I felt like the walls were closing in on me. I had to do . . . something."

At that, she slumped onto the corner of the cot and buried her face in her hands, body shaking with suppressed sobs. Suddenly feeling guilty for my earlier judgmental lapse, I promptly sat beside her and gave her a comforting pat on the back.

"I can't guess how hard this is for you," I told her, "but I under-stand needing to keep busy when something terrible shakes up your life."

"You're right," she wailed through her fingers, "but it's not just that. I'm having to do financial stuff that I don't know anything about, just to make sure I don't end up on the streets before the estate is settled. I called one of Len's money managers a minute ago, and he treated me like I don't know anything . . . which I guess I don't!"

That last ended on another wail. Not that she'd sounded help-less on the phone from what I'd overheard, but then I hadn't been privy to the full conversation.

"Why don't you go ahead and finish packing," I suggested, "and in the meantime I'll bring you some homemade chicken salad since you missed lunch. And when you finish getting everything rounded up, I can help you carry it upstairs to your room if you like."

Susie lifted her tear-stained face from her hands and managed a quavering smile. "Oh, Nina, that would be nice. Both the chicken salad and the help."

I left her to resume packing and went back to the kitchen, returning a few minutes later with the promised meal. As for the conversation I'd overheard, I dismissed it once I recalled something similar from when my ex–father-in-law had passed away. His body hadn't even been cold before my then mother-in-law had hurried off to the bank and emptied their safe deposit box.

She'd explained later that the bank would have frozen even that joint asset upon learning of her husband's death. That, in turn, would have meant she'd be unable to access their stashed cash and other items like their passports for some time. Especially with a pre-nup in place, Susie was probably simply being prudent in making sure she had access to sufficient funds while the lawyers and government got their ducks in a row.

With Susie temporarily settled, I retrieved my abandoned muffin and wine and finally headed outside. As the mosquitoes had already begun their assault, I bypassed the hanging swing near the front door. Instead, I barricaded myself inside the screened porch off my room, where I'd recently added a lighted ceiling fan to make the spot more conducive to evening use.

But that wasn't the only upgrade I'd made. In a nod to Georgia tradition, I'd also repainted the ceilings of all the porches haint blue. The practice dated to the early nineteenth century, originating with the African slaves who believed the sky-blue color warded off unwelcome spirits from a home. These days, the superstition part of the practice had given way to simple Southern custom. I grimaced. Hopefully, it still would work on Len should the man decide to make a ghostly curtain call.

Mattie joined me, happily catching a few muffin crumbs tossed her way before settling at my feet. Meanwhile, I finished my wine and made progress on a paperback mystery I'd left out there for downtime moments like this.

So absorbed in my book was I that I didn't realize darkness had fallen. In fact, I didn't look up until the sound of a drunken chorus drifted to me from the street. With Mattie barking an accompaniment, I set down my novel and hurried out the screened door to the main porch. Then, grinning and gesturing Mattie to follow, I started down the dimly lit front walk toward the sidewalk.

The returning troupe was singing what sounded like sea chanties, based on a few bellowed *yars* and *heigh-hos*. My grin broadened. While not exactly the repertoire I'd have expected from a Shakespeare troupe, doubtless this was the closest they could come, given a likely limited Elizabethan songbook. The pirate tune ended as they reached the front gate, the final notes followed by laughter and a few drunken cheers.

"Let's get inside," I told them, opening the gate and waving the players in the direction of the front door. "We don't want the neighbors complaining, and I'm sure Harry will want to get an early start tomorrow with rehearsals. Besides"—I paused and slapped at my arms—"another couple of minutes and we'll all get bled dry by mosquitoes."

"Not me," Marvin chortled, loud enough to be heard all the way down at Peaches and Java. "Heck, I've got enough booze in me to drop any mosquito that tries to bite me in its tracks."

"Me, too!" Radney bellowed. He threw his beefy arms around Bill and Tessa in what was more a headlock than a hug, though from the pair's sloppy grins they apparently were fine with his manhandling.

Chris trailed behind them, carrying what appeared to be the remains of a large, whipped cream–covered ice cream sundae. I smiled, knowing this was the closest the youth could get to over-indulgence, as he wasn't old enough to drink. Though if he managed to finished the whole thing, the sugar high would likely rival the buzz the adults in the group were feeling.

Harry brought up the rear, along with Mattie. I held the door open for them both. Then, while the rest of the troupe dispersed to their rooms, I turned to the actor.

"Looks like everyone had a good time. Do you think they'll be up to going through with the play?"

He nodded. "We had a few nice toasts to Len, then gossiped about him and Susie a while before eating the best that Cymbeline has to offer . . . not counting Daniel and Gemma's breakfasts, of course. I'm pretty sure everyone is going to regret it in the morning, but they're not feeling any pain right now."

"What about you?" I asked, since it appeared to me that he'd not indulged like the rest of them.

He raised a brow. "You mean pain? Don't worry, Nina, I'm fine. Now, do you mind rustling up a big pot of boiling water? I'm going to make everyone drink a cup of rooibos before they go to sleep. Detox, you know."

I went to the kitchen and put on my largest kettle, then pulled down a stack of cups and saucers that I left there on the counter. The rest was on Harry, I thought with a grin. I'd tried his rooibos tea last time he stayed at the B&B and had not been a fan. My guess was his troupe wouldn't be either.

Leaving the kitchen, I made a stop by the parlor. I found the room empty when I flipped on the overhead light, though Len's luggage sat neatly in one corner. I'd strip the cot and store it away in the morning, I told myself. But recalling my promise to Susie, I hauled the luggage upstairs.

As I could hear the unmistakable sound of snoring from within—apparently, she'd finally taken one of her pills—I left the suitcases outside her door and then headed back downstairs to my room. It was barely nine, but given the exhausting day I was ready to make an early night of it. Besides, I'd likely need to brew double the usual amount of coffee come morning if there was to be any hope of keeping the troupe awake for that day's rehearsals.

I checked my phone once I got to my room and saw that the good reverend had returned my earlier call. His voice message indicated that I should stop by the church office any time after nine AM and ask Sister Malthea to track him down. Perfect. And then, to quote Radney, it was lights out the minute my head hit the pillow.

Chapter Fourteen

"Number Nine, you got any more coffee? We about drained this pot."

Marvin held his head in one hand and waved an empty coffee cup with the other, looking as green as the pale plaid of his shirt. Tessa, Bill, and Radney appeared to be similarly suffering, drooped over their respective breakfast plates, which this morning were conspicuously empty.

Chris, however, had no such problem. Radney gave a dramatic groan as the youth sauntered past with what I guessed was a deliberately overflowing collection of burritos and quiches on his plate. Taking a seat, he began stuffing himself while the others queasily keep their gaze averted from him.

As I'd expected coffee would be in high demand this morning, I already had another insulated carafe of fresh brew ready, with yet another backup pot at the ready. I brought in the refill and, since the coffee drinkers all looked too weak to manage it themselves, grandly refilled everyone's cups.

Harry, of course, had his usual tea in lieu of coffee. He looked none the worse for the previous night's outing. I didn't know if it was because he hadn't indulged at supper to the same extent as the others, or if his rooibos tea was really the miracle beverage he claimed it to be. Yorick was in his familiar spot in front of Harry's plate, also looking relatively rested.

As for myself, I had slept surprisingly well. Even so, I'd barely made it out of the shower in time to throw on white jeans and a jaunty blue-and-white striped boatneck top to answer the door for Jasmine at seven.

Not that I could have overslept. Harry had made sure that everyone was out of bed by seven sharp, channeling his inner drill sergeant with a little door pounding and whistle-blowing to roust everyone. I'd heard the protests issuing from the hungover troupe members all the way downstairs as I got breakfast ready. I'd felt bad for Susie, who I was sure needed the additional rest, but hopefully her sleeping pill had allowed her to snooze through Harry's approximation of reveille.

Now, with everyone's coffee replenished, I poured a cup for myself and loaded up my own breakfast plate. I suspected no one would protest my hanging out with the troupe for a bit. For I was curious to learn if I was correct about how Harry planned to recast the play with the loss of Len.

I didn't have long to wait.

"My lords and ladies," he began with a dramatic flourish of one hand as I took the empty seat on the other side of Marvin, "I need not remind you that we suffered the loss of one of our troupe members yesterday. As we discussed at supper last night, we're all of the opinion that Len would want us to continue on."

"And there *is* the matter of the contract," Tessa broke in, clutching her coffee cup to her kaftan-draped bosom and looking as limp as her drooping gray braid. "Don't forget that."

Harry nodded.

"Tessa is correct. We do have a signed contract with the Shakespeare on Cymbeline Square Committee that commits us to performing for the festival. Breaching that agreement could prove unpleasant for all concerned, so the reality is that we have little choice but to uphold the contract despite our tribulations. But I am confident that the Georgia Amateur Shakespeare Players will rise to the occasion."

That should have been the moment when everyone clapped and huzzahed . . . except that none of the troupe save for Chris looked capable of summoning much more than a nod. Harry obviously realized this, for he quickly moved on.

"To get us back on track," he continued with a tap on Yorick's bony head, "our first step will be recasting Len's role of Hamlet."

"Me, me," Chris promptly piped up, waving his arm as if waiting to be called on in class. "Choose me!"

"Thank you, Chris. I appreciate your enthusiasm," Harry replied with an approving expression, "but we've talked about this before. Maybe next season, when you've got a few more performances under your belt, we can consider a more prominent role for you."

Then, while Chris muttered under his breath, another voice spoke up beside me.

"I'll do it," Marvin said. "I know the part, and it would be a dream come true for me to play Hamlet. Heck, I'll even shave off my whiskers for the role."

I shot Marvin a look of mingled surprise and respect as he stroked the whiskers in question. I knew that sacrificing a beard that had obviously been cultivated for years wasn't something a man did lightly. Then I suppressed a smile. Of course, if he were to play Hamlet, it might take some doing to find princely tights and a doublet that would fit him . . . and that wasn't plaid.

Harry, meanwhile, gave him a considering nod.

"Marvin, your dedication to the play puts many professional actors to shame. But I won't require such a sacrifice from you. Because you are so versatile, you're too valuable to me in other roles to recast you."

The man nodded and took a long drink of coffee. From his expression I couldn't tell if he was disappointed or relieved not to be playing the Danish prince, but he did seem accepting of the decision. Then Harry's gaze traveled to Radney, who raised both hands in a gesture of mock surrender.

"Don't worry, I already know I don't know the part," he said with a wry shake of his bald head. "So don't feel you need to make up an excuse."

"None needed. You're right . . . you don't know the role."

Then, tempering the bluntness, Harry smiled and added, "But you're the best swordsman of the troupe, so we shall see you shine as Laertes. No, I'm casting someone who knows the tragic prince backward and forward."

Backward and forward.

I glanced at Bill, surprised. That was how the older man had described his knowledge of the lead role. And now, hearing that same phrase from Harry, Bill looked up from his empty plate, his expression brightening and bleary eyes suddenly hopeful.

"You mean . . .?"

"Exactly," Harry replied to him with a satisfied nod. "I shall follow in the footsteps of Branagh and Welles and Chaplin, and direct myself in the role of Hamlet."

Bill's expression sagged like the aged brown batik dashiki he was wearing today. Seeing his reaction, I couldn't help but feel a bit sympathetic to his disappointment. Obviously, he'd thought that, as none of the other men was up to Harry's standards, the Hamlet role was his by default.

Just as obviously, he'd forgotten that Harry had been an actor before he was a director.

No one else seemed to notice Bill's dismay, however. Harry's announcement had done what the coffee couldn't and roused the rest of the troupe into a semblance of enthusiasm.

"That's wonderful," Tessa gushed, never mind that she'd privately suggested to me that her husband should take the role from Len. "Not only will we have a famous actor as our director, but we'll get to play opposite you as well. This is so thrilling, and such a boost for our resumes!"

"Great decision, Spiel—er, Harry," was Marvin's opinion, while the others nodded their agreement. "I can't wait to see you and Rad-man crossing swords . . . literally."

"We'll concentrate on that tomorrow. For now, we have one more casting change to make. Unfortunately, someone also will need to take over the role of Ophelia from Susie."

I nodded along with the rest. It made sense that she wouldn't be able to carry on with something as frivolous as a play while trying to cope with the aftermath of her husband's death. But the ranks were thinning rapidly. Pretty soon Harry would be drafting me!

He went on, "I realize we're already doubled up on some roles, but that's what a Shakespeare troupe does. And so, for Ophelia, my thought was that the part should be played by—"

"Me, of course," finished a familiar voice from the doorway.

Smile tremulous, Susie walked into the dining room. She looked different, I thought . . . and it wasn't just how her hair was caught up in a messy bun, or the dark circles around her eyes, or the fact that her full lips were free of lipstick.

I realized after a moment that it was her clothes. Instead of the carefully matched trophy wife summer outfit complete with coordinating jewelry and sandals she was wearing tight faded blue jeans, a black silk T-shirt, and what appeared to be discount-store running shoes. I had to admit that, stressed features aside, she looked far younger and fresher than she had the day before.

Marvin and Radney both leaped up to pull out a chair for her and help her into her seat beside Bill, who gave her an approving smile. Even Tessa deigned to lean across her husband's plate to give the younger woman an approving pat on the arm. Only Chris seemed unimpressed by Susie's return, attention studiously fixed on the breakfast burrito he was devouring. I got up and poured Susie a cup of coffee. She gave me a grateful nod, then swept her gaze around the table.

"Thank you, all y'all, for your kindness," she said in a quavering voice. "This is the most difficult thing I've ever had to face, losing my first and only love. You've been true friends. I just know that Len is looking down everyone and smiling at you for taking such good care of me."

"Looking down?" I heard Marvin mutter as I resumed my seat, voice loud enough for my ears only. "I woulda figured he'd have to look up."

I shot him a disapproving look, the effect of which was marred by my involuntary snicker, which I hurriedly disguised as a cough. Fortunately, everyone else was responding with encouraging words, so that our moment of irreverence went unnoticed.

Harry let the chatter go on for a minute, then tapped his water glass for silence.

"Susie, I'm happy you've decided to rejoin us. But are you really sure you're up to a week of rehearsals and then three performances?"

"I am. I can't sit around doing nothing while waiting for them to . . . you know, let Len come home. This will keep my mind occupied. Besides, I know Len would want me to do it."

All of which made sense. Moreover, she had gotten through this emotional speech without tearing up or breaking down, which boded well for the rest of the week. And she was right. Without the rehearsals, what would she do with herself while waiting for Len's body to make it to the front of the ME's autopsy lineup? Better to keep her mind occupied with lines and stage directions and such.

"Fine," Harry decreed, and then glanced at his Rolex knock-off. "As several of you did not take my advice to drink a cup of rooibos last night, I've left a few teabags on the sideboard. I strongly suggest that you avail yourself of a cup, since we have a long day ahead of us. Finish your breakfast, and be sure to hydrate well. We'll meet promptly at 8:30 on the front porch to begin rehearsal."

The front porch, not the back patio, I thought in relief. While the latter best approximated the stage area at the festival, it would have been too much to ask the troupe—particularly Susie—to rehearse a few feet from where Len had only recently met his end.

The troupe had groaned and staggered their way out of the dining room by 8:29, and I got to work in the kitchen. As I loaded the dishwasher, from outside I heard a familiar sputter from a defective muffler. I looked out the window to see a decrepit compact black pickup creaking its way up the drive. It was Hendricks, arriving for his usual Monday cleanup of the grounds.

I considered going outside to explain the situation with the broken hedge and the ruts in the lawn, but in the end chickened out. I'd let him find the damage himself and wait until after he'd taken off again to leave him a voicemail of apology and explanation. It was almost ten by the time I'd finished the guest rooms and was loading the last of the linens into the washer. By then, Hendricks's pickup was gone, and so I ventured a look outside.

As Harry had predicted, the ruts in the lawn were filled with clean sand. As for the broken hawthorn, it took me a minute to pinpoint the spot where Len had fallen into it. Somehow, with a bit of pruning and clever weaving of the remaining branches, the gardener had managed to disguise the worst of the damage to that particular bush. In a few more weeks, and with a little more growth, the hedge would be good as new again.

But returning to the house I noticed that a note had been left on the patio bench. It was written in black marker on a page torn from a gardening catalog. In stark contrast to the elegant penmanship, the unsigned message was blunt.

Ms. Fleet, do not let this happen again.

"Believe me, I won't," I muttered and headed back inside to my room. Mattie had been lounging on the foot of my bed. She heard the car keys jingle as I pulled them from my oversized purse. She whined, then leaped down and launched into the little dance on her hind legs that meant, *Please take me with you, Mom.*

I gave her a pat and an indulgent smile even as I shook my head.

"Sorry, girl, where I'm going they don't allow dogs. And you know it's not safe to leave you in the car in this heat, even with the windows open. You hang out here and make sure that Harry doesn't burn the place down while I'm gone."

A few minutes later, I had eased the Mini out of the garage and around Harry's beater of a bus, heading to the Heavenly Host Baptist Church. The champagne flute in its potato chip canister was safely tucked into my purse. It would be a relief to have it off my dresser top and in the reverend's hands. And hopefully, once he'd examined it, he could even return it to me so my glassware set remained whole.

I consulted my GPS as I drove beneath the mature live oaks overhanging the street. The green canopy added welcome shade to a day whose temperature was rapidly climbing toward the nineties. Turning just beyond the town square, I could see crews already setting up there for the festival. Traffic was a bit heavier too, no doubt because of the out-of-towners already arriving for the big weekend.

The church and funeral parlor were located about a ten-minute drive away in the so-called new part of town, meaning the houses there had been built in the first decade of the 1900s. (Of course, Cymbeline had its own suburbs too, but those were located beyond the original city limits and dated back only twenty years or so.)

Homes here were smaller than in the historic area near the square where I lived. The predominant style was one that was popular in this part of Georgia and known as Folk Victorian. These were simple one- or two-story houses, but with the porches and roof gables "fancied up" with the same detailing found on Queen Anne homes like mine. Of course, like any good small-town Georgia abode, most homes featured a tomato plant or ten somewhere in the yard . . . or, failing that, in a tin bucket on the porch alongside the ubiquitous potted ferns found practically everywhere. (I'd not gotten around to getting any tomato plants of my own this year but had big plans for doing so next spring.)

Almost as many houses featured a full-sized statue of a squat English bulldog, sometimes wearing a black-and-red sweater, somewhere in the yard. No, they weren't members of some cult-like dog fanciers association. Instead, they were fans of the University of Georgia football team and showed their pride by displaying the team's bulldog mascot, Uga. (University of GA— UGA—get it?) Once the college football season was in full bloom, those same houses would sport black-and-red flags and pennants with big G's on them.

Okay, so maybe it *was* kind of a cult.

My Mini took me right to my destination. The church and the funeral parlor each held down a prime bit of corner real estate on the same street, right across from each other. Both establishments had been converted from neat cottage homes and were painted identically, bright white with matching white shutters and trim. The only splash of color, mostly shades of pink, came from narrow strips of flower gardens edging the buildings' foundations. Not that I knew my flowers—as I've said, I leave that up to Hendricks—but I still recognized chrysanthemums and asters and begonias, all garden favorites here in our part of Georgia.

Parking was in the former homes' backyards, which had been paved over and striped and could each hold probably fifteen cars the size of mine. I eased into a spot behind the church one space over from the only car currently in the lot, a champagne-colored Cadillac that had to be at least twenty years old. Probably not the Reverend's, I told myself. I pictured him driving something more like a late-model Mercedes, most likely black and almost certainly with a moon roof. Tucking my purse with the glass safely under my arm, I followed the sidewalk around to the front.

The Heavenly Host Baptist Church had a large wooden sign in the front yard ringed by a small garden of the same surprisingly frivolous blooms. Painted the same white as the building, the sign sported curlicued corners and fancy black lettering proclaiming the church's name. Beneath that name was that of the Reverend. At the very bottom of the sign were the office hours (9 AM *to* 5 PM *Mon–Fri*) and service times (*Sundays* 8 AM *and* 11 AM, *Wednesdays* 7 PM).

But what really got one's attention was the blood-red cross that appeared to be electric and was mounted smack in the middle of the sign like a rogue Christmas decoration. I suspected that it was turned on at night for the benefit of those having the sort of spiritual crises the Reverend had referred to in his voicemail announcement.

A green awning stretched halfway down the walkway, adding a welcome bit of shade as I made my way to a pair of wooden double doors. I stepped inside the single-story building and was immediately hit by a blast of arctic-level air conditioning.

One wall of what might have once been a living room had been removed so that the space combined with the original short hallway now served as a foyer. A few chairs lined the front and far-right walls, while coat pegs and an oversized bulletin board stuffed with notices took up most of the rear wall. The faded braided rug on the gleaming wooden floor muffled my footsteps as I stepped closer to read a couple of postings.

My curiosity only partially satisfied (what *did* a single women's group that was part of Dr. Bishop's church actually do? And what exactly was a Holy Moly Rummage Sale?), I checked out the rest of the area.

A closed door directly in front of me led to what I assumed was the worship area. I poked my head in and saw rows of what appeared to be vintage wooden theater seats, currently empty, filling the rear two-thirds of the converted open space. Beyond the seating was a low carpeted platform with an ornate wooden podium mounted front and center, where Dr. Bishop likely preached on Sundays and Wednesdays. A large wooden cross was mounted on the back wall directly behind the podium, serving as a stark backdrop. The place was silent now save for the hum of the AC, but I imagined that during services the very walls shook with enthusiasm.

I eased the door closed again. To my left, opposite the foyer area, was another closed door leading to what might have once been a front bedroom. A small white-painted sign on that door had curlicued corners and fancy writing identical to that of the church's exterior sign. As this one proclaimed *Office*, I gave a quick knock and then opened the door.

Most of the room was filled with a very large wooden desk behind which sat a very tiny and very elderly African American woman wearing very red lipstick. Her yellow knit suit with its white pussy-bow blouse had probably been fashionable thirty years earlier, but the bright color gave the outfit a timeless appeal. Likely she was the owner of the vintage Caddy, though she appeared to be far too short to see over its steering wheel without the benefit of a pillow to sit on.

She looked up from a stack of papers and studied me over the top of narrow horn-rimmed glasses. "May I help you?"

"Yes. I'm Nina Fleet, here to see Dr. Bishop. He said in his voice mail last night that Sister Malthea could direct me to him."

"That would be me," she agreed with a gracious nod. "You just missed him. The Reverend is across the street at the funeral parlor now if you'd care to walk over."

Indicating the rotary dial telephone at her elbow, she added, "I'll be happy to call him and let him know you're on the way."

I thanked her and left her dialing as I headed outside again. After the sub-zero AC inside the church, the ninety-degree temperature outside felt even more oppressive. I was already sweating by the time I reached the curb to cross the street. Fortunately, another green awning also shaded the walkway to the funeral home's front door.

Whoever had done the church's signage had obviously also made the large sign in front of the Heavenly Path Funeral Home, though a yellow dove that probably glowed golden at night had replaced the scarlet cross. The business hours listed were the same, though amended with an, *And also by appointment*. But the funeral home was quite a bit larger, a two-story building with a front porch that ran its full length. I assumed that the Reverend lived on the second floor, though for all I knew he had a McMansion out in the suburbs that he called home.

I stepped inside to equally frosty temperatures and the soft sound of gospel music. Similarly to the church, the original home's floor plan had been opened so that I walked into an open foyer area. The vestibule took up the full front of the house, with a couple of love seats and a half-dozen upholstered chairs arranged around low tables to form two seating areas.

A curtained archway—drapes currently tied open—led to a hallway that ran the remaining length of the house. I could see a door at the end that I suspected opened onto the parking lot beyond. To one side of that door I glimpsed what appeared to be an enclosed staircase. Opposite that stairway was a closed door. And just beyond the main entry where I stood were four smaller alcoves, two on either side of the hall. Assuming that one of these rooms was where Dr. Bishop was, I started my search.

The first alcove appeared to be the official display area. Sections of caskets in various styles were mounted trophy-like on the wall, while a series of large binders was arranged on a long countertop. The far wall supported a lineup of actual headstones, while in the corner was a table holding urns of different sizes and materials.

The other three rooms were viewing rooms, each dimly lit with rows of folding chairs arranged six deep. They faced the far wall, with a broad aisle dividing them. Beyond the chairs in two of the rooms were biers that supported closed caskets. Empty, I hoped, though I suspected not. The giveaway was the proliferation of flower arrangements in each room, along with a large framed photograph propped on a stand beside each casket.

I found the Reverend Dr. Thaddeus Bishop in the third visitation room dressed in a stark black suit and leaning into an open casket. As the mellow tones of Elvis Presley singing *Joshua Fit the Battle* softly spilled from the sound system, the Reverend raised the mallet he was holding and began to swing.

Chapter Fifteen

I must have gasped, for the Reverend abruptly halted and turned to face me.

"Ah, Ms. Fleet," he said with a smile. Then, glancing at the mallet he still clutched, his smile broadened.

"My apologies," he said, and lowered the rubber hammer. "I have a display unit here that has a problem with one of its hinges. I was attempting to facilitate a repair."

He stepped aside from what I could see now was an empty casket. The flowers and photo of the deceased were noticeably absent from this room, giving me a clue I should have picked up on right away.

"Of course. That's what I figured," I lied blandly, though his soft chuckle told me he knew differently.

I felt myself blush but forged ahead.

"Thanks for seeing me, Dr. Bishop. As I told you in my voice-mail message, I found the champagne flute that Mr. Marsh—Len—had been drinking out of just before he died. There seems to be some sort of residue left in it. I thought you might want to have it tested just in case whatever that substance is has some bearing on Len's death."

"Certainly." He set down the mallet on one of the folding chairs and gestured me to come forward. "I presume you brought the glass in question with you?"

I reached into my purse for the potato chip cannister and handed it to him. The Reverend chuckled again, but nodded his approval as he popped off the top and pulled out the bagged flute. Leaving it inside the plastic, he handed me back the chip can and raised the glassware so that what little light there was in the room reflected through it.

"Interesting," he murmured. "Can you tell me what was in the drink you served?"

I gave him my recipe, and he shook his head. "None of those liquids should leave a residue of this sort. Definitely worth taking a look at."

"Harry said that you have your own lab here," I told him as he returned the glass to the canister and set the unorthodox package beside his mallet. "Can you do the tests yourself or do you have to send this to the state laboratory?"

His expression stiffened a bit at the mention of Harry's name. Still, his tone was mild enough as he replied: "Since the sample is relatively sizeable, I will reserve a portion here to test and send the rest to the gentlemen and ladies in Atlanta. Of course, they tend to have a backlog of several weeks, so I should have a preliminary determination long before they do."

"Wonderful! So, how quickly can you find out what's in the glass?"

The Reverend gave me an indulgent smile.

"Unfortunately, Ms. Fleet, this is not CSI Cymbeline. One cannot pour random chemicals into a random sample and have a full analysis pop up five minutes later on one's computer. It is a tedious process that requires we have some sort of idea of what we are searching for."

When I frowned in disappointment he added, "Fortunately, Sheriff Lamb provided a list of medications that Mrs. Marsh said her husband took. In addition to the typical prescriptions for high blood pressure and cholesterol, he apparently was prescribed Oxycodone for an injury he recently suffered. Knowing that gives us a starting place in attempting to identify this substance."

Then he gave me a considering look. "It's not often that civilians show such keen curiosity regarding autopsy results . . . not unless they are members of the decedent's family. May I ask why you have such a vested interest in the outcome?"

I hesitated. Part of my interest was concern for my B&B's reputation. But more compelling was my unsettled feeling that there was more to Len's death than a bad heart. Cliché as it might sound, practically everyone in the troupe held a grudge against the man. And with all the anonymous pranks that some unknown person had been pulling, it didn't seem too farfetched a theory that maybe the trickster had taken the joke—deliberately or not—too far this last time.

But as I had absolutely no proof of the latter, I stuck with the former.

"I know this sounds terribly selfish," I told him, "but having someone die at my B&B is pretty bad for business. If I could say that he passed away from natural causes, that would be better."

"I understand. Believe me, as a small businessman myself I know the rigors of maintaining one's corporate reputation."

With a glance at his watch, which, unlike Harry's, appeared to be a genuine Rolex, he added, "Actually, you are in luck, Ms. Fleet. I don't have to start work on my next, er, client, for another hour. I should have time to set up a few simple panels on the sample, just to eliminate some of the more obvious possibilities. How about I phone you in a few hours when the tests are complete?"

At my eager agreement, Dr. Bishop escorted me back to the foyer while Mahalia Jackson quietly belted out *Amazing Grace*.

"Oh, one last thing," I said as I stepped outside. "Would I be able to get my champagne flute back when you're finished with it? It's crystal and part of a set."

"Most assuredly. And as I said, I will telephone you when my tests are complete."

I left feeling far lighter than when I'd walked into the funeral parlor. Once back in my Mini, I cranked up the AC full blast as I drove the few miles back to the square. I still wanted to chat with Gemma about the whole dead body and business thing. Besides, as far as I knew, she hadn't heard that Harry was part of the troupe staying at my place. As his former babysitter and informal life coach and cheerleader, I could guarantee that she'd want to know that Harry was back in town.

*   *   *

"So, girl, when were you going to tell me that Harry was back in town?" Gemma greeted me at the door of Peaches and Java as I walked in a few minutes later. "Jasmine told me she saw him at your place this morning. I can't believe I had to hear about it secondhand. Is something going on between the two of you that you don't want me to know about?"

Her tone was mock angry, but I could see she was somewhat serious too. Of all the people in town, she was the one who would defend the actor against all comers, mostly because she knew what he'd been through growing up.

I'd heard fragments of the *Harold A. Westcott III, the Early Years* saga from both her and Harry and was moderately sympathetic. A lonely childhood with summers spent living with his great-aunt in what was now my tower room . . . real-estate magnate father who was verbally abusive . . . same dad who cut his son out of the will because of his chosen career. Sure, he'd had a tough time, but not so much compared to some people I knew. Moreover, I didn't see how any of this excused his sometimes questionable actions, but Gemma apparently did.

"I swear, there's nothing going on with me and Harry . . . now or ever," I hurried to assure her. "But there's lots of crazy stuff going on in general. I'm dying of the heat. How about a glass of ice water first, and then I'll tell you everything?"

With all the festival construction, I'd had to park down the block near Weary Bones, the local antique shop run by my friend Mason Denman. I had waved through the window as I'd walked past, earning a wave back of his trademark handkerchief and a bobble of his distinctive black pompadour. Fortunately, he'd been waiting on a customer. Otherwise, he'd have popped out to the sidewalk in a flash, and what would have been a quick walk from car to diner would have dragged out an extra fifteen minutes while he gossiped. But even the short walk had been long enough for me to break a sweat.

For her part, Gemma didn't look convinced by my excuses. Shaking her graying locks, she went behind the counter. Her husband, Daniel, spied me and threw me a shaka sign—the Hawaiian twisting wave with middle three fingers folded over the palm, pinkie and thumb stuck out to either side.

I smiled and shaka'ed him back. It was just a little after eleven, and the lunch rush rarely started until eleven thirty, and so Gemma had a few minutes to chat. Returning with two glasses of ice water, she led me to my favorite table for two, a pair of former flat-topped school desks with built-in chairs bolted front-to-front. She took the seat across from me as I drank.

Peaches and Java was a cross between your typical small-town diner and your funky urban hangout. The food and the friendliness of both customers and owners definitely fit the first category, as did the diner counter and pastry case backed by a double-stacked commercial oven and an open grill. The artisan coffee and fun, mismatched fixtures like the school-desk table fit the second. That and the ukuleles in various colors and sizes hanging on the far wall. Not only were the stringed instruments a tribute to Daniel Tanaka's Hawaiian roots, he occasionally pulled one down and played for his customers. Though I had to admit that my favorite bit of decor had more of a Georgia flair . . . the anthropomorphic male and female peaches painted on the restroom door indicating it was a unisex facility.

"Ah, better," I said once I'd drained most of the water. Then, as Gemma stared at me expectantly from over her own glass, I went on, "I meant to tell you that Harry was back, but things got away from me. And it's not like I knew he was going to show up in town. It turns out he's the director of this year's Shakespeare festival's troupe, the same troupe that just happened to have reservations at my B&B."

While Gemma tsk'd and shook her head, I gave her a rundown of the actors' arrival. Next was a quick description of the troupe members and their various foibles.

"I was already wondering how I was going to put up with all of them for almost two weeks," I told her, "and then Len went and croaked on us yesterday."

"That was you?" Gemma's exclamation was loud enough to draw looks from the diner's only other customers. "I heard from one of my RN friends that someone had dropped dead in the historic district, but I had no idea they were talking about your place."

"Right. Lucky me."

I described how Mattie and I had found Len past help, and how Sheriff Lamb and the coroner, aka Dr. Bishop, had both made appearances.

"Everyone is pretty sure it was a heart attack, as he fits the pattern. You know, mid-fifties, high-stress job, high blood pressure and cholesterol, smoker."

Gemma nodded, and I caught the glance she sent Daniel. He towered over his five-foot-two wife by a mere five inches but outweighed her by a good two hundred pounds. And he pretty well fit the other criteria himself, except for the smoking.

Then Daniel dispelled the morbid mood as he rounded the counter and headed toward us, plate in hand. "Check it out, Nina. I came up with something new for the Shakespeare festival. Peaches and Java is now P&J's. This is the new logo I designed," he proclaimed, puffing out his barrel chest to better show off the peach-colored T-shirt he was wearing.

I nodded. "I like it."

He had taken the old Peaches and Java design, a fat cartoon peach plopped in a cartoon coffee cup, and made it smaller. Now a caricature of the Bard, drawn from the waist up, cradled that peach-filled cup in his arms. The slogan, *P&J's . . . a Peach by any Other Name* was emblazoned below the Shakespeare figure.

"And even better," Daniel went on, holding out the plate, "I've created a special PB&J sandwich for the festival. Peanut butter, thinly sliced cooked peaches coated in peach jam, and a layer of cream cheese all grilled between two slices of cinnamon pound cake."

The aroma of peaches and cinnamon wafted enticingly in my direction. Daniel handed me a clean fork, so I obediently cut off piece of the freshly grilled sandwich and took a bite.

"Wow," I managed a moment later through the sticky mouthful. "I'm not a big peanut butter fan, but this is fabulous."

"It *is* pretty good," Gemma agreed, reaching with a second fork for a bite of her own. "We've already made arrangements with the SOCS committee to set up a grill station on the square right across from here. We'll be selling Shakespeare's Peachy PB&J sandwiches during the festival."

"I'll be your first customer," I promised.

Satisfied, Daniel left the rest of the sandwich for Gemma and me to finish off and returned to his spot behind the counter.

"So, where were we?" I asked as I took another bite.

Gemma finished chewing and swallowed. "The dead guy. You said Dr. Bishop was there to pronounce him. Did he mention having an autopsy done?"

At my affirmative response, she gave a satisfied nod. "Good. Nothing against the Reverend, but he's a funeral director, not a trained medical professional. Though I suppose hanging out with dead people all the time qualifies him for the job to some extent."

"Actually, I just came from the Heavenly Path Funeral Home," I told her. "I found the glass Len was drinking out of before he died, and there seemed to be some sort of residue in it. I brought it to Dr. Bishop so he could have it tested."

Gemma set down the forkful of PB&J she was about to eat and frowned.

"I thought you said everyone thought the man had a heart attack. But it sounds like maybe an overdose, or a drug interaction."

"That's what they're going to find out. But as I told Dr. Bishop, I know it's horrible, but I'm really worried about what people will do if they find out someone died in my garden. What if no one ever wants to stay at Fleet House again?"

Gemma snorted and raised her fork.

"Actually, there are plenty of folks who'd love to stay at a B&B where someone died. People who think they're psychic, paranormal groups. Wait until we get close to Halloween and you'll find plenty of takers. Heck, regular hotels have folks die in them all the time, and it doesn't affect business."

When I gave her a doubtful look, she persisted, "Let it go, Nina. Just plant something nice in the garden in the poor man's memory and be glad you don't have to throw out a mattress."

I winced a little at that final blunt advice. What Gemma said made sense—except that I couldn't let it go. Not until I knew whether Len's death was a result of natural causes or something else. And despite Gemma's blithe assurances that a little thing like a dead body wouldn't hurt my business, I wasn't so sure. Especially since everyone else involved seemed a bit too eager to rubber-stamp the man's death as your garden-variety (no pun intended) heart attack.

But because I knew Gemma would try to talk me out of pursuing the matter, I merely nodded and took another bite of Daniel's gourmet PB&J. By then diners were beginning to trickle in with the start of the lunch rush. Gemma reached for the now empty plate and stood.

"Back to work," she declared. "I'd love to drop by the B&B and say hi to Harry, but things are busy for us all with the festival coming. So let him know I asked about him and that I'll be in the front row on opening night."

Once outside on the square, my ears were again assaulted by the sounds of hammers and electric saws as construction on the main festival stage moved along at rapid speed. Despite the noise and heat, I paused a moment to watch the workers' progress. This was no simple platform, but a full-blown stage with roof, backdrop, and wings that was going up. I was surprised as well—though perhaps I shouldn't have been—to recognize one of the carpenters who was busy cutting a series of planks on a table saw.

The lean, dark-haired man in question was Jack Hill. He was owner with his wife, Jill, of the Taste-Tee-Freeze Creamery on the square next door to Mason's antique shop. I'd gotten to know the couple because of Harry and the unfortunate incident with the penguin mascot suit earlier in the summer.

Like me, Jack had worked at a different career before buying the creamery. He'd been a professional carpenter and still did occasional woodwork on the side. I'd already spoken to him about the fancy wooden arbor I wanted constructed for future outdoor weddings at the B&B. But apparently he also worked as a volunteer for the Shakespeare festival.

I caught Jack's eye and waved. He waved back, but it was obvious he was too busy to chat. Which was just as well, because I suddenly had another place I needed to be. And that was the Cymbeline Public Library.

I turned and headed in the opposite direction. My destination was a three-story Queen Anne that was almost an architectural twin sister to my house. Located a block off the main square, it had been converted decades earlier from a private home into Cymbeline's first true library. Of course, a modern main branch had long since been built not far from the suburbs and shopping mall, but I enjoyed the charming vibe of this red, white, and blue painted lady.

I already had a library card, so once I slipped inside the blessedly cool building it was simply a matter of taking a seat at one of their half-dozen computers. Of course, I could have waited and done my research at home, but I didn't want to be interrupted—or, worse, accidentally leave any incriminating browser history behind. Besides which, if my search proved fruitful, I might need to access the library's periodicals archives.

I spent the next hour or so doing web searches for all of the GASP troupe members, starting with the Benedicts. The expected academic references as far as papers and conferences came up, along with a few articles that featured the pair in various GASP productions over the years. The only hit that raised any flag had to do with Bill. He had managed—probably purposefully—to get himself arrested during a handful of campus protests over the past few years. All the better for that professorial cred, I thought with a snicker. But my amusement faded when, scrolling down, I read that one charge against him had been battery. Apparently, he had punched some counter protester at a recent climate-change rally. The charge had been dropped, but it did indicate that good old Professor Bill could be provoked to violence.

Mentally filing that information for future reference, I moved on to Susie. I found the expected references to Atlanta society events and charity functions, along with a few mentions of GASP performances. Nothing about her past working at a sports bar, but then, I didn't know her maiden name to do a more detailed search.

Chris proved a bigger puzzle. For one thing, my search brought up any numbers of Chris, Christian, and Christopher Boyds. For another, someone his age didn't typically have much of a Google presence. Knowing that Twitter, Snapchat, and Instagram were the preferred social media for college students, I gave those platforms a try. But either he had his privacy settings locked down or else didn't use his real name, because I couldn't find an account that seemed to tie to him.

Radney's online presence held no real surprises. He had the expected LinkedIn page with numerous endorsements and an impressive list of awards and recognitions listed. He was mentioned in a few electronics magazine articles and in press releases put out by Atlanta International Communications Group, otherwise known as AICG—apparently, the company he and Len both worked for. As I'd not known that company name before, I mentally filed that info too and kept searching. I smiled at a couple of ancient photos from his University of Georgia days. Radney had gone in on a wrestling scholarship and left with a mechanical engineering degree. Back then, the bulging biceps had more resembled stovepipes, and he'd sported a full head of hair. But there were no blotches on his record that I could see.

Marvin was a different story.

I stopped short at the first result, a several-years-old article about Peachtree Communications going into Chapter 11 bankruptcy. That hadn't been part of Marvin's story that Harry had told me.

I did a quick check of Wikipedia, finding a generic piece on the company's history and founders. What caught my eye, however, was the paragraph that read, *A year after the partnership between Lasky and Marsh was dissolved, leaving Lasky at the helm, Peachtree Communications lost a lucrative contract with Atlanta International Communications Group. Eighteen months later, the company filed for bankruptcy protection. One year later, Peachtree Communications was acquired by AICG, with all of Peachtree's personnel, including Lasky, subsequently let go.*

So much for Marvin's supposed millions he'd got when he had sold the company. Chances were he'd ended up with pennies on the dollar. Worse, I had a bad suspicion that the lost contract and subsequent bankruptcy and acquisition had Len Marsh's neatly manicured fingerprints all over it.

And that could give someone quite the motive for murder.

Feeling suddenly shaky inside, I checked out the references at the bottom of the listing. Several articles from the *Atlanta Business Monthly* seemed pertinent, and so I scribbled down the numbers of the issues containing them. Hopefully the library would have copies in their magazine archives.

But before I could make it to the information desk, my phone rang. I checked the caller ID to see that it was our friendly neighborhood coroner-slash-funeral director on the line. Shoving my note and pen into my purse, I hurried out the door while answering the call.

"Ah, Ms. Fleet," came the Reverend Bishop's dulcet tones on the other end of the line. "I am glad I caught you. You may drop by anytime it is convenient to retrieve your champagne glass."

"That's wonderful," I replied. "Does that mean you've finished your analysis?"

"I have. And let us just say that the results were not what we were expecting."

Chapter Sixteen

Was that good news or bad? Still feeling a bit unsteady, I sat on the library's front steps and asked, "Can you tell me what those results were?"

The Reverend was silent for a moment before replying, "Technically, I should keep this information to myself, as the lab in Atlanta will have the final word. But as my findings are not official, I do not think there would be any harm in sharing. Though I do ask that you keep this between us."

"I understand. So what was in the drink?"

"As I told you, there is not a single magical test that can determine an unknown substance. And so I began with the list that Sheriff Lamb provided to me to see if the specimen proved to match any of those chemistries."

He rattled off the names of several prescription drugs: Oxycodone, and others that I recognized from television ads. "Interestingly," he said, "there was no match."

"No match?" I echoed, picturing Harry's *I told you so* look when he found out. "So you're saying there wasn't any sort of drug in the glass after all?"

"I said there was no match with any of the medications on the list. However, it occurred to me that perhaps that list was, shall we say, incomplete. And so I tested for a few other common pharmaceuticals. Once I eliminated the usual illicit substances, I decided to test for other common but legal drugs. To my surprise, I was successful in my first attempt."

"So what was the drug?"

"Benzodiazepine," he replied, and then clarified, "It is a sedative. You might know it by trade names like Xanax or Pazaxa."

I reached for my pen and the piece of paper where I'd written down the magazine issues for reference. I'd heard of Xanax and Pazaxa before, but . . .

"Benzo-what?"

The Reverend repeated the word and spelled it out, adding, "That is the class of drugs. They are known more colloquially as benzos. Oh, yes, there was colorant still remaining on a bit of the crumbled coating, so from that I narrowed my guess to Pazaxa as the medication in question."

I jotted all that on my paper and then asked, "But aren't those drugs for anxiety or depression? Why would Len take one without it being prescribed?"

"I am afraid I cannot answer that," the man intoned. "Moreover, all I can confirm is that the drug was in the glass. Of course, I'll mention my findings to Sheriff Lamb, but we won't know until the toxicology results come back whether or not that same drug was actually in Mr. Marsh's system."

Which will take weeks, as the lab in Atlanta is backed up, I silently finished for him.

"Thanks, Dr. Bishop. But I wonder if—"

"I am afraid I have shared everything with you that I can, Ms. Fleet," the coroner smoothly cut me short. "And now, you must excuse me. I have a client waiting in my office who has been more than patient. Be sure to drop by and see Sister Malthea for your glass."

And with that, the line went dead.

I stuck my phone back in my purse and stood, uncertain whether this was progress or not. Because until the autopsy was complete, no one would know for sure how Len died. And even if the drug in question was found in his system, there was no way to prove that he hadn't purposely taken the pill himself.

"Not unless someone confesses to spiking his drink," I said aloud as I headed back toward the square to retrieve my car.

And the chances of that happening were slim and none, I grimly told myself. Which left me with two choices. I could forget what I knew about the drugs in Len's peach mimosa and leave the investigation up to Sheriff Lamb. Or, I could poke around and see who of the troupe had access to that particular drug.

I hadn't yet come to a decision when, a couple of minutes later, I was back at the square. The stage had continued to take shape, with Jack and his crew still hard at work. This time, however, when the man spotted me passing by, he flipped off his saw; then, with a word to a retirement-aged gentleman standing nearby whom I didn't recognize, the pair headed in my direction.

"How's it going, Nina?" Jack asked as they approached, reaching out a sawdust-covered hand in greeting. "You're looking good, but then you always do."

He was wearing a dark-gray Taste-Tee-Freeze logoed T-shirt. As usual, he'd rolled up the sleeves almost to his shoulders, displaying a respectable set of tanned biceps for a guy in his late fifties. Away from his wife, he tended to be chummy with the ladies. However, I knew that Jill—who bore an uncanny resemblance to the current Duchess of Sussex—kept her man on a tight lead.

Indicating his companion, Jack went on, "Have you met our SOCS committee chair, Professor Joy?"

A flash of panic swept through me. This was the guy Harry had to report to about the Len situation. As far as I knew, he hadn't done that yet. And it wasn't my job to spill the beans, particularly if the man hadn't heard about the death.

Praying that the professor wasn't much for Internet neighborhood gossip, I managed a casual smile and shook hands with him. With his rumpled red vest and collar-length gray hair tied back in jaunty pirate style, Joy reminded me of a taller, bluffer version of Bill Benedict.

"The pleasure is mine," the man insisted, sounding as if he meant it. He vigorously pumped my arm with an oversized hand better suited to manual labor than pedagogy. "I understand that not only are you one of our town's chamber members, but you are also a sponsor of our little event."

"Only indirectly, but next year you can count on me for more. And I must say how impressed I am by everyone's hard work. That stage could be on Broadway when it's finished. I can't believe how quickly you put it together."

The men chuckled, and Joy explained, "Actually, we built that behemoth a few years back. We just break it down after every festival and store it in Mayor Green's barn until the next year."

Mayor Green being Melissa Jane Green, a hard-charging sixty-something businesswoman who'd been running the town for more than a decade and a major force behind Cymbeline's resurgence. She'd also been responsible for fast-tracking the paperwork for my B&B, but her assistance had been contingent on a favor on my end. Fortunately, it had worked out well for all of us.

"Still impressive," I told him. "Well, lots to do at the B&B, so I'd better let you gentlemen go. Nice to meet you, Professor."

I gave the pair a nod, pleased that I'd dodged the issue of Len's death. Jack thumbs-upped me in return and headed back to his saw. But I'd barely made it a dozen steps away when, from behind me, Professor Joy called, "Ms. Fleet, one moment."

Grimacing, I turned again. The man's expression was flustered now as he said, "I realize this is an indelicate subject, but I really need to ask. What is the situation with the gentleman who passed away at your establishment yesterday? My understanding is that he was one of the Georgia Amateur Shakespeare Players . . . which is the troupe headlining our festival."

I gave the professor a somber nod.

"Unfortunately, yes. Mr. Marsh suffered what we believe was a medical incident and passed away. Haven't you heard from Harry Westcott yet about this?"

"I haven't, which is of even greater concern," Professor Joy replied, features sagging in dismay. "With all I have on my plate right now, I'd appreciate some reassurance. Not to sound callous about the situation—certainly, we send our condolences to the poor man's family—but we do have a contract with GASP. The

Shakespeare performance is the festival's big draw, and it is vital that they put on the play as scheduled."

I hesitated. Should I toss this hot potato Harry's way? Or should I be a lamb, to quote the actor, and try to mitigate the damage on his behalf?

B-a-a-a, I answered myself.

"Of course, I can't speak for the troupe officially," I told the professor, "but I do know that they will be performing as planned. Unfortunately, Mr. Marsh was the lead player, so they are minus a Hamlet. But Harry is going to do double duty and play that role himself as well as directing the troupe."

"Indeed? How very Orson Welles of him."

He didn't exactly sound convinced, however, so I found myself strangely compelled to defend the actor.

"You do realize that Harry has appeared in numerous major motion pictures. Plus he just finished filming a brand-new cop show for Netflix. Frankly, having someone of his caliber both acting in the festival play and directing it is sure to increase attendance. If you hurry, you can even update the festival website with that information."

Joy rubbed his gray-stubbled chin. "Perhaps you're right. Lemonade from lemons. Thank you, Ms. Fleet."

"Nina," I corrected him with a smile. "See you opening night."

Feeling rather proud of how I'd managed, I headed to where I'd parked the Mini. Hopefully, by the time I made it home the troupe would still be busy rehearsing. And that would give me an opportunity to do a bit of snooping in their rooms under the guise of housekeeping.

Because, yes, that's what I'd decided to do.

But when I pulled into the drive Harry was the only one of the troupe on the front porch. I left the Mini in the garage and walked around front.

Harry was sitting motionless on the porch swing, Yorick beside him. Both wore pensive expressions. Mattie had joined them, sprawled on the Adirondack chair beside the swing and keeping a stern doggie eye on the skull.

"Everyone still on lunch break?" I asked in surprise, as it was already well after two.

Harry shot me a weary look.

"More like a mental-health break. Susie collapsed halfway through the second scene, so she's out at least for the rest of the day . . . and probably for the duration. I let everyone go for a long lunch while I figure things out."

Susie was out permanently? I thought back to Harry's casting choices. Not much there.

He continued, "And now we're down to one woman in the show, and she's already playing Queen Gertrude. No way can she play dual roles, as the queen and Ophelia appear in scenes together."

"What are you going to do?" I asked, squeezing into the Adirondack chair next to Mattie.

He shrugged. "Best I can come up with is having Tessa put out a call to the full GASP company for any Ophelias who can fill in last minute. If not, I can give the Cymbeline High drama club a shot. There's got to be at least one girl in town who knows the part."

"I know it."

The confident voice came from behind the screen door.

I glanced over to see Chris walking out to join us. For once, the omnipresent earbuds weren't stuck in his ears.

"I know it," he repeated, slipping into the other Adirondack chair. He leaned forward, elbows propped on knees, and gave Harry an earnest look.

"I know the role. I could play Ophelia."

Harry frowned back at the youth, his expression considering. I knew that boys and men had taken on female roles during Shakespeare's time simply because women had been forbidden to set foot on the stage. And Chris did have an androgynous look that, with the right costuming, could allow him pass for a young woman.

"Please, Harry," he persisted. "This is my big chance. I'm not afraid to play a girl's part. I'll do good, I promise."

"If I say yes—which I haven't yet," the actor replied, raising a cautioning hand, "what do we do about your other parts?"

"How about me? I could play his roles," I blurted impulsively.

From his expression, my offer surprised Harry almost as much as it did me. But in the next moment, I found myself warming to the idea. When else would I ever get a chance to perform Shakespeare? And, besides, being part of the troupe would make it easier for me to learn more regarding their respective relationships with Len.

"It's not that crazy an idea," I went on. "I've seen *Hamlet* performed a lot of times, and Chris doesn't have that many lines. What I can't memorize, I could always write on my arm or something."

Chris grinned at that and reached out for a fist bump. We tapped knuckles, and then he and I waited while Harry considered our proposals.

After a moment, the actor stood, gathering up Yorick and tucking the skull under his arm.

"Fine," he said. "We'll give it a try, at least through today's rehearsals. But I'd better see some stellar work out of both of you."

Then, as Chris and I eagerly nodded, he finished, "I'm going inside to call in my lunch delivery order. Let the rest of the troupe know that I expect them back here on the porch in fifteen minutes so we can resume rehearsing."

*　*　*

"That was fine, Tessa," Harry said, rapping with his pencil on his binder to call a halt in the action. "That is, if your intent was to portray a soccer mom angry about a tie-up in the carpool lane. But if you were attempting to communicate the outrage of a wronged queen, then you failed miserably. Let's try again."

We'd been rehearsing for almost two hours. Harry and Yorick had resumed their spots on the porch swing, the former wearing one of those battery-powered neck fans to keep him cool. The remaining porch furniture and fixtures that weren't screwed down had been temporarily relocated to my screened-in porch. This left a small but suitable open area to serve as the stage for the performers.

Given the afternoon's blazing temperatures, everyone was wearing the minimum amount of clothing required for modesty. Even Tessa had abandoned her usual yards of flowing skirts and kaftans for a more practical pair of shorts and a moisture-wicking Atlanta Falcons T-shirt. As a group, we'd already gone through two pitchers of ice water plus a jug each of iced tea and lemonade. On the bright side, I told myself, I'd probably lost two or three pounds just from sweating.

Rather than rehearsing the play from beginning to end, Harry had been running through the major scenes, coaching the troupe member who had the most significant role in each. I'd already survived my debut as the hybrid gentleman renamed Rozencrantz Guildenstern, reading my first scene, which included both Tessa and Harry. When it ended, Harry had given me an approving nod.

"A bit rough, but not at all bad considering this is your first attempt. Brava."

Scant as the praise was, coming from Harry it was the equivalent of an award nomination, and so I'd basked in the momentary limelight.

Of course, being on the actual stage in front of an audience would be a whole different thing. Fortunately, Harry already had come up with a solution to the obvious problem of memorizing all my lines in time for the performance. He decreed that each of my characters, Rozencrantz Guildenstern and the Gravedigger, would have an oversized cap as part of their respective costumes. My script pages would be pinned to the cap's underside, and while I would appear to be servilely clutching my headgear before me, I'd actually be reading my part.

But Chris in the Ophelia role was the performer that all of the troupe was watching. So far, the scenes we'd gone over had required only a few lines from him. But Harry had already announced that coming up next was the second act scene where Ophelia confides in Polonius that she's afraid of a crazed Hamlet. We all knew without it being said that this would determine if he did or didn't have the skill to pull off the role.

"Much better, Tessa," Harry decreed once the woman had repeated the scene that Harry had previously dissed. "I now feel your pain."

Glancing down at his binder again, he went on, "All right, act 2, scene 1. As you know, we've lopped off that unnecessary first portion where Polonius and Reynaldo are plotting to spy on Laertes. We begin with Ophelia confessing to her father her fear for . . . or is it of? . . . Hamlet. Marvin and Chris, take your places. And action."

"*How now, Ophelia? What's the matter?*" Marvin as Polonius asked, rushing to his "daughter" and rather ineffectually patting her on the shoulder.

Chris as Ophelia—and minus the oversized black glasses—assumed a brave if piteous expression. "*O my lord, my lord, I have been so affrighted!*"

"*With what, in the name of God?*"

The scene continued with a few more speeches between the pair, until Marvin's world-weary Polonius ended with, "*Come, go we to the King. This must be known; which, being kept close, might move more grief to hide than hate to utter love. Come.*"

"And, *exeunt*," Harry called. Then, with a nod, he added. "Do it just like that on opening night, and we've got a hit on our hands."

"Woohoo!" Marvin decreed, breaking character to slap Chris on the back, which sent the youth staggering.

Chris was grinning, however, as he began an exaggerated bow that he switched in midstream to a curtsy, complete with holding out imaginary skirts. The rest of us, meanwhile, applauded enthusiastically.

"Gotta admit, the kid's good," Radney said beside me, while I nodded my agreement. "I wasn't expecting this. If we're not careful, he might just show up the rest of us."

Tap, tap, tap.

"Keep in mind that we have two-thirds of the play still to rehearse," Harry said, cutting short the congratulations. "I suggest we wait until the end before we sprain our arms patting ourselves on the back."

And on that note, rehearsals continued. By the time Harry the Taskmaster called a final curtain, it was seven PM.

"Whew," Marvin declared in understatement, mopping the sweat from his face. "Number Nine, you got any more of those cookies you put out earlier?"

Tessa sniffed. "I believe that Radney ate the last one approximately two hours ago. And if my count was correct, that made at least three more cookies than anyone else got."

"Hey, I'm a growing boy," Radney protested, toweling off his bald head, which was literally streaming sweat past his ears and onto his shoulders. Flexing a bicep, which bulged alarmingly, he added, "You don't want me wasting down to nothing, do you?"

I laughed harder than everyone else, but that was only because I'd seen pictures of Radney at his wrestling weight.

"Don't worry, there's more where those came from. But maybe we should think about supper first?"

Harry nodded. "If no one has objections to Chinese again, I'll place an order with the Dancing Tiger . . . my treat."

The cheers at this were heartfelt if subdued as everyone started going inside, presumably off to their respective rooms. I waited a moment on the porch with Harry, my own mood sobering. Busy as we'd been with rehearsal, I hadn't had time to mull over what I'd learned about the GASP members at the library. And I definitely hadn't had a private moment with Harry to tell him about my conversation with Dr. Bishop. Before I could broach the subject now, however, he said, "You really did do a good job today, Nina. Not Broadway caliber, mind you, but good for a rookie."

"And I'll take that," I replied with a smile. Not wanting to spoil the mood—or delay our takeout delivery, since I was as hungry as everyone else—I decided to talk to him later tonight about the Reverend's findings. And so I switched back to innkeeper mode.

"While you're phoning in that order, how about I check on Susie and see if she's up to eating with us."

I left him on the porch, phone to ear, while I headed inside. But when I reached the second floor, I saw that Marvin was already tapping at Susie's door.

My first impulse was to step back toward the landing so that he wouldn't see me—why, I wasn't certain. But before I could, he was already inside the room, closing the door after him. And if I wasn't mistaken, the metallic click of the door being locked followed.

"Looks like the widow won't be alone for long," came a voice behind me, causing me to jump.

I whipped around to see Bill right behind me. Apparently, given the glass of iced tea he was holding, he'd made a stop in the kitchen first.

"I'm sure Marvin's just making sure she's okay. I was on my way up to do the same thing, myself," I told him, feeling a little creeped out by the man's observation. Though whether that was because it was a creepy thing to say, or because I suspected there might be some truth to it, I wasn't sure.

Bill merely smirked a bit and passed me on his way to his room.

Throwing up figurative hands, I returned downstairs for a badly needed shower. Once sweat-free, I changed into a fresh white linen top and denim shorts. I even had Mattie fed before the Dancing Tiger delivery guy rang the bell.

Supper in the dining room a while later was companionable if subdued—and, for once, Yorick-free. Marvin was there, but minus Susie.

"I'm kinda worried about that girl," he said as he dug a fork into a big plateful of chow mein. "I checked on her before I came down, and she was still kinda out of it. Maybe someone can bring her up some food after we eat."

"I'll do it," Chris piped up, surprising us. Shrugging a little, he added, "I'll let her know that her part as Ophelia is covered so she doesn't have to feel like she's letting the troupe down."

Harry nodded his approval. "Good idea. As for the rest of you, I suggest once you're finished eating that you retire to your rooms to study your lines. You did good work today, but we cannot afford to slack off this close to opening night. Your wake-up call tomorrow will be at the same time as this morning."

This announcement brought a groan from everyone. Still, once they'd shoveled down their dinners—the heat having made everyone doubly hungry—the troupe obediently filed upstairs.

Except Harry. He remained stretched out in his chair, presiding over the empty table rather like the lord of the manor. The difference was that instead of a snifter of brandy or an oversized beer stein in his hand, he had a steaming cup of rooibos at his elbow.

"Just so you know," I told him, "I might be filling in for one of your troupe members, but I still have a business to run. Those bathroom floors don't mop themselves. So I might be late to the party tomorrow."

Then, glancing about to make certain none of the troupe had slipped downstairs for leftovers, I asked, "Do you want to hear how things went with Dr. Bishop?"

"I was wondering if you were going to bring that up. I figured since you hadn't said anything that it turned out to be pollen, like I told you."

His smile was smug, so I took particular pleasure in replying, "You figured wrong. There *was* something in the glass."

Pulling out the notes I'd made during my call with Dr. Bishop, I gave Harry a swift recap, repeating the names of the medications the man had specified. When I had finished, Harry nodded.

"So the Rev says that it was some sort of benzo in the glass. Does he think that's what killed Len?"

"No one will know until the toxicology results come back from Atlanta, which will take weeks," I said, repeating what was rapidly becoming a mantra. "The thing is, Susie gave Sheriff Lamb a whole list of drugs that Len was taking, and nothing like Xanax or Pazaxa was on it. And I don't know about you, but that sounds kind of suspicious."

Harry shrugged. "Maybe she didn't know. Maybe he went doctor-shopping and had a secret 'script. Or maybe he bought a few tablets off someone in the troupe."

The way he said this made me wonder just how many of the GASPers had their own prescriptions. Guessing what I was thinking, he shrugged again and said," Half the actors I know are on antianxiety meds. Think of it as an occupational hazard."

"And, no," he added, easily guessing my next unspoken question. "I'm not part of that half. But just because these guys are amateurs doesn't mean they aren't quivering bundles like us pros. I bet you one or two of them are packing pills in their bags right now."

Which could support my suspicion that Len didn't take the med on his own, that someone in the troupe had slipped it into his glass. But I wasn't ready to share my thoughts with Harry at this point . . . not until I'd snooped around some more.

Instead, I changed the subject. "I meant to tell you earlier, but while I was out on the square this afternoon I ran into Professor Joy from the SOCS committee. He'd heard about Len and wanted to know if the play was in jeopardy. I told him you had everything under control, that you were going to take over the role of Hamlet. I even put in a plug for you as being a major draw for the show."

"So he said." Harry picked up his phone off the table and swiped a couple of times. "And I quote, *Ms. Fleet thoughtfully reminded me of your star power. We shall update the website tonight so that your name is prominently featured as both director and headliner for the play.*"

"That's good . . . right?"

Harry shrugged. "If the play is a success, yes. If it bombs, I would prefer my name not to be associated with it."

"Then we'll just have to make sure it's a success," I declared.

We chatted a few minutes longer about the upcoming performance and then joined the rest of the troupe in calling it an early night. But weary as I was, I still had difficulty falling asleep thinking about what I'd learned from Dr. Bishop. Worse, despite agreeing to keep the results of the champagne-glass testing confidential, I was starting to feel guilty keeping the information a secret from Susie. Was it right that I, a veritable stranger, knew more about her husband's death than she did?

Slumber finally claimed me well after midnight. I awakened with a groan less than six hours later when my alarm went off. Figuring I could skip the morning shower as I'd showered the night before, I hit the snooze button a couple of times. I managed to be dressed and at the door by seven to greet Jasmine, and had breakfast set up by seven thirty as usual.

Radney made it downstairs and into the dining room first.

"Sucks getting old," he muttered. "Ten years ago, I coulda hung out in the heat all day and be rarin' to go at dawn. But yesterday kicked my butt."

"I'm sure you're not the only one," I replied, pointing him to the coffee while covertly studying him.

Nothing alarming had appeared in my web search about the man. Still, I hadn't forgotten the look he and Susie had exchanged when Len had mocked him about his ruined notes. That, and Radney's assertion that Len had tossed up roadblocks in his, Radney's, career path. Either could be a motive for seeking revenge.

By now the rest of the troupe minus Susie was trooping in. By seemingly mutual agreement, everyone pretty well kept to themselves. That was fine by me, as it gave me the chance to quietly observe.

Now that I knew more about what had happened between Marvin and Len, I found myself looking hard to see if I could read any guilt behind that beard of his. I'd still not laid hands on those business journal articles yet, but it seemed—to quote Marvin—that Len really *had* done him wrong.

And I found myself giving Bill the Brawler a bit of extra scrutiny too. His comment about the widow had struck me as odd, almost as if he thought *he* should be the one providing her comfort. The only thing I could hang on Tessa was her desire for Bill to have the Hamlet role. Maybe she'd thought slipping Len a mickey would take care of that, never actually meaning him permanent harm. I couldn't come up with a motive for Chris, which, had this been a television cop show, would probably have meant he was the guilty party. Though the drug thing did seem rather Generation Z. Frankly, at this point I couldn't afford to dismiss any of the troupe as suspects, not even Susie.

I frowned into my rapidly cooling coffee. Susie's shock and tears in the face of her husband's sudden death had seemed genuine to me. Then, again, she was an actor like the rest of them. Besides, wasn't it usually the spouse that the real-life police always looked at first when they suspected foul play?

I'd checked in on her after I'd laid out the food and before everyone else came downstairs. Somewhat to my surprise, she had answered the door looking freshly showered and dressed, and even with a bit of makeup on.

"Thanks, Nina," she said when I reminded her about breakfast. "If you don't mind, I think I'll wait until everyone else has eaten and then I'll pop down and grab a bite. Tell Harry I'll try to rehearse today too."

So had Chris not told her that her role had been recast, or had she chosen to ignore that bit of news? Figuring that problem was between actor and director, I merely nodded and agreed to pass on the message. Which I did when Harry came strolling in at 7:45.

At promptly eight, Harry gave the troupe their ten-minute warning. "And a slight change to our rehearsal space. With Nina's permission, today we'll be moving onto the front lawn. We need to block out some big scenes, including the final sword fight. Radney, I'll leave it to you to haul the weapons downstairs."

"Do me one favor today," I told Harry as the troupe dispersed and I began stacking dishes. "Try not to chop up the front yard with your sword fighting. I'm already in Hendricks's bad book over the backyard and the hawthorn. He'll be livid if he has to repair anything else on the grounds."

"We'll leave the golf cleats behind," he wryly promised. Then, with a sigh, he continued, "For the moment, I'm more worried about dealing with Susie. I know she wants to try rehearsing again, but I think I've got to cut her loose."

I sighed too. "I know it stinks, but you're doing the right thing for the festival."

Harry nodded. "Bottom line, we're too close to opening night. I know she's going through a lot right now, but the play is too important to risk her falling apart on stage. I feel like a jerk replacing her, but I've got to do it."

"If it helps, I'm right with you in the jerk club," I reassured him. "I tossed and turned all night, thinking about the whole situation with the champagne glass. I kind of told Dr. Bishop I wouldn't say anything, but I've already told you. You know, barn door and horse and all that. So, don't you agree it's only right that Susie should be told, too?"

Harry gave me a quick head shake, but it was too late. I heard a little gasp from the open dining room doorway, and then a familiar voice demanded, "Susie should be told what?"

Chapter Seventeen

I had momentarily forgotten that Susie planned to come down to breakfast after the rest of the troupe had finished theirs. And so, of course, she had walked in on my conversation with Harry. And while I meant what I'd told Harry, I had also wanted time to decide how best to broach the subject. Unfortunately, it seemed like I was going to have to organize my thoughts on the fly.

I managed a weak smile. "Really, it's nothing. I just—"

"Please don't patronize me, Nina," the woman cut me short.

She marched into the room on high-heeled sandals, grabbed an empty coffee cup off the sideboard, and started pouring. "I might be a blonde but that doesn't mean I'm a half-wit. You said that Susie should be told. That must mean something about Len. So please tell me."

I exchanged a quick look with Harry, and then I nodded.

"You're right, Susie. You have the right to know. I was just trying to decide how best to break it to you. So here it is. The afternoon after Len, uh, after he . . ."

"After Len died," Susie sharply prompted, dumping a few teaspoons of sugar into her coffee.

I blinked, and then frowned. If Susie wanted blunt, then that's what I'd give her.

"Right. After Len died, I realized that the champagne flute he'd been drinking his mimosa out of was missing. I remembered he'd carried it off when he went for a smoke, so I went outside to search for it. I actually found it hung up in the hawthorn, not far from where he fell."

"Oh, well, I guess that's a good thing for you," she said, sliding a triangle of quiche and some sliced peaches onto a plate and settling at the table. "There's nothing worse than an uneven number of glasses. It makes it so hard when you're entertaining. But, seriously, is that what I needed to know?"

"Not exactly," I told her. "When I found the glass, it still had some of the mimosa Len was drinking left in it. It turns out there was some sort of residue, as well."

"Residue? You're saying Len was drinking out of a dirty glass?"

She gave a dismissive wave of one hand and then dug into her quiche.

"That's real sweet of you, Nina, but it's okay. I know you worry about things like that, but I promise I won't put anything about that glass in the online review. Just wash it out real good and no one will ever know the difference."

"It wasn't dirt, Susie," I said with a sigh. "Yesterday, I took the glass to Dr. Bishop—he's the coroner—to get it tested. What we found out is that the residue in the drink was actually Pazaxa."

Susie set her fork down with a clatter.

"What do you mean, Pazaxa?" she demanded, giving me a sharp look. "That's some sort of antidepressant, isn't it? Len didn't take anything like that. Your Doctor-Whatever-His-Name-Is has to be mistaken."

She gazed down at the half-finished slice of quiche on her plate. "You know, I thought I was hungry, but I guess I'm not. Harry, I'm not sure I can make rehearsal today after all. I thought I was doing better, but Nina's got me all upset now talking about Len and drugs. I think I'd better go lie down again."

With that, she abruptly shoved away from the table, high-heeled sandals clicking on the wooden floor as she hurried out of the dining room. I could hear the echo of her shoes on the stairs, and the faint sound from upstairs of a slamming door.

Harry slid back his own chair and rose. I noticed that, along with the untucked gray cotton shirt he wore, he was sporting a pair of ankle-length black tights in lieu of the usual jeans. Obviously ready for swordfight practice, I told myself, trying not to notice that the black tights were definitely tight and that they showed off some well-developed glutes.

"I'd say thanks for running off my actor for me," he said as he tucked Yorick under one arm and his binder under the other, "but you saved me the trouble of telling her she's out. And I guess I'll see you after you finish all the housemaid-ery things you do."

"Sure," I told him, but my thoughts already were elsewhere. I watched him leave the dining room, followed by Mattie, who'd apparently been bitten by the show-biz bug. Since the entire property was fenced in, I had no problem letting her hang out with the gang. And besides, for the moment I was mentally replaying my brief conversation with Susie.

Talk about the lady protesting too much, as Hamlet's mom would say. The blonde had been quick to claim that no way had her husband been taking any antianxiety meds. Had Susie known all along that Len was taking Pazaxa and been keeping his secret safe? Unless the meds were hers, and Len had been pilfering her stash.

I glanced at my watch. Once I turned on the dishwasher it would be time to give the rooms a quick run-through. As I changed the linens every other day, today I'd only be remaking beds and wiping down counters and sweeping floors. And while I cleaned, I could do something that I had never yet, as an ethical innkeeper, done to my guests. I could take a look at their stuff.

The notion made me a little queasy. In fact, a whole lot queasy. After all, that was one of the unwritten understandings between innkeeper and guests, the idea that one's possessions were sacrosanct while under the B&B's roof. Not that I'd be digging through their suitcases.

What was that discreetly admonishing sign in Cymbeline's one art gallery? *Look With Your Eyes and Not With Your Hands.* If something pertinent—say, like a prescription bottle—was sitting out in plain sight, I'd simply take a hands-free gander at the label.

Conscience only a bit eased, a few minutes later I was pulling my wheeled bucket with my cleaning supplies out of the upstairs linen closet. The door to Susie's room was closed, so I assumed she was still barricaded within. I'd start with Bill and Tessa's room. Just in case, I gave the usual courtesy knock and called, "Housekeeping," before letting myself in.

Even a few days into their stay, the pair kept a relatively neat room. They'd availed themselves of the vintage highboy dresser and had unpacked all their clothes into it. Their suitcases were stowed in a similarly neat tower on the folding rack in the corner. Tessa had claimed the top of the dresser, leaving Bill the small desk as his drop zone. The only disorder was the clear plastic tub beside the highboy from which spilled bits of costuming and wigs and what appeared to be a leather codpiece.

Taking a prudent step back from that last, I made quick work of straightening everything else, visually searching for anything that looked like medication. But no incriminating plastic cylinders dropped out of the sheets as I remade the bed, and none were neatly lined up on either desk or dresser. Since the desk and dresser drawers were firmly closed, I declared them off-limits.

Finishing the bedroom, I moved into the shared bathroom between their room and Susie's. Her connecting door was shut. Just to be sure, I put an ear to the door. Faint sounds from what sounded like a movie drifted to me, so chances were she was watching something on her laptop.

I gave the fixtures and floor a quick cleaning while doing my best to peer into Bill and Tessa's unzipped toiletry bags. Nothing . . . that is, not until I spied one of those plastic pill organizers alongside a well-worn bamboo toothbrush on the hanging shelf.

Bingo.

Except that (a) I had no idea whose pills they were, and (b) loose in their individual day-of-the-week sections as they were, I could only guess at the medications' identities. It didn't help that the *Sunday* through *Saturday* slots were filled with more than one size and colored pill. For all I knew, they could be vitamins or perfectly benign supplements. More importantly, I wasn't sure what Pazaxa actually looked like.

I finished in there and moved to Radney and Marvin's shared room. As their bathroom was down the hall, I'd have to catch it later. For now I concentrated on the bedroom.

Despite the "girly" decor, as Marvin had put it, anyone could see that a couple of guys were sleeping there. From Day One, I'd had to tiptoe around their open suitcases and piles of electronic accoutrements. Now their bordering on slovenly ways made it easy for me to do my stealthy observation. Even so, I almost missed the amber-colored plastic pill bottle sticking out of the leather shaving kit on the small table next to Radney's bed.

I squinted at the bottle's label, which was half concealed by a deodorant stick tossed on top of it. My earlier queasy feeling returned with a vengeance as I made out the letters PAZ.

I glanced around me even though the door was shut. Then, telling myself that this fell into the "out in the open" category, I bit my lip and pulled the bottle out of the leather bag.

Pazaxa XR 3mg Tab, according to the label, which also included Radney's name and the address for an Atlanta pharmacy chain. There were instructions, too, that read, *Take one tablet once daily, preferably in the morning. Do not be chew, crush, or break tablets. Do not take with alcohol.*

No alcohol. Which would include champagne. I thought back to the night after Len's death, when half the troupe had come back from their evening at Brutus Burgers pretty well snockered. Did that mean Radney didn't take his meds daily—which might also mean he wouldn't notice a tablet or two missing? Or was he setting himself up for trouble by mixing booze with his meds? I wondered, too, about the whole chew-crush-break thing before realizing the XR on the label might mean *extended release.*

Carefully sticking the pill bottle back where I found it, I pulled out my cell phone and did a quick search to find that the antianxiety medicine also came in a dissolvable form. If Len was used to the chewable version but had swiped a couple of tablets from Radney's stock, maybe he'd crushed them up in error. And according to what my search results said, breaking up what was meant to be an extended release medication could prove dangerous.

I was shaking a little as I left the men's bedroom. I now knew more about anxiety meds than I had ever wanted to know. Worse, I had learned more about the private lives of some of my guests than I should. Never would I have guessed that Radney required Pazaxa, but the truth was that anyone was susceptible to mental health issues

Certainly, I wasn't judging, but I *was* beginning to wish I had heeded Harry's advice and kept my nose out of the whole situation. Or that I hadn't found that darned champagne flute in the hawthorn. But since I still had a final room besides Susie's to clean, I would finish what I'd started.

I entered Chris's room, needing the tranquility of the decor's cool yet earthy tones. The youth's luggage consisted of two backpacks and a duffle bag. Everything was neatly laid out on the second bed, including a heavy pink vinyl box with black polka dots that looked surprisingly like a woman's makeup kit.

What were you expecting, camo? I asked myself. The box's lid was closed but the heavy-duty zipper was unzipped. And as I straightened the bedspread around it, I managed to bump it hard enough (okay, it took two or three times) that the top flipped open, revealing the contents.

I sighed. Lying atop the expected hair gel, toothpaste, comb, and what looked like a manicure kit was a familiar skinny bottle made of amber plastic. The medication name on the label, and even the dosage and warning were the same as for Radney's meds. Even the pharmacy chain that had filled the prescription was the same.

Poor kid.

Being eighteen or nineteen and needing that sort of medication to get through life had to be rough, I told myself. On the other hand, the fact that the youth's issues had been diagnosed at such a young age definitely was a positive. His treatment apparently was working too. Of all the troupe, he actually appeared to be the most balanced despite a certain tendency toward snarking and ignoring his elders.

I went to flip the kit's lid closed again, then frowned as I noticed something else. The surname printed on the medication label belong to the youth, but the first name wasn't Chris. At least, not exactly.

"Christina Boyd?" I puzzled aloud. Had Chris swiped the meds from a sister, or maybe his mother? That could explain why he didn't seem to need the prescription . . . but not why he had the drugs tucked away in his luggage.

Then a possible answer for at least one of those questions occurred to me. Just as quickly, however, I told myself that it was way too Shakespearean a scenario to even consider. Putting that theory on ignore—at least until I had enough mental bandwidth to deal with it—I left the room and rolled my way back to Susie's door. I could still hear the faint sounds of the movie or whatever it was that she was watching.

"Hey, Susie," I called, knocking, "it's Nina. Do you want me to straighten up?"

I waited for an answer, but none came. I gave another knock and then tried the knob. The door was locked from within. Maybe she'd fallen asleep, I told myself. Or maybe she was simply ignoring me.

"Fine, clean your own room," I muttered, but without much real heat.

I stuck my cleaning bucket back in the closet and headed downstairs. Since there was no laundry today, I was pretty much finished with the chores portion of my morning. That meant I could head outside and join rehearsals with Harry and the gang.

Or, I could take a nice air-conditioned car ride over to the Heavenly Path Funeral Home and Crematorium for another chat with the Reverend Dr. Thaddeus Bishop.

I smiled to myself. For the moment, that sounded like the more enjoyable choice. Of course, I'd use the excuse of picking up my champagne flute to explain why I'd stopped by, and I would even bring him a slice of Daniel's cobbler as a thank-you. Then I sobered. Since we'd be chatting in person and not over the phone, maybe I could convince him to tell me a little more about drug interactions, particularly those that involved Pazaxa.

First, however, I plated the remaining fruit and pastries from breakfast and added some of Marvin's favorite cookies, then made a fresh pot of coffee. This I set up as usual in the dining room for my guests' late-morning snack. When everything had been arranged to my satisfaction, I went out to let the troupe know it was ready.

I immediately saw that the restaging of my front porch had continued. Someone had moved both of my Adirondack chairs out into the yard and under the magnolia. Harry slouched in one, looking very directorial wearing mirrored sunglasses and with his omnipresent binder propped in his lap. Mattie had commandeered the other chair, sitting so that she was rolled back on her rump with all four legs sticking out, virtually mimicking Harry's pose.

Since the players appeared to be re-setting themselves between scenes, I took the opportunity to go over and talk to Harry.

"I see you found your assistant director," I told him, indicating the pup.

Harry smiled in Mattie's direction, and for a moment twin Aussies were reflected in his sunglasses. "She's a lot smarter than most of the ones I've worked with, I'll give her that. So, are you here to work?"

"Actually, I'm here to let you know that everyone's morning snack is laid out in the dining room. And, if you don't mind letting Mattie hang out with you a while longer, I need to run a quick errand. I'll join everyone after lunch if that's all right."

Harry gave me a look over the mirrored shades. "It's pretty bad when your dog is more dedicated to the arts than you. Tell Dr. Bishop that I said hi."

I considered protesting that the funeral home wasn't where I was headed, but both of us would know I was lying. So instead I said, "No way am I bringing up your name. I mentioned you yesterday and about got the deep freeze from him. So apparently you're still in the good Reverend's bad book."

"I can't think why."

"No, seriously," he protested when I snorted in disbelief. "The only thing I remember is that whole disappearing coffee-cup hoopla I told you about the other day. My theory has always been that Sister Malthea broke it and hid the evidence."

My snort became a snicker. The elderly church secretary would have been merely middle-aged at the time, and her champagne-colored Cadillac fresh off the showroom floor. I could readily picture the tiny woman sneaking pieces of the broken mug out to her ride, and then driving far out into the country to some bridge at midnight and tossing the shards into a fast-moving stream.

"Fine, I believe you," I told him. What I didn't say was that, depending on how well the cobbler worked as a bribe, I might ask the pastor outright why he was still holding a grudge against one Harry Westcott.

Chapter Eighteen

"Dom Perignon?"

I smiled a little as I stared at the matte-black gift box that Dr. Bishop had just handed me there in the foyer of his church. The gold shield label on its front said *Vintage 2006*. Probably a good year for champagne, not that I drank Dom on a regular basis. In fact, I'd not had any since celebrating one of the ex's first tournament wins several years earlier (I'd toasted my divorce with margaritas instead).

I grinned inwardly. Perhaps it was meant to be a swap for the cobbler I'd brought for him and Sister Malthea, and which the latter had already carried off to the church office for later. If so, I definitely was getting the better part of the deal.

But, of course, the sturdy yet elegant box I held now was far too light to contain a bottle of the iconic sparkling wine.

"The packaging was left over from last night," the Reverend explained with an answering smile. "Mr. Murphy's wake was quite the celebration of a long life, and we opened more than one bottle in his honor."

"I thought the box would be a more fitting receptacle for your stemware than a potato chip canister," the pastor went on. "And you can be assured that Sister Malthea carefully cleaned your glass before packing it. Now, unless there is anything more I can do for you . . ."

He trailed off on a questioning note and with an elegant gesture to the door behind me, both of which translated to, *Why don't I see you out now?* It had been merely bad luck on his part that he happened to be in Sister Malthea's office when I stopped in. But as this was likely my last chance to chat with the man—unless someone else checked out in a more figurative sense from my B&B sometime in the near future—I had to seize the opportunity now.

"Thanks again, Dr. Bishop," I told him, keeping my feet firmly planted. "But maybe you can help relieve my mind a bit more concerning this unfortunate situation. You see, it turns out that a few of the people staying with me actually do take Pazaxa, so it's possible that Mr. Marsh did too. But I would have thought it was a safe drug, with all those people having prescriptions for it. Why would it factor into Len's death?"

The coroner hesitated. I suspected he was weighing the enjoyment of lecturing on a subject he knew well versus giving me, the civilian, too much info. After a moment, he apparently decided to indulge his scholarly side.

"At the directed dosage, Pazaxa and similar antianxiety medications have minimal side effects and seem to be quite beneficial to those who take them properly. But at too high a dosage, or mixed with certain other medications—most particularly opioids—the interaction can prove injurious . . . or even deadly."

"But shouldn't he—or shouldn't his doctor—have known all that?"

He nodded. "Yes, which is why I would guess that this drug was not specifically prescribed for Mr. Marsh. No competent physician would prescribe benzodiazepine to someone taking opioids."

"And now," the pastor finished with a smile, "I really must say goodbye. Thank you again for the cobbler."

A few moments later I pulled the Mini out of the church parking lot and barely missed hitting the ginormous SUV that zipped through the intersection in front of me. Which reminded me that Len had recently been the victim of a hit-and-run accident. An accident that, given this new information, maybe hadn't been so accidental.

Meaning that perhaps one of the GASP troupe—all of whom lived in Atlanta—had been behind the wheel of the hit-and-run car.

And also meaning that the whole drug in the mimosa thing could actually have been a second—and finally successful—attempt by one of his fellows to murder Len Marsh.

During the short drive back, I tried to recall where everyone had been while the mimosas were being served, and how everyone had reacted when Len's body was found. But my mental spreadsheet flew right out of my mind when I turned down my street to see twenty or more people in my driveway crowded around my wrought-iron gate. Worse, a sheriff deputy's car was parked in front of the house.

The frantic refrain of, *Don't let it be someone else dead*, looped through my brain at supersonic speed as I cut over to the opposite lane and screeched the Mini to a halt nose-to-nose with the cop car. Leaving purse and champagne box on the front seat, I grabbed my keys and rushed down the sidewalk to the gate.

The deputy on scene was again the red-haired Mullins. He stood with the crowd who were pressed up against the bars of the gate, apparently intent on something happening beyond it. I halted alongside the deputy.

"What's wrong?" I breathlessly demanded, as from my angle I couldn't see through the gaggle of bystanders. "And please don't tell me there's another body lying around!"

Mullins turned and whipped off his omnipresent amber-lensed sunglasses. Wire-framed and vaguely aviator in style, they bore a strong resemblance to those worn by the red-haired actor on that CSI show from a few years back. Deliberately, I was sure.

Deadpan, he said, "Ms. Fleet, we received a call about men fighting and weapons being drawn. Do you know anything about this?"

Before I could reply, a cheer rose from the group beside me. Mullins glanced toward the gate and broke into a grin. Realizing what must be happening, I muttered a few swear words and shoved my way through the three-deep crowd for a look myself.

Radney sprawled face-up on the grass beneath the edge of magnolia's canopy. Harry posed dramatically over him, the point of his sword at Radney's throat. And then, with a final poignant cry of, "I am justly killed with my own treachery!" Radney twitched for a moment and then lay still.

The crowd around me burst into enthusiastic applause. After holding his pose a moment to allow those with cell phones to get a picture, Harry straightened. He thrust his sword into the grass beside him (another thing for Hendricks to complain about!), then reached a hand down to his vanquished foe. Radney leaped up, miraculously healed, and both men took sweeping bows.

"Thank you, lords and ladies," came Harry's infamous English accent over the sound of clapping. "We appreciate your kind attention. Remember that you may witness *Hamlet* in its entirety beginning this Friday eve, again on Saturday eve, and a final time on Sunday afternoon. And now, you must excuse us as we break for our noon repast. Farewell."

The crowd grumbled good-naturedly at the end of this free entertainment but obediently dispersed, chatting excitedly among themselves. I waited until all the tourists had continued on down the sidewalk before turning a sour look on Mullins.

"Thanks for the heart attack," I told him.

Gaining control over his grin, the deputy soberly replied, "Sorry, Ms. Fleet. I was driving past and saw some folks peering in your gate, so I stopped to make sure everything was okay. It turned out it was Mr. Westcott and his people practicing for the show. I don't normally go for that Shakespeare stuff, but all that sword-play was pretty good. I stuck around, and the next thing you know, we had a whole crowd watching."

"Well, I'm glad you enjoyed the show, Deputy Mullins," I wryly replied. "And thanks for not slapping us with a citation for swashbuckling in public, or whatever."

He shrugged. "There's no law against sword fighting on private property, as long as you practice safely. But you might want to

197

move your car so I don't have to ticket you for parking facing oncoming traffic. There *is* a law against that."

With that, he gave me a crisp nod and put his sunglasses back on, then headed back to his car. Since he appeared to be waiting for me, I muttered a few more bad words and pulled open the gate. Getting back into the Mini, I carefully signaled and pulled around Mullins, then signaled again and pulled into the drive. That must have satisfied him, for with a wave out the driver's window the deputy drove off.

By the time I had reclosed the gate, parked, and walked back around to the front, the rest of the troupe except for Harry and Mattie had gone back inside. Harry noted the box I was carrying and gave an approving nod.

"A little something for opening night? That's kind of you."

"Sorry, it's just the box with my glass in it," I told him as I gave Mattie a skritch behind the ears. "Mr. Murphy's friends finished off all the good stuff last night. But you do seem to have accumulated a few fans here in town. Even Deputy Mullins is a convert."

"The applause *was* gratifying," Harry agreed, tucking the binder under his arm and then liberating his sword from the turf. "And I must say I'm starting to feel more positive about the situation. The troupe is coming together quite nicely. I trust you'll take part in this afternoon's session?"

I nodded.

"Excellent," he replied. "Then that entitles you join us in the dining room. A sandwich platter was delivered from the grocery-store deli a while ago. We'll have a quick lunch, and then we're back to work again."

"Sounds good," I told him. But when he made as if to head for the house, I put out a restraining hand. "Harry, wait. I really need to talk to you before we join the others."

He gave me a quizzical look but nodded.

"Step into my office," he said, and gestured to the Adirondack chairs. We each settled in, though Mattie gave me a side eye for hogging what had been her seat. Harry set down his binder beside him and laid his sword across his lap. "What's on your mind?"

I hesitated. I'd planned to tell him about my conversation with Dr. Bishop. But it was too much to discuss in the space of a few minutes, so instead I settled on something else that had been bothering me ever since I'd conducted my "hands-free" sweep through the guest rooms.

"It's about Chris," I told him. "But first, I have to confess something. Remember at breakfast, when you told me that chances were some of the troupe had prescriptions for anti-anxiety meds? Well, later on, while I was cleaning the rooms, I poked around a little to see if anyone did."

Harry gave me hard look. "Hold on. You're saying you searched your guests' luggage? Does that include mine?"

"No! I mean, I didn't search anyone's luggage. Especially not yours. I didn't even go up to the tower room."

"Then what exactly did you do?"

Now, I was *really* regretting sticking my nose into things. But since I couldn't undo that, let alone undo this conversation with Harry that I'd started, I forged on and hoped he'd agree that the end justified the means.

"All I did was keep my eyes open while I was fixing the beds and straightening the counters in case someone had left a pill bottle lying about. I didn't touch anything."

Well, didn't touch much, I silently amended.

"But I promise it wasn't idle curiosity," I went on. "After that call from Dr. Bishop, I felt I owed it to Len to see if I could help figure out what really happened to him."

"I see," Harry replied, but from his cool tone I could tell that he wasn't exactly convinced my motives were pure. "And did you find any benzos on display?"

"Actually, I did. Both Radney and Chris had prescriptions for Pazaxa."

"Interesting." The actor nodded, expression growing thoughtful. "I could see Chris, but Radney's a bit of a surprise. You actually saw their names on the labels?"

"Both of them, yes. And that's why I need to talk to you about Chris."

I hesitated again. In this era of hash tags and pronouns, how did one ask a question that could be construed as insensitive at best, hostile at worst . . . and, *noneofyourbusiness* either way? But some sixth sense—or maybe it was Len whispering in my ear from the Great Beyond—was telling me that the answer had some bearing on what had happened to Len.

"I don't know a polite way to put this," I finally said, "but is Chris a guy or a girl?"

"What?"

The look Harry gave me was one of pure astonishment, though that expression promptly morphed into uncertainty, and then disapproval. "Have you been living under a rock the past few years? You've got to know that it's considered really bad form to ask a question like that, don't you?"

"Of course, I do. And as far as I know, everyone has been going under the assumption that he is . . . a guy, I mean. But I think he might actually be Christina, which happens to be the name on his prescription bottle."

Harry's expression promptly switched back to astonishment. "Interesting. It's actually on the label?" At my nod, he went on, "You're sure Christina isn't his mom, and he swiped the pills from her?"

"I thought about that. But then there was the pink make-up kit in his luggage."

Harry rolled his eyes. "You're going to condemn a guy for liking pink?"

"I'm not condemning anyone!" I shot back, feeling like one of those beleaguered politicians whose comments were constantly taken out of context. "I'm trying to find out what, or who, is behind Len's death. And I really need someone to bounce my thoughts off of."

He shook his head and glanced in Mattie's direction.

"Poor dog, is this what you have to put up with on a regular basis? Okay, okay!" he interrupted himself as I landed a kick on his tights-covered shin. "I'll be your sounding board, just not your punching bag."

"Thank you. So, can we start with the possibility that Chris is actually Christina?"

Harry shrugged. "Sure, let's go with that. Which means what . . . the kid is transgender? And which is it, Chris to Christina, or Christina to Chris?"

I gave him a stern look, pretty sure he wasn't taking the matter seriously but also sure that, until further notice, he was the only troupe member I could trust. Or, rather, trust a little.

"Not a clue," I told him. "For all we know, Chris just prefers the name Chris and likes gender-neutral clothing. It doesn't have to mean anything. I'm more interested in the name on the prescription bottle. With a different name and gender in the doctor's records, the prescription would probably be harder to trace."

"And that's an issue because . . ."

"I don't have it all figured out yet, but I've been thinking about those tricks someone in the troupe has been playing. Maybe that's all Len's death was originally meant to be . . . a trick. Maybe someone thought it would be funny to slip the benzos into his drink to make him sick. You know, payback for being a jerk. And they didn't know that the combination with Len's painkillers could actually be deadly."

Harry abruptly straightened in his chair, which is hard to do in an Adirondack and with a sword in one's lap.

"Whoa. So now we're moving from Chris going all Viola on us"—referencing, I knew, a female Shakespearean character who'd disguised herself as a male—"to accusing him . . . er, her . . . er, they . . . of murder?"

I shook my head. "I'm not saying anything about murder. And I'm not even saying that Chris did anything. Maybe the only secret he's keeping is the gender thing. But he sure was upset about Len's death for only knowing the man a few months."

And then, channeling my best inner Detective Columbo, I went on, "Plus there's one more thing. Remember how Len was hit one night while riding his bike, and the case is still unsolved?

What if that had been an actual attempt on his life, and the whole benzo in the mimosa was act 2 . . . only this time it worked?"

I could see from Harry's expression that he was beginning to consider the possibility, and that he wasn't liking it at all. And so I continued. "What sort of process do you have for bringing on new GASP members? Would someone have checked Chris out before letting him . . . her . . . into the troupe?"

"That's Tessa's bailiwick as the GASP secretary. If you're interested in joining, all you do is fill out an application and attach an acting resume and headshot. She does the preliminary vetting, and then the application goes up before a committee that consists of me, Tessa, and three others. Majority approves, and you're in for a six-month trial period."

He shrugged and added, "Of course, I didn't have to go through all that red tape myself. I told Tessa I was available, and she overnighted me my membership card that same day."

Of course, she did. Heck, Tessa probably sent him his own personal red carpet while she was at it. But all I said was, "Obviously, Chris made the cut. How long has he been in the troupe?

"Close to five months, I think."

Which meant that either Chris was really good to have landed a role in the traveling troupe, or else no one else in the main group wanted to perform *Hamlet* in Cymbeline in the dead of summer. I suspected it might have been the latter.

But before I could make a reply, Harry went on, "You're not going to confront Chris on this whole gender identity thing, are you? It could really blow up in your face, and I'm not sure it has any bearing on the Len situation, either."

"I think it does, Harry. I won't say anything yet, but I want to check into Chris's background. Do you think you could get his . . . her . . . application package from Tessa so I can do some research online? You know, see if there are any social media pages that might prove if Chris and Christine are the same person?"

I didn't want to ask Chris that question directly. He'd likely deny whatever I said, and that would be an end to it. But if I could somehow get him to admit the truth about his identity on his own—as in, being confronted with incontestable evidence as to who he really was—then I would. Because even if Harry didn't agree, I still felt in my gut that this deception, deliberate or not, somehow was tied to everything happening within the troupe, including Len's death.

Harry hesitated, then finally sighed and nodded.

"Let it go on the record that this is against my better judgment, but I'll see what I can manage. In the meantime, I need you to swear that everything we've talked about is Secret Squirrel, Top Secret, Scooby-doo-y—"

"Hey, Spielberg . . . Number Nine!" Marvin bellowed from the porch, cutting Harry short. "Y'all want to get in here? Emo Boy ain't looking so hot."

Chapter Nineteen

I scrambled out of the lawn chair and hurried to the house, Mattie bounding after me. Harry followed more slowly, having to juggle a sword along with his binder. Once inside, I saw that the dining room door was open and the troupe gathered within.

It was apparent the minute I walked into the room that something was going on. A deli platter of mixed sandwiches, along with two quarts each of potato salad and coleslaw and a bunch of little plastic condiment containers took up the center of the table. Plates sat at the usual spots, though for the moment they sported half-eaten sandwiches and dollops of sides. Everyone had left their chairs to gather around Chris.

The youth was still seated at the table but had pushed away his plate, which held what was left of a turkey and Swiss on rye. He rested his upper body upon the now empty spot, head pillowed face-down on his skinny arms. The rest of the troupe stood a respectful few steps back, but were staring at him in concern. Susie was there too, I saw in surprise, apparently having ended her embargo with the arrival of lunch.

My first fleeting thought was that this might be some sort of trick on Chris's part. He was, after all, an actor. But the concern on the faces of the rest of the troupe definitely appeared to be genuine.

I hurried over to the youth. For rehearsals, he'd removed the omnipresent knit cap, so his black hair flopped untidily around his skull.

"Chris, are you okay?'

"G'way," came the muffled groan as I lightly touched his shoulder. "M'fine."

"You don't sound fine to me." I glanced over at Radney, who was closest to him. "What happened?"

Radney frowned. "We were just sitting here eating when the kid suddenly said he didn't feel good. A couple of minutes later, he does this."

"Probably heat exhaustion," Marvin opined. "Get him something to drink, put a wet rag on the back of his neck, and he'll be fine in a couple of minutes."

I nodded. "I've got a couple of sports drinks in the refrigerator. Can you get those, and some ice water and a towel?"

"On it," the man replied and headed to the kitchen.

"I'll help," Susie echoed and followed after him.

By now, Harry had made his way inside. He took one look at Chris and said to me, "Why don't we get him into the parlor. He can stretch out there."

"Good idea," I agreed. To Chris, I said, "If Harry helps you stand, do you think you can make it into the other room?"

"Try," he mumbled, raising his head.

By now, Marvin was back with the sports drinks, while Susie had brought a bowl with the ice and towel. Between Radney and Harry, they pretty well carried the youth into the parlor, with everyone following after. I had hurried ahead and spread a blanket over the threadbare light-blue velvet of one sofa so they could settle Chris there. Tessa grabbed a throw pillow and tucked it beneath his head while Bill moved one of the side tables closer to hold the drinks and bowl. Once the youth was as comfortable as we could make him, with a wet rag on his forehead, I turned to the others.

"Thanks, everyone. Now, why don't you go back into the dining room and finish your lunch. I'll stay with Chris and make sure he's okay."

I expected a protest or two, or even a volunteer to be official Chris watcher, but the troupe dispersed as quickly as they'd come. Apparently, in the acting world lunch trumped any crisis. Only Harry stayed with me.

"He doesn't look good," the latter murmured as he eyed the moaning youth. "You think we should get him to the ER?"

I hesitated, staring at Chris with equal concern. If he was acting, he deserved an award, especially if he could fake that pallor and the sweat that was dripping onto the throw pillow.

"Let me try to cool him down with the ice pack and the sports drink. If he doesn't bounce back in a few minutes, we'll put in him the Mini and take him to the emergency clinic."

Harry nodded. "All right. I'm going back to the dining room to make sure no one else is on the verge of collapse. Yell if you need help."

"Will do."

While Harry left to ride herd on his rapidly dwindling troupe, I wrung out the cold towel again in the bowl of icy water and replaced the cloth on Chris's forehead.

"This will help cool you down," I told him, earning a nod and another groan. I let him stay settled like that for a couple of minutes, keeping an eye on his breathing. Then, picking up the bottle of neon-blue sports drink, I went on, "If I prop you up a little higher, do you think you can manage a few swallows of this? We need to get some electrolytes back into you."

"I'll . . . try," he choked, and scooted up a bit while I added another throw pillow behind him. He grabbed hold of the plastic bottle and took a few small swallows.

"Slow down," I warned as I re-soaked the towel and draped it over the back of his neck. "Chug it down too fast and it will come right back up again."

He nodded and handed me back the bottle. "I–I don't know why . . . I feel so bad," he moaned. "We were in the shade . . . the whole time. I drank . . . plenty of water."

"Sometimes that heat just sneaks up on you," I reminded him, though my attention was more on his appearance than his words. By now he should have started to come round, but he still looked like something Mattie had dragged out of a ditch. If he didn't perk up in the next few minutes, we'd be making a run to the ER.

He managed to drink a bit more, then handed me back the bottle. "I–I'm not sure this is helping," he whimpered. "I feel pretty sick."

And then he clamped a hand over his mouth.

"Wastebasket!" I exclaimed and leaped up, running to snatch the metal can tucked under the desk in the corner.

I made it back to him in time to thrust the receptacle into his hands just before he began throwing up a bright-blue stream of liquid.

"You okay?" I gingerly asked a few moments later once he'd quit coughing and gagging.

He nodded and set down the can, then used the wet towel to scrub his face. Looking up at me again, he said, "Yeah, I feel, like, a hundred percent better."

And, indeed, his voice sounded quite a bit stronger. Sighing in relief, I carried the trash can at arm's length to the porch door and left it outside to be dealt with later. I came back to find Chris sitting up and drinking the rest of the sport drink.

"Uh, you think you should be chugging that stuff down after what just happened?"

He managed a wan grin. "Seriously, I'm, you know, really good now. That was weird. I don't know why I felt so bad all of a sudden, but now that I've thrown up I feel a lot better."

I shook my head. "No one else got sick from rehearsing outside, so maybe it was the deli food that didn't agree with you. Maybe there's a spice or something in it that you're allergic to."

Then I hesitated as another though hit. *Or maybe someone put something in his food to make him ill.*

Surely not, I protested to myself. Chris's getting sick was too much like the Len situation to be believed. "It had to be the food," I persisted aloud. "Maybe we can narrow it down. Do you remember what you ate?"

He shrugged. "I don't know, turkey on rye. I think there was roast beef too, but I didn't eat that. Bill was making a big deal about everything though."

If I'd been Mattie, my ears would have pricked up. "Really? How?"

"Oh, you know, giving everyone a job. I mean, it was just a stupid lunch, but he and Susie had to take everyone's orders and serve them, and Radney had to pour all the drinks. I got to put out the silverware, yay," he added with a mocking wave of his fingers.

"What about Marvin?"

"I think he just sat around. Oh wait, no. He had to give everyone a serving of potato salad and coleslaw. I hate potato salad, so I didn't eat any."

"But the sandwich tasted okay?" I prompted.

He shrugged again, looking a little puzzled now at my continued questioning. "Yeah, I guess. I mean, it had some sort of funky spicy mayo stuff on it that wasn't the best, but the turkey and cheese were fine."

Funky spicy mayo stuff. Maybe funky and spicy enough to hide the taste of some sort of meds?

So that could explain how only Chris's food had been tainted. Someone could have added something to one of those individual condiment containers and then spread it on just his sandwich. Though there was another possibility.

Maybe Chris was trying to deflect suspicion from himself and had deliberately made himself sick.

Harry would say I was going into Secret Squirrel territory with that theory, but somehow it almost seemed the more logical explanation. I couldn't think of a reason why any of the troupe members would target Chris—not when he was the one running around with a bottle of Pazaxa in his luggage. He might have a whole pharmacopeia in that pink box for all I knew. And if he *was* guilty of tampering with Len's drink, no matter his actual intent, how better to throw off any suspicion than to taint his own food?

A smart kid could go online and do a search for some substance that would make him temporarily sick but wouldn't actually hurt him. Heck, there were probably YouTube videos out there that told exactly how to do it. Would Dr. Bishop analyze the uneaten half of a turkey sandwich, I wondered?

But all I said aloud was, "How about I fix you some plain buttered toast until you're sure you can keep anything heavier down?"

"Seriously, I'm fine. You don't have to treat me like a kid," he replied, sounding more like his whiny self again. Dropping the towel in the bowl, he got to his feet. "Thanks for looking out for me, but I think I'll go back with the troupe now."

"If you're really sure you're up to it. The toast is no trouble."

"I don't want toast. I'm fine. Really," was his impatient response.

I nodded. There was still the matter of the name on the pharmacy bottle label. And while Harry was right that I couldn't just come out and ask him, a scene from an old World War II movie that I'd watched with my dad had flashed through my mind while I was thinking about disguises. The tactic had worked for the movie's bad guys.

Still, I found myself hesitating. What I was about to do could go wrong in a very different way if Chris really was transitioning.

Calling out his female birthname—*deadnaming*, it was called—could be hurtful, at best, and seen as threatening, at worst. No way did I want to do either to him. But a man had been murdered on my property, and discovering who'd killed him was equally important.

And so, sending the youth a mental apology in advance, I waited until he was almost to the door to call, "Hey, Christina!"

"Now what?" he replied with a long-suffering sigh and turned to face me.

Abruptly, his—her!—eyes widened in horror. Sputtering, he cried, "What's wrong with you? That's not my name."

I was about to point out that he'd just answered to it, but seeing the youth's expression begin to crumple, I hurriedly tempered my tone and added, "Don't worry, no one else knows you're really Christina."

Well, except for Harry. And since he hadn't believed me, he didn't count.

"I didn't answer to anything," Chris shot back, seeming to rally. "I wasn't paying attention, that's all. I don't know any Christina. My name is Chris, period."

What about the prescription label with Christina's name on it? I wanted to say, but that would reveal that I'd snooped. Instead, I replied, "I won't say a word to anyone about how you identify until you give the all-clear. But I think you'd be happier if you got all of this out in the open."

Chris gave me baleful look. "Seriously, this is so not cool. You'd better quit making up stuff about me or I'm going to tell Harry."

I raised my hands in mock surrender. "Fine, consider the subject dropped. But if you change your mind, I'm a good listener."

The offer earned me a rude gesture before the youth stalked a bit unsteadily from the room. I sighed, knowing I deserved that. I was 99.99 percent sure that I was correct, but without a confession or DNA test it was my word against his . . . hers. The problem was that if I kept pushing the matter, things could get unpleasant for all of us. So my only option right now was to sit tight until I had something more to go on.

In the meantime, I'd be keeping an eye on Chris as I still hadn't eliminated her . . . him . . . as the anonymous jokester. But I'd also be watching out for him too. If someone else in the troupe was the prankster, another of the actors might fall ill, or worse. And as far as I was concerned, three strikes would be it for whoever was responsible. If necessary, I'd lock the whole darned lot of them in the parlor and make them watch the *Gilligan's Island* version of *Hamlet* on a continuing loop until someone confessed.

More fired up than I wanted to be, I returned to the dining room to find that the rest of the troupe was about finished with lunch. Fortunately, none of the other players were sprawled out on the table as Chris had been. But they all seemed glad to see him (I decided for now to use male pronouns) relatively healthy and back with them again.

Except for Susie. While the others greeted him as if he'd been gone for days instead of minutes, I saw her glance Harry's way. The actor give her a nod in return.

I frowned as I served myself a sandwich, careful to avoid the funky spicy mayo stuff. What had the pair been scheming about in the short time that I'd been gone? I found out quickly enough, however, when everyone had resumed their seats and Harry tapped his water glass for order.

"We're happy that our youngest troupe member appears to have recovered from his illness. But we don't want to take chances with anyone's health, particularly this close to opening night. So for the rest of today, Chris is sidelined. Susie will resume the role of Ophelia."

So much for Harry taking a hard stance with Susie.

I heard a few murmurs from the others, but mostly it was heads nodding in agreement at the casting change. Even Chris didn't pipe up with a protest, so apparently he had the good sense to realize he still wasn't fully recovered from whatever had made him ill.

Harry, meanwhile, went on: "Chris, if you're up to it, you can hang out and act as my assistant director today. Nina, can you still read Chris's original lines this afternoon?"

"Sure," I mumbled through a bite of turkey on rye. At least that way, I could keep an eye on everyone all in one place. "But can I talk to you about that before we go back out again?"

Harry gave a regal nod. "Certainly. As for everyone else, if you've finished your lunch, you have another ten minutes before we assemble again under the magnolia."

He remained kicked back in his chair, idly drumming his fingers atop Yorick. As for the troupe, they gathered their binders and notes and started moving in the direction of the door. I'd finished my sandwich by now, and as the others left I began gathering the dirty lunch dishes . . . careful to keep the plate with Chris's half-eaten sandwich on top of my growing stack.

Not that I was going to go crazy and run it over to Dr. Bishop demanding that he test it, too. But, just in case, I'd toss what was left into a plastic bag and stick it in the freezer. That way, if something else happened later that pointed to tampering, I could bring out the sandwich as Exhibit B.

I carried the dishes into the kitchen and set them next to the sink, then returned to the dining room. By now, everyone except Harry had already left. Still, for good measure, I slid the pocket door between the dining room and hallway shut in case someone wandered back in our direction.

Harry waited until we were closeted away and then gave me a sideways look. "Don't tell me, you have a Secret Squirrel report to file already, don't you?"

"Actually, I do," I admitted, "but I can't share it. At least not yet. I promised someone I'd keep my mouth shut."

"Fine by me," he replied with a shrug and stood. "Then I guess this meeting of the Scooby-Doo club is adjourned."

"Hold on. That's not why I wanted you to wait. Did you ask Tessa to send you those applications on all the troupe members?

"Already done. She's going to e-mail me everything after we finish rehearsals for the day. As soon as I get them, I'll forward them to you."

Since I knew from past e-mails he'd sent regarding the ownership of Fleet House that he already had my addy, I nodded. "Thanks, I just wanted to be sure. Now, give me five minutes to toss the dishes in the dishwasher and I'll be right out to rehearse."

While he went out the hall door, I surveyed the leftovers. The containers that had held the sides were pretty well scraped clean, and all that was left of the condiments was a single spicy mustard, which I'd toss just to be safe. The sandwich platter was pretty well decimated too, but there was enough left that I decided to find a smaller container that would fit in my refrigerator. Between Marvin and Radney, they'd finish off the remaining sandwiches by mid-afternoon.

I pushed open the swinging door to the kitchen intent on my search mission for plasticware, only to hear the distinctive sound of running water and a grinding motor.

The last person I'd expected to see at my sink was Bill. But there he was, along with the pile of dishes I'd left there a few minutes earlier, busily scraping and rinsing them, and sending the food scraps into the running garbage disposal.

And, of course, those scraps included Exhibit B, the half-eaten sandwich that might or might not have almost poisoned Chris!

Chapter Twenty

"Wha–What are you doing?" I choked out over the clashing sound of the garbage disposal.

"Oh, Nina, there you are."

The man met my disbelieving look with a smile and flipped off the disposal.

"I had to come back in for a fresh glass and saw all these dirty dishes waiting to go into the dishwasher. I knew you were busy talking with Harry, so I thought I'd help out as you're pulling double duty. You know, your regular job plus rehearsing with us."

Bill's smile wavered as he finally noticed my shocked expression. "Like I said, I was just trying to help. That's okay, isn't it?"

I took a deep breath. Either he'd craftily gotten rid of any evidence that someone had tampered with Chris's food, or Tessa had trained him well as far as household chores went. Before I'd found out about his battery arrest, I might have been inclined to go with the second explanation. But he had been the one in charge of serving the sandwiches. That fact, and knowing he could be pushed to violence if someone messed with his agenda left Bill squarely on my suspect list. All I needed was a plausible reason for him to target Chris.

For the moment, however, I managed a smile and said. "No problem. I was just a little startled to find someone in the kitchen when I thought it was empty."

"Well, I'm finished rinsing. I'll let you stick everything in the dishwasher. I know everyone has their own way of doing it."

While he left with his glass of ice water, I went looking for a container for the sandwiches. I'd put away the food and leave the cleaning for later. Maybe running lines with the troupe would help settle my brain.

Though, of course, by an hour into rehearsals my brain felt like *it* had gone through my garbage disposal. Tomorrow, Harry promised, we'd be doing dress-dress rehearsals—no costumes, but complete run-throughs of the play—but today was the final blocking of scenes.

Better late than never, Professor Joy finally had texted him the festival stage dimensions during lunch. And so, at Harry's direction, Marvin and Radney had commandeered a quartet of decorative pots from the front gardens. Pacing out the measurements Harry gave them, they set the pots at our virtual stage's four corners so that we had a visual of our limits.

I prayed that Hendricks wouldn't make an unexpected swing by the house and see this desecration of his landscape artistry.

Rehearsal continued, but in increasingly boot-camp mode. We repeated each scene multiple times, with Harry clapping out the rhythm and calling stage directions. While I continued to read from my script pages, the rest of the troupe had long since memorized their lines. They spouted slightly modernized Elizabethan dialogue with pathos or vigor, as the moment required, and I had to admit that for amateurs they were pretty darned good.

Early on with the rehearsals, I'd been a bit surprised when Harry had decreed that no one, including himself, would attempt an English accent for their role. Though, apparently, he bent his no-accents rule when addressing the audience. But other than that, we all spoke in our normal accents.

As our characters are Danes, he'd pointed out, *they wouldn't be speaking the Queen's English anyhow. Consider our play a translation. When you translate something from another language into English, you don't throw on an accent, and so neither would we.*

In his role as Hamlet, Harry was in the majority of scenes. Seeing him at work, I acquired a new admiration for the skill it took to direct and act at the same time. I didn't even want to know how much time and effort it had taken to condense the play into its foreshortened length but still retain its integrity. And though Harry's classic speeches were constantly interrupted by directions to the troupe—*Gertrude, stage right . . . Polonius, I want another beat between lines*—I still found myself sucked in by his portrayal of the Melancholy Dane.

Susie, I was surprised to see, held up for the entire rehearsal. Never once did she succumb to any of the histrionics that could have been forgiven under the circumstances. In fact, in my opinion, she more than rivaled Chris with her slightly more fragile but equally powerful take on Ophelia. From his vantage point in the Adirondack chair next to Harry, Chris could see it too. When I glanced over at him during Susie's version of Ophelia's mad scene, his baleful expression spoke folios.

By the time we finally broke for the day, it was after six. All of us were exhausted and dripping with sweat. Except for Mattie, who had found a nice cool spot in the dirt beneath the magnolia tree and had been lounging on her belly all afternoon. And Yorick, who didn't feel the heat much.

A couple of hours earlier, Harry had scheduled a delivery from my favorite Mexican food place. Right as we were gathering our notes and props, the Tino's Tacos delivery van pulled up, earning a subdued if sincere cheer from us all. Worn out as I was, I was still determined to keep an eye on everything, and everyone. On my watch, no one was going to slip anything except Tino's handmade salsa into anyone's food! And so I personally walked the delivery guy into the house and stood guard over the food until everyone had washed up and joined me in the dining room.

Fortunately, the brief yet tasty meal proceeded without drama. The only groans came from Marvin, who ate one too many bean burritos. And from Radney, who lamented aloud that, as Marvin's roommate, he would be subject to any side effects from the other man's culinary overindulgence.

I was gratified to see that I didn't have to recruit any cleanup help once we were finished. Everyone carried their own dishes to the kitchen, while Radney and Tessa made efficient work of consolidating the leftovers into a couple of the takeout trays. There was enough for lunch tomorrow, I judged, which meant more time for rehearsals.

In a few minutes, most of the mess was cleared away, and the troupe had dispersed— I assumed, to their rooms for more study and then an early bedtime. Which left me with only a dishwasher to load and breakfast to prep for morning.

Harry was the last to quit the room.

"I'd stick around, but I've got Secret Squirrel business pending," he stage-whispered as he passed me on the way out. "You know, files to send one of my agents."

The files. Sure, I'd asked for them, but after an afternoon spent in the heat, and breakfast prep still ahead of me, doing online searches for Chris and the other troupe members wasn't exactly an enticing prospect. And so I grimaced a little but nodded.

I rushed through my final cleanup and the setup for tomorrow, merely stacking the breakfast plates and coffee cups and silverware instead of setting the usual fancy morning table. I hadn't even had time to pick another batch of fresh peaches off my tree, so I sorted through what I had left from the previous day, slicing and plating the ripest fruit before refrigerating it.

That accomplished, I switched off all but the usual lights and headed to my room. I'd make the formal final rounds of the place before I went to sleep.

Even though it was barely seven thirty, Mattie was already lounging on the foot of my bed, blue eye and brown eye both firmly closed. I grinned at the way all four fuzzy feet stuck straight up, while her body was twisted about like a croissant. The posture hardly looked comfortable, but judging from the snores emanating from the pup she was apparently deep in blissful sleep.

I took a brief but satisfying hot shower. Feeling human once more, but with wet hair still in a towel, I pulled on a gray T-shirt and pair of matching gray cut-off sweats. Since I was off the clock as far as my innkeeper role, I didn't need to look good for the guests. Comfy for me was all that mattered.

I checked my e-mail and answered a couple of reservation requests for the week after the festival. Harry's expected message, sent from *harrywestcottactor,* was in with my spam where I'd previously relegated any correspondence from him. The subject line, of course, was Secret Squirrel. I shook my head and moved that e-mail to my in-box, then clicked on it.

A zipped file was attached that I assumed contained all the applications and backup documents for the GASPers. The message simply said, *Will be awaiting your report. ~Agent Harry Westcott.*

And then a *PS* a few lines down, which read: *Seriously, this is confidential troupe information that is not to be shared beyond the GASP executive board, let alone with anyone else. Get whatever you need to do your web search and then permanently delete this file and message. I'm trusting you to follow through. If anyone discovers you have this information, I will claim that you hacked my computer. ~HW*

And then a final *PPS* below that: *Do not under any circumstances reply directly to this email. ~H.*

I grinned a bit at the melodrama, even as I recognized that he was indeed violating troupe policy by sending me this information.

I was a bit touched that he actually said he trusted me . . . but then again, I'd saved his bacon before, so he kind of owed me. But as all I needed was the pertinent data for each troupe member in order to do a search, I'd simply copy off that information into a separate file and then permanently delete everything else.

Had I not been so tired, I likely would have succumbed to nosiness and spent time actually reading each member's acting resume and, in some cases, clicking links to their reviews. As it was, I did spend a moment looking their headshots.

Susie's, of course, was pure glamor, professionally made up and dramatically backlit against a black background, so that her blond hair looked almost blinding. Len was Brooks Brothers handsome, a three-quarter profile against a black background that made him look quite dashing. Bill and Tessa each had emphasized the character-actor image in their photos, chin on fist (Bill) and finger to cheek (Tessa), expressions serious. Radney's headshot looked like something out of a corporate publication, dressed as he was in a suit and tie, expression stern yet thoughtful. Chris had opted for full emo, hair spiked and combed to one side, angry eyes outlined in black, and looking more androgynous than ever. Only Marvin was smiling in his headshot, though he'd eschewed the usual flannel for a plain dark-blue button-down, giving him an appearance that was everyman appealing.

I did a quick cut-and-paste of each actor's name, DOB, and current address into a document. Going full Secret Squirrel, I named my new doc *Mattie's Feeding Instructions, Updated*. I saved said document into my personal miscellaneous file before permanently deleting Harry's message.

Then, feeling virtuous, I composed a new e-mail. *Mr. Westcott, be advised that requested information has been received and dispositioned per your instructions. Sincerely, Nina Fleet.*

With the preliminaries done, I started my online search for Chris aka Christina Boyd. Immediately I was swamped with results, finding Christinas who ranged from lawyers to teachers to truck drivers. LinkedIn alone had more than three hundred possibilities, as did Facebook and Instagram. I narrowed my search to Georgia, and then Atlanta. That cut down the results significantly, and with that, I started searching the images, looking for her headshot.

Apparently, she'd never posted it online. And as for the various social media accounts, she'd done a good job of locking down her privacy. The one Instagram account that might have been hers had a profile picture that was a close-up of what appeared to be a tiger's eye . . . definitely not identifiable as male or female.

After a few more minutes of this, I pushed back from my laptop and simply stared at the screen. Exactly what I was trying to accomplish, I wasn't certain. Stumbling over incriminating comments on Twitter? Finding a Pinterest page with memes illustrating how to mix prescription drugs for very bad reactions?

I shook my head. Somehow, everyone else managed to find obscure twenty-year-old quotes from politicians and sports figures. Yet I couldn't discover anything about Chris/Christina that would qualify as dust, let alone incriminating dirt! And certainly nothing that would tie her into a crime that might or might not even exist.

I pulled up my "Mattie" document again. *Address and phone number.* Why not try searching the old-fashioned way?

I typed in her name and address, and immediately got results from several of those public records pages. You know, the ones that promise to spill everything about bankruptcies and criminal records and so forth . . . for a fee, of course. I even found a listing with an address match, except that the age was at least ten years too old.

I frowned. The age difference wasn't enough that this could possibly be her mother, assuming both had the same first name. But given the address match, this had to be the right Christina Kimberly Boyd. Maybe the records site had made a mistake?

An *aha* moment hit me, and I typed in the name of my teen-aged nephew. His name and city immediately popped up—this despite the fact that, at seventeen, he shouldn't have any records yet, let alone ones that were public. Sure enough, his age as listed on the site was twenty years off.

I nodded. The boy had had social media accounts since he was twelve or thirteen, despite technically being too young for sites such as Facebook. Which had meant he'd fudged his online age in order to create his accounts. Chances were that Chris had done the exact same thing; hence, the reason her purported age didn't match.

Feeling rather proud of my online sleuthing abilities now, I retyped Chris's name. The entry popped up again, and I took a closer look. No bankruptcies or arrests that I'd have to pay to find out about were noted. And then I checked the list of possible relatives.

Only one family member's name was shown . . . Amanda Christina Boyd.

Her mother, I presumed. And, possibly the owner of the prescription I'd seen, if the older woman also went by the name Christina. Maybe still a reach, but worth checking out. And so I typed *Amanda Christina Boyd* into the search block.

Among the listings for that name was one at the same address as the person I assumed was Chris. The age shown was forty-seven, which fit for having a child who was nineteen or twenty. Unlike her daughter, Amanda had several lawsuits and even one criminal activity that the site teased was available for review.

The section listing possible relatives was longer, with Chris as well as five others—male and female—with the surname Boyd. Likely siblings and parents, possibly other children, though Chris has never indicated whether or not she was an only child.

That, however, wasn't what interested me.

The final public section of the listing was "also knowns," names the listed person might also go by. Thus, Amanda Christina Boyd was also *Amanda Boyd* and *Amanda C. Boyd*. But apparently the woman had gone by yet another name . . . *Amanda C. Marsh.*

My heart suddenly began racing as it occurred to me what this might mean. Still, I wasn't ready to believe it until I did more Googling. Finally, I located a few archived documents—by this point, only a few sentences each, as the original links had long since gone cold—that confirmed my suspicions.

Twenty years earlier, Amanda Christina Boyd had married Leonard Quayle Marsh at Holy Grace Episcopal Church in

Atlanta. Their divorce had been finalized eight years later, with Amanda resuming her maiden name. In the interim, however, the once-happy couple had welcomed a child, Christina Kimberly Marsh.

All of which pointed to the incontrovertible fact that our GASP troupe member, Chris Boyd, was actually Christina Marsh, the late Len Marsh's daughter.

Chapter Twenty-One

"Incontrovertible?" Harry echoed a while later as he scanned the screenshots from my laptop that I'd printed out. "I'm not going out on that limb. Not yet."

It had taken a moment for my initial shock at discovering that Chris Boyd aka Christina Boyd aka Christina Marsh was Len's daughter to subside enough for me to react. Next had come a bit more Googling. Finally, I'd texted Harry to tell him I was headed up to see him, pronto.

I hadn't been up in the tower room since Harry had taken up residence following the troupe's arrival. Somehow, between rehearsals, he'd managed to turn what had been a sparsely furnished open area into a quite livable suite that I almost didn't recognize—mostly because the new accessories weren't mine.

A three-paneled wooden screen complete with carved tigers now separated the sleeping area from the rest of the octagonal room. Several splashy batik throws in Woodstock hues were draped across the bed and other furnishings. But what made me roll my eyes was the bright-yellow happy-face pillow beside the yoga mats that were propped against the wall. Doubtless all this decorative flair had been stashed somewhere in Harry's bus along with the trio of suitcases that he'd stacked to make a quirky table.

I was perched on one of the throw-covered ladderback chairs in the sitting area, while Harry enjoyed the comfort of the room's single upholstered chair. As he had studied my screenshots by the light of a vintage floor lamp, I recounted my conversation in the parlor with Chris, including my only partially successful attempt to get the youth to admit his true identity. Harry had listened to it all with interest if not a little skepticism.

Now, setting down the pages on the suitcase table, he opined: "It does appear that an Amanda Boyd was married to a Len Marsh. And it also appears that the same couple had a daughter named Christina. But the whole 'Chris is Christina' scenario is a stretch. For all we know, this is some sort of identity theft. Unless the kid admits outright to being someone else, we've got nothing."

"And, no," he cut me short when I opened my mouth to protest, "pulling a trick you saw in *The Great Escape* doesn't count as firm evidence. And while I applaud your ingenuity, I hope you realize that was so not cool."

Hearing echoes of Chris and knowing Harry referred to the possible deadnaming, I winced and nodded. "But even if he doesn't admit anything, it's pretty evident he . . . she . . . is up to something even if it doesn't have anything to do with Len's death. So we can't just turn a blind eye to it."

"Aha!"

He jumped to his feet and pointed a dramatic finger heavenward.

"And there—to paraphrase my very close friend Hamlet—is the rub. Or the eye, more accurately. If we go with your theory about Chris being Christina, why after all these months in the troupe together didn't Len recognize his own daughter? And wouldn't Susie have known her too?"

I'd already asked myself those questions. So while Harry leaned against the dresser, arms crossed and waiting expectantly, I was able to lob this one back at him pretty easily.

"If the public records are right," I began, "Len and his first wife divorced when their daughter was eight or nine. And Susie said she and Len had been together for about ten years. So if the daughter is around nineteen . . ."

". . . then that's not a lot of time in between wives," Harry finished for me.

I nodded. "Right. And Susie didn't say if the divorce was finalized or not when she took up with Len. But I'd guess either way that he probably didn't have much time to spend with his little girl at that point, not when he had a hot new girlfriend to worry about."

"Okay, so maybe your timeline works," Harry conceded, somewhat to my surprise. "But between the name and the face, I don't see how a parent wouldn't recognize his own kid."

"The name part is easy. Len probably didn't even know that she dropped his last name for her mother's after the divorce. And even if he did, Christina Boyds are a dime a dozen. You wouldn't believe all the hits I got when I typed in that name, even when I narrowed the focus to Georgia."

The actor nodded. "And the face?"

"Think about it. If Len had been slacking on the visitation pretty much from the start, his mental picture of his daughter would have been that of a little girl. Not an adult who had dyed black hair and wore unisex clothes and was passing as a male. So chances are that meeting a Chris Boyd who was a guy probably never even rang any kind of familiarity bell with him."

Harry was silent for a moment. Finally, he said, "I love a good Secret Squirrel conspiracy as much as the next person. But there's still a lot of *supposing* and *chances are* for me to totally buy into your theory."

When I started to protest, however, he held up a finger. "Let's say for the sake of argument that you're right. What's the point? Assuming that it's not merely a case of transitioning, why would Chris go through such a charade and hide his identity for all this time?"

Now it was my turn to go silent. I'd come up with a few theories while I was doing all that Googling. As I ran through the list in my head again, they all sounded like rejected plotlines from one of those after-school specials I'd watched when I was a kid. But because Harry was waiting, I tossed them out there.

"Maybe she was spying on Len for her mom. Or maybe she wanted to renew contact with him but didn't know how he'd react, so she was scoping out things first. Maybe she really wanted to join the troupe but was afraid he'd veto her if he knew she was his kid."

While I was talking, Harry had resumed his seat across from me. The time was closing in on nine PM, meaning with the shortening summer days that it was long since dark outside. With only the floor lamp and the meager stairway bulb throwing out any light, the tower room was heavy with shadows now, making it hard to read the actor's expression.

But when he finally replied, his response was not what I'd expected.

"Forget the whole Chris or Christina situation. If someone did deliberately spike Len's drink—whether or not they actually planned to kill him—then someone in this house is a murderer. And if Chris didn't just have a bad reaction to a deli sandwich, then there's a good chance he was almost the second victim. Which begs the question, is our prankster-slash-killer going to go after him again . . . and is there going to be a third victim, and maybe a fourth?"

I whooshed out a big breath, feeling the stereotypical shiver run down my spine. I'd been so busy looking at the details that I hadn't considered a bigger picture. And the picture that Harry was painting was nothing short of ginormous.

Then I shook my head.

"I can't believe someone is planning to kill off the whole troupe. That's a little too Agatha Christie even for me. If Chris really was targeted, it has to be that he knows something about Len's death . . . or else the killer thinks he does. Maybe it's time to call Sheriff Lamb?"

"And tell her what? That a kid got sick over supper? You said Dr. Bishop was going to let her know about the benzos in Len's mimosa. Connie's a pro. If she thinks there's anything to investigate, she'll be investigating it. But if we bring her over here on a wild-goose chase, all we're going to do is let the prankster know we're onto them."

"So what do we do in the meantime?"

Harry gave me a hard look. "We keep our eyes open, our mouths shut, and lock our respective doors at night. And then, we put on the best version of *Hamlet* that the town of Cymbeline and the state of Georgia has ever seen."

"Agreed," I told him, gathering my notes and getting to my feet. True, he'd just ramped my paranoia level to a full ten out of ten, but I felt better now that he'd validated my suspicions.

"I think that's enough detective work for tonight," I told him. "I'm going to do a final lockup downstairs and then work on my lines before I go to sleep."

"Eyes open, mouth shut," he reminded me.

I nodded and started down the ladder stairs, then paused to call back up to him, "And thanks for not thinking I'm crazy."

"I never said that," I thought I heard him reply.

I slipped out of the tower-stair closet and quietly closed the panel behind me. The hallway was dark except for the small lights I usually kept on at either end of the corridor. I could hear the murmur of voices from behind Bill and Tessa's door, but otherwise all was quiet. Still, I hustled downstairs a little faster than usual.

Once back in my own room, I debated a moment, then stuck the screen captures that I'd printed into my shredder. If any prying eyes made their way into my suite, the only incriminating evidence they'd find would be nice diamond-shaped confetti.

"We're done playing detective for the night," I told Mattie, who was still lounging on the foot of my bed where I left her. "Time to get back into innkeeper mode. C'mon, let's lock up."

The Aussie knew the routine, so she leaped from bed to floor and followed me back out into the hallway. And this night, I definitely appreciated her stalwart presence as I flipped on the usual nightlights and front porch light, and turned out the rest as I made my sweep of the parlor and dining room and kitchen. I turned the deadbolt of each exterior door after first looking outside to make sure that no one was hanging about on the darkened porch. Mattie patiently served as my double-checker, detecting no errant guests afoot until we reached the back door. There, she halted and stared at the windowed door, giving a soft *woof.*

"Good girl, is someone outside? Let's take a look," I said, my tone braver than I actually felt as I peered through the glass.

I moved to one side of the window so that the fountain wasn't blocking my view. And when I did so, I could see a small shadowy figure crouched atop the steps that led from the garden to the yard beyond. With only the solar garden lights and a sliver of moon above, I couldn't make out the person's identity; still, I had a feeling I knew who it was. And so I opened the door just a bit.

"Go on," I whispered to Mattie.

The Aussie obediently padded outside, trotting around the fountain and making a beeline for the seated figure. I heard a soft cry of surprise as the pup plopped herself down, then saw a thin arm reach around to hug the dog closer.

I quietly closed the door again. I'd check in a bit to make sure that both pup and human were back safely inside, and the door locked after them. But for now I'd leave Mattie to her fuzzy comforting, since after debating the matter with Harry, I was pretty sure now that the youth was not responsible for Len's death.

But barely had I reached my bedroom again than another explanation hit me—one so obvious that I couldn't believe it hadn't occurred to me before. For now I clearly recalled that the tainted peach mimosa had first been served to Chris. Not wanting to be responsible for a minor drinking alcohol, I had swooped in and handed off the drink to Len before Chris could take a sip. And then Len had polished off most of the mimosa, not suspecting anything was wrong with it.

But if I'd not been paying attention, it would have Chris who ingested the overdose of the benzo drug . . . perhaps also with fatal consequences. Which, combined with the sandwich incident, told me one thing. Forget Chris being the second person in the prankster's sights. There was a very real chance that Len's daughter, and not Len, had been the true target of whoever had sabotaged that drink.

Chapter
Twenty-Two

I slept fitfully that night, worried about Chris. Mattie had come scratching at my bedroom door sometime after ten, so I'd taken her on a quick check of the garden again. The grounds proved empty this time, and the upstairs hall was quiet too. Figuring that Chris was safe enough behind closed doors for the night, I'd retired to my room again.

I'd wait until morning to run my latest theory by Harry. As for warning Chris to be careful, I knew that likely wouldn't go well, not if our last conversation was any indication. The best I could do would be to keep an eye on the youth until the end of the Shakespeare festival's run . . . or until Sheriff Lamb and her deputies stepped in.

My alarm clock woke me a little after six. I felt slightly more revived after a long blast of hot water, so that I had breakfast ready to go by seven thirty. My time under the pulsating shower had also given me a chance to rethink my theory from the night before.

Try as I might, I hadn't been able to come up with a reason for Chris to have been the prankster's original target. He'd only been with the company a short while, and everyone apparently accepted him at face value. Moreover, despite the significant age difference and omnipresent earbuds, he'd seemed to fit in well enough with the other players.

But that didn't mean he wasn't still at risk of becoming collateral damage. And so I'd come up with a new plan to foil any future attempted poisonings.

"Uh, Number Nine, we're missing plates," Marvin blearily observed as he led the other equally groggy troupe members into the dining room.

I indicated the tea cart beside me. Instead of the usual fancy china, or even the less formal stoneware-style crockery, I'd pulled out a set of vintage children's dishes that I'd found at an estate sale a few weeks prior.

"Don't worry, all the plates are right here. I thought as we've got a tough day ahead of us that I'd do something a little fun for breakfast. Now, everyone line up to get your set."

I handed Marvin a matching trio of brightly painted plate, bowl, and cup, which he studied in ill-concealed bemusement.

"The theme today is circus animals," I explained. "Marvin, you get the dishes with the lion on it. Radney, you're the tiger. Tessa, you're the zebra."

"Can I have the dog?" Chris asked with a hopeful look as he reached the front of the line.

I smiled. "Sure. And Bill—"

"Uh, I'd really like the giraffe, if you don't mind," that man shyly interrupted. "That is, if you have one."

"You bet. And Susie—"

I paused and gave the woman a quick look. This morning, her hair was pulled back in a tight, business-like French braid, though she was dressed more casually than I'd yet seen, wearing jean shorts and a University of Georgia T-shirt. As for her expression, the usual look of vulnerability was once again gone, replaced by a neutral mask. I gave her a pleasant smile and went on, "Here you go, Susie. The circus pony is for you."

She shot me a tight smile as she took the dishes. "Thanks, Nina. They're real cute."

Harry was last in line. He raised a brow, giving me an expectant look and said, "I'm afraid to see which animal you've reserved for me."

"Oh, that's easy," I answered brightly, and handed over the set emblazoned with a long-armed chimpanzee.

He smiled a little as he glanced from the plates back to me. "Clever," he murmured, just loud enough for me to hear.

I wasn't sure if he was alluding to the chimp thing, or if he recognized there could be no swapping of dishes with the distinctive plates assigned to each troupe member. From the look he gave me, I was inclined to think both. And so, with a satisfied nod, I took my own set, painted with a colorful parrot, and joined the others at the buffet.

I kept my birdy eye on everyone as we ate a mostly silent breakfast. Whether it was the dishware or simply the fact that everyone was still exhausted from the previous day's practice, no errant plates ended up in the wrong hands.

Today would be something of a marathon, for Harry had decided that we'd run through the entire play twice. The first time would be in the morning, followed by a session reviewing the actor's notes he had for the cast (thankfully inside in the air conditioning). The second was actually to be held at the festival site and was what I'd learned was a technical rehearsal—basically, going through our paces for the benefit of the lighting and sound crew so that they could figure out, well, light and sound. The one other difference between today's rehearsals and the dress rehearsal on Thursday was that, in addition to not wearing costumes, we would be minus the drama students who were serving as the actors in the play-within-the-play.

Harry had also made the final casting decision, permanently restoring Susie to her role as Ophelia and returning Chris to his minor roles. Which also meant that I was out of an acting job. I wasn't yet sure whether to be relieved or disappointed by this decision. But that didn't mean I wasn't going to watch with Mattie from the sidelines.

And so, once everyone had eaten, I swiftly gathered the left-overs and loaded the dirty dishes in the dishwasher. That done, I pulled out fresh jugs of lemonade and tea from the refrigerator, and joined the rest of the troupe beneath the magnolia.

The morning went by quickly. After thirty minutes or so of reviewing final stage direction and blocking, we—or rather, they—launched into their performance. As before, I saw everyone else dutifully jotting down final comments on their scripts. I learned in an aside from Radney that formal notes—instructions for each individual actor—were given only by the director. He'd gone on to warn me that, unless actively solicited, giving notes to your fellow actors was a major protocol violation. He had also revealed what he claimed was the biggest secret about acting.

"When it comes to stage fright, everyone gets it," he'd confided. "I might look pretty tough, but you know what I have in my suitcase? A bottle of Pazaxa, because otherwise I'm about to cry like a little girl every time I have to do any sort of public speaking."

Which explained the prescription that I'd seen in his shaving kit.

As for the note thing . . . that, I didn't need to worry about. What I was scribbling on the back of my script pages didn't fall into that category. Instead, now that I'd returned to my original theory of Len as primary victim, it was time to get serious about evaluating the likely guilt of each troupe member.

It's always the spouse . . . or significant other . . . or child/sibling/ parent. That much I had gleaned from watching true-crime shows and reading the newspapers. And so I started my list with Susie.

Motive: Len was a jerk and she wanted out, but there's a pre-nup if she divorced him.

Which was pretty much a strong motive, except that I had no clue what the terms of the presumed pre-nuptial agreement were. They'd been married long enough that chances were she met any minimum requirements for a hefty divorce settlement. Which would certainly offset the risk of being caught in a crime while trying for all his money. Besides, in the short time I'd known Len, I had never seen his jerkiness extended to his wife. In fact, they had seemed like a relatively well-matched couple. And so I moved on to Marvin.

Motive: Seemingly got shafted by his one-time business partner, resulting in lost contracts followed by bankruptcy and a forced sale of the company. And might have the hots for his ex-partner's wife.

To my mind, this was a far more compelling motive . . . unfortunately, because I really liked Marvin. But the opportunity definitely was there. He would have known that Len was on some sort of opioids for his knee. Moreover, with Radney as his roomie for the duration, he'd have easy access to that man's Pazaxa prescription. And there was one other thing. Marvin seemingly had a nickname for everyone he came across, but I'd yet to hear him call Susie by anything other than her given name. Which could be significant when it came to the secondary motive. I added that observation to my list and turned my attention to Radney.

Motive: Said that Len was standing in the way of departmental funding and promotions.

A legitimate gripe but, in my opinion as a former corporate drone, hardly worthy of such tactics. Better to take a new job elsewhere than go to the trouble of trying to eliminate the guy. On the other hand, Radney did have that Pazaxa prescription, so I couldn't quite let him off the hook yet.

Bill and Tessa seemed relatively motive-free save for their mutual dismay that Len had been cast over Bill as Hamlet. In fact, Tessa had even hoped aloud that a fortunate accident that might put Bill back in contention for the role. Could she have engineered that accident herself? As a bonus, Bill—like Marvin—seemed more than a little interested in Mrs. Marsh. Maybe he'd thought that if Len were out of the way his professorial charms would win her over.

With that last note made, I took a quick survey of my list. The only troupe member left was Chris, whom I'd pretty well eliminated from the list. Unless my theory about Chris being Christina being Christina Marsh was correct, in which case there could be a whole slew of Shakespearean motives for offing a parent.

Tucking my notes safely into my pocket, I returned my attention to the play's final scene in time to watch Harry succumb to his stage death alongside Randy, Bill, and Tessa. My applause when Harry called, *And close curtain!*, was genuine.

"All right people, good work," Harry exclaimed as he lithely got to his feet and extended a hand to his fellow corpses, who rose more slowly. "Let's take five and then meet in the dining room to go over our notes. After that, we'll break for a while and have lunch at noon. Our tech rehearsal will begin at one-thirty."

The note reading went relatively smoothly, with most of the commentary constructive. Lunch was from Romeo and Juliette's Pizza: salad, chicken fettuccine Alfredo, and garlic bread. I broke out the animal dishes again, and everyone stuck to the script, so to speak, as far as keeping their plates to themselves.

The full troupe helped with the cleanup, so that at a few minutes after one we were all loading into the Uber van that Harry had called to take us to the town square. I'd considered bringing Mattie along to help me keep an eye on things, but given the heat I decided she'd be better off lounging in the AC rather than broiling in the sun like the rest of us.

We arrived at the site to find burly young men and women dressed in bright-blue festival T-shirts busy putting the finishing touches on the stage. As the festival didn't open for two more days, a temporary fabric privacy screen now surrounded the stage area so that the crew could work without interference from passersby.

A professional-looking light bar hung from the canopy-styled roof system made of canvas and metal rigging, while speakers on tall tripods stood at either side of the stage. Two sets of portable aluminum bleachers were arranged in front of the stage, each with enough benches that perhaps a hundred people could squeeze in. Those bleachers were separated by an aisle, at the end of which was set up what Radney explained was the control booth.

Rather than an actual enclosed booth, however, it was a waist-high box-like platform similar to what I'd seen at small outdoor concerts, with lots of wires and metal panels covered in switches and indicator lights. That was where the technical crew handled the light effects and the audio mixing.

The tech rehearsal pretty much lived up to its name. Tessa had warned me that it could be boring, and she was right. While the actors walked their way through the various scenes, Harry coordinated with the stage manager, Mrs. Constance O'Malley. In her late fifties, with a flawless white complexion and the reddest curly hair I'd ever seen, she had a no-nonsense air about her that even Harry seemed to respect. From what he'd told me earlier, they'd been conferring back and forth now for more than a month regarding the script and casting, plus she had served as stage manager for all the previous festivals.

I noticed that her binder was just as thick as his.

Between Harry and the stage manager and the sound and lighting designers, they determined what lights would hit us when, and how loud we would be. I also learned that, except for a few large props—thrones, sections of wall, and a curtained panel—we had no backdrop scenery per se. Instead, the lighting director would project the appropriate scenes of mountains, castle walls, and so on onto a false wall that stood up against the rear stage curtain.

We repeated the critical scenes until the technical folks were satisfied, which took a big chunk of afternoon. Fortunately, Harry had arranged an Uber for the return trip home too, since none of us wanted to make the short but hot trek back to the B&B on foot.

After the long day we'd all had, no one seemed very interested in calling in a new order for supper either. Sufficient leftovers remained from lunch for another round, however, and everyone agreed that supper could be a repeat. So we gathered in the dining room again at six, with Tessa and Susie insisting that, given the fact we had just enough to go round, the ladies serve themselves first.

"Because there's always someone"—Tessa shot a stern look at Marvin while spooning up a sizable portion of fettucine herself—"who will take more than his share."

"Nope, not the night before dress rehearsal," Marvin genially protested, and gave his broad belly a fond slap. "No extra garlic bread for me tonight. Don't wanna have to let out the seams of my doublet."

"Yeah," Radney echoed, giving his own somewhat convex stomach a rueful look. "I'm sticking with salad."

"A sensible suggestion," Harry agreed, forking greenery from the half-filled salad bowl onto his plate. "But tomorrow's a different story. You'll want to carb up a bit more than usual for the dress rehearsal. I don't want anyone passing out on stage from low blood sugar."

Then, shifting the subject back to Marvin's comment, he went on, "Speaking of costuming, Nina, we need to get you an appropriate ensemble too."

"Me?" I echoed in surprise as I grabbed the extra slice of garlic bread that Marvin had passed on. "You mean, as an actor? But I thought I was out."

"We can use you as an extra. You don't have to worry about lines, you'll just follow Radney or Marvin around and look subservient."

"Oh, go ahead and do it, Nina," Susie spoke up with a smile. "It'll be fun."

Bill nodded his encouragement. "And you'll get to see the play up close and personal."

"C'mon, Number Nine," Marvin urged. "Think about it. You can put it in your annual Christmas letter that you got to perform *Hamlet* onstage . . . and with the great Harry Westcott, no less."

Plus I'd get to keep an even closer eye on Chris and the others.

The last of which being what decided me, though the suggestion about my Christmas letter was almost as compelling. I nodded. "Okay, I'll do it."

Which is how the next morning, while the others were finishing breakfast, I found myself in the parlor with Harry and what he called his *trunk o' costumes.*

Said trunk was actually a ginormous wheeled red suitcase, the zippers of which appeared strained to their limits. I was already familiar with it, in a sense, given that I'd seen Harry assume more than one costume in the past. But when he unzipped it there on the parlor floor, it was rather like flinging opening a cram-packed steamer trunk found in your grandmother's attic.

All manner of costume pieces, from hats to jackets to monk robes to practically anything else spilled out of the suitcase. The actor knelt and riffled through it, pulling out a pale-yellow jacket with poufed sleeves and a dark-green cloak, both of which he tossed to me.

"You've got black leggings, don't you, or maybe some heavy-weight black tights? You'll wear the doublet over them. It'll be big on you, but that's okay. You can pad it with a throw pillow and that will flatten out your figure. The cloak will cover everything else."

He dug around a bit more and extracted a flat black cap with a scarlet feather coiling from it. "This will work. Blow-dry your hair so it's straight and curled under, and wear the cap at a rakish angle. We're not costuming to look like Danish courtiers, we're going for the more traditional Elizabethan look."

"What about shoes?" I asked him as I juggled my new wardrobe.

He frowned. "If you have some ankle-high black boots, preferably with heels, wear them. Nothing cowboy, please. That, or lace-up black shoes with a chunky heel."

Since I had two of the three in my closet, I nodded.

"And when we go for rehearsal," he went on, "you'll need a bag for your civilian clothes and any personal items. Susie or Tessa can help you with stage makeup, so you won't need that. Leave as much of your personal stuff at home, but bring your script with you. No cell phones allowed onstage . . . and that includes backstage. We'll have some sort of lock box or locker for all that."

"Got it," I managed.

Surprisingly, I could feel an incipient attack of stage fright creeping up as he literally piled all this on me. Knowing that I really was going to have to get up in front of an audience, I was beginning to have second thoughts about letting myself be volunteered. Unfortunately, it was too late to back out now.

Harry must have read all that in my expression, for he gave me an understanding smile. "Feeling a bit shaky? That's okay, a little bit of nerves is good for you, keeps you on your toes. As long as you don't fall off the stage, you'll do fine."

"Besides," he added, with a shrug, "no one will even notice you. The audience will be focused on the acting brilliance of that marvelous actor Harry Westcott."

I knew he'd thrown in that bit of braggadocio for my benefit, and so I smiled back. "I'm sure they will. Let me run all this to my room, and then I need to get breakfast cleared up. I'll be sure to try everything on before we head out to the festival."

"Remember what I said about the throw pillow," he told me as he started repacking the suitcase.

Then, from outside the parlor, I heard a frantic shout from Chris, "Nina, come quick! Mattie's sick!"

Instantly, I tossed the costume pieces onto one of the blue-velvet loveseats and rushed into the hallway. Chris stood near the back door alongside the Aussie, who was choking and gagging. By the time I reached the pair, the dog had thrown up what appeared to have been a breakfast burrito.

"Mattie, what happened?" I asked the pup, suddenly feeling a bit like choking and gagging myself.

She stared up at me with guilty eyes, and her bobtail gave a small wag as if to say, *Sorry.* Then I turned to Chris, whose expression was equally guilty.

"I promise, I didn't feed her anything . . . at least, not on purpose," the youth protested. "After you went off with Harry, I got another breakfast burrito. I wanted lemonade too, so I went into the kitchen to see if there was any in the fridge. I swear I was gone thirty seconds, max. When I came back, Mattie was eating the burrito right off my plate. I figured it wasn't that big a deal, so I just went and got another one. And then five minutes later she starts heaving."

"Well, at least she had the decency to do it in the hall," Harry observed as he rolled on past with his suitcase on his way to the kitchen and back out to his bus. "Though I must say I've never seen Daniel's food get anything other than stellar reviews."

I frowned at that and gave Mattie a comforting pat.

It wasn't like her to snatch food from anywhere but her bowl. I'd left a whole baked chicken on the counter before, and though she'd whined longingly at the smell of it, she'd never tried to steal it.

And Harry was right. Daniel's burritos were light and tasty, made with scrambled eggs and potatoes and cheese, with just a hint of his famous jalapeno bacon. Nothing in his food should have made Mattie sick.

Unless some had added something to the burrito she'd chowed down on . . . the same burrito that Chris had planned to eat.

My previous suspicions that had been allayed for a time came rushing back. I'd kept an eye on breakfast again this morning, but had left before everyone finished, which could have given someone the chance to slip a little something into Chris's food.

Torn between guilt and fear, I dropped to my knees and gave the Aussie the once-over. Already she seemed perkier than a moment ago. Her eyes were bright, and she wasn't drooling or staggering, which was a positive. Plus, her gums and tongue were pink, not white or bright-red. Still, when it came to the possibility of poison, I wasn't going to take chances.

"Chris, please take her to her water bowl in the kitchen so she can drink. If you can watch her for a minute, I'll clean up this mess. Call me if she acts at all strange. And don't let her eat anything else!"

I made quick work of the cleanup and then returned to the kitchen to find Mattie and Chris going through the former's repertoire of tricks. Chris looked up and gave me a hopeful look. "She seems fine now, don't you think?"

Mattie gave a quick *woof* of agreement.

Relieved, I called the Aussie over to me for another look. Whatever might have affected her a few minutes ago seemed like it was out of her system now. But I'd keep her close for the rest of the morning in case a visit to the vet was called for.

"I think everything's okay," I told the youth, who looked as guilty as I still felt. Which was why I added, "Don't worry, the jalapeno bacon probably didn't agree with her. We'll just have to be a bit more watchful next time she's in the dining room. Why don't you go ahead and finish your breakfast while Mattie and I take care of the dishes."

I waited until Chris had left the kitchen, then knelt and gave my pup a big hug.

"Such a good girl, Mattie," I exclaimed, not caring as she licked me back. "You're a true heroine, aren't you? You knew someone tampered with that burrito, and you ate it so Chris wouldn't get sick."

"You really think that's what it was?" came Harry's voice from behind me.

Startled, I swung around. The actor had come back in through the door that led out to the driveway, empty-handed now that he'd stowed away the red suitcase again. He bent to give Mattie a scratch behind the ears, adding, "Don't you think it's more likely the burrito didn't agree with her?"

I shook my head no. "She's eaten the exact same thing before and never gotten sick. Besides, there's something you don't know about her."

I gave her a final pat and stood. "You see, Mattie is a rescue dog. I'm pretty sure her first owner"—I put that last word in finger quotes—"equated beating with training. When I brought her home from the shelter, she was afraid she was going to be hit anytime she did . . . well, anything. It took a good year for her to get over the worst of that. But one thing she still won't do is steal food off the table."

Harry frowned, and I could see from the expression on his face that the light was slowly dawning. "So you're saying . . .?"

"I'm saying there's no way would she have swiped Chris's burrito. Not unless it was a matter of life and death."

Chapter
Twenty-Three

Harry considered my words for a moment. "Did Chris say who else was in the dining room right before he went into the kitchen? That might narrow down the field as to who our mysterious poisoner is."

I shook my head. "I was so worried about Mattie that I didn't think to ask."

I hurried over to the swinging door between kitchen and dining room and pushed it open a crack. "Everyone's already gone back to their rooms, it looks like."

Then, my voice teetering on a quaver, I went on: "I can't believe I let that happen. I'd been so careful watching everything these past few days."

"Don't beat yourself up," Harry replied. "Thanks to Mattie, Chris is okay, and that's the most important thing to remember. We'll just keep doing our best to keep an eye on things."

Then he brightened up. "How about I assign Chris to help you out with getting ready for the dress rehearsal this afternoon as this is going to be your first official appearance onstage? That way it'll look like he's sticking to you instead of vice versa. And no one will have any reason to ask questions."

"The buddy system," I agreed. "That makes sense. And, to be truthful, I wouldn't complain about having someone hold my hand through all this."

"Don't worry. I promise you're going to be tired of hands on you by the time we're done today."

I learned what he had meant that afternoon, as the troupe and I gathered at the front door with our costumes and props a few minutes before four, waiting for the Uber van to arrive.

According to Harry's description of the festival stage, while impressive it had minimal dressing-room amenities. For that reason, we'd all done our stage makeup in advance, the ladies setting up with lights and mirrors in the dining room and the men in the parlor. As promised, Tessa and Susie had helped me with the heavy pancake foundation and the rest of the makeup. Chris, minus the earbuds and already wearing what looked like a cosmetics aisle's—worth of products, looked on.

"As you're playing a man," Susie had explained as she dabbed pale-pink spots on each of my cheeks, "we can't pretty you up too much. But plain old everyday makeup won't cut it. The idea is for people to be able to see your features from the cheap seats."

"Exactly," Tessa agreed as she drew on large red lips many shades brighter than the brown-hued lipstick Susie had used on me. "Otherwise, your face is just a big white blob once the lights hit you."

I'd felt more than a little conspicuous once Susie had finished, as I was also wearing plenty of eyeliner and mascara. But that feeling faded a bit when we joined the men at the door and I saw their kohl-ed eyes and lipstick similar to mine.

Marvin noticed my scrutiny and grinned.

"And just when you thought the Rad-man and I couldn't get any prettier," he said, nudging Radney in the ribs.

Radney shrugged and nodded toward the stairs. "We might be pretty, Marv-man, but Harry's got us all beat."

I looked in the same direction to see what he was talking about. Harry was coming down the steps, garment bag in hand and Yorick tucked under his arm. Like the rest of us, he'd already done his makeup. But rather than looking like a refugee from the musical *Cabaret*'s Kit Kat Klub like the other men did, he looked . . . well, rather awesome.

His foundation was flawless, with subtle contouring and minimal cheek and lip color since, as the Melancholy Dane, he was supposed to appear fashionably pale rather than robust. He'd spiked his dark hair, too . . . not all crazy and Mohawk-y, just enough to look edgy. But what really did it were the eyes.

In the fashion magazines and blogs, they called the look "smoky"—lots of smudgy gray and black with heavy liner and mascara. You'd think that on a man the effect would be over the top, even feminine, especially with eyes as blue as his. But on him, that whole dark gothic look was pretty darned sexy.

"Wowza," Marvin agreed with a low whistle. "I'll never admit saying it, but that Harry is one good-lookin' fellow. There's gonna be a line of ladies at the stage door every night, and they won't be lookin' for you or me."

"All right, listen up, people," Harry announced as he reached the bottom step and paused, free hand on the baluster. "I've got a surprise for you. Our rehearsal this afternoon will be an invited dress."

"What's that?" I whispered to Tessa standing beside me.

"It's a gypsy run!" Tessa exclaimed, while the rest of the troupe murmured their approval.

Since I had no idea what either term meant, I was relieved when Harry went on: "For Nina's benefit, an invited dress, or gypsy run, means that we will have a specially invited audience watching our dress-rehearsal performance. Professor Joy and I agree that the downtown square merchants, as well as the festival volunteers and crew, all deserve this special privilege. And we're counting on their support and enthusiasm to add energy to our final rehearsal before opening night."

There was cheering and as much clapping as could be managed with all the gear everyone was juggling. Harry's phone, meanwhile, was chiming.

"Our transport awaits," he declared, and headed for the rolling bag he'd already stowed near the door.

In addition to my own small bag with the costume Harry had loaned me, I had Mattie. After the scare that morning, I didn't want to leave her alone. And as it was an outdoor venue, Harry had agreed that she could tag along.

We arrived at the square soon afterward. I admit I gawked a bit at the transformation. In addition to the curtained-off stage area that took up one corner of the quadrangle, tented booths had been set up along three sides of the square's perimeter.

Additional tented seating areas dotted the square's center. Obviously, the festival's show runners were expecting a great crowd for opening day.

As we trooped from the van toward the stage, Professor Joy came trotting in our direction, waving his broad hands.

"Ah, Mr. Westcott—Harry—we are so excited to witness the dress rehearsal this afternoon. The drama club is already here and in costume. Of course, our stage manager has gone over the notes from yesterday with them, but perhaps you can give them some final instructions?"

By then we were ducking around the privacy curtains at a gap between the bleachers and the stage. For this performance, only the front rows were filled with our invited guests. Close to forty people, I guessed, spying Jack and Jill Hill, as well as Mason Denman and a younger man I presumed was his date sitting among them, Mason's black pompadour gleaming under the lights. The Tanaka family was there and had managed to grab a front-row spot.

Waving at the Hills and Mason, I rushed Mattie over to where Daniel, Gemma, and Jasmine were sitting.

"I'm so glad you made it," I exclaimed to the trio, all of whom were wearing matching yellow logo P&J's T-shirts. I added to Gemma, "You got my text about watching my big fluff-ball?"

The woman nodded. "Jasmine agreed to be dog wrangler for you."

Though Jasmine had already answered the question herself. The girl had left her seat and squatted down next to the pup. Now she was vigorously scratching her behind the ears and giggling as Mattie responded by licking her face. I grinned and handed a reusable grocery bag to Gemma.

"There's a bottle of water in there for Mattie, and a little bowl, so Jasmine can give her a drink if she seems hot. Oh, and a couple of crunchy treats if she gets restless during the play."

Daniel, meanwhile, was grinning too. "Hi, Nina. Looking good. I really like that new makeup look of yours, though I don't think you used enough eyeliner."

As the black liner around my eyes was a good eighth of an inch thick, I stuck my tongue out at him. "Thanks, Daniel. I'm thinking of starting a makeup blog."

Both Gemma and Jasmine snickered at that, with the former adding, "It's so exciting that you're actually going to be in the play. You might not realize it, but we've had some famous people stop by the festival before. You know, sports figures and authors and even Hollywood types."

"Yeah," Jasmine exclaimed. "You might even get discovered!"

I grinned. "Well, since I don't have any lines, that's pretty unlikely. And speaking of which, I'd better get into costume. See you afterward."

I hurried behind the closed stage curtains to find the rest of the troupe and Harry there on the main stage. With them was the stage manager from yesterday, Mrs. O'Malley, who I'd learned from Tessa was also Cymbeline High's drama teacher. Alongside her were perhaps eight teens in Elizabethan peasant garb . . . obviously, the high school drama-club recruits.

"And our latecomer is Nina Fleet," Harry announced to the teens with a gesture toward me, having apparently been doing the introductions between the two groups. "She's an honorary member of our traveling GASP troupe as she happens to own the bed and breakfast where we all are staying. Now, while they finish getting costumed, why don't Mrs. O'Malley and I take the rest of you through your marks for our "play-within-a-play," *The Murder of Gonzago*."

While Harry and the drama coach ushered the drama students downstage, the rest of us took a shortcut through the wings—the curtained alcoves on either side of the stage area where we actors would wait to make our entrances—and headed to the dressing rooms.

There were two of them, situated end-to-end at the rear of the stage platform and taking up its full width. A gap between them and the stage's rear curtain formed a hallway of sorts that was just large enough for two people to pass. Tessa told me that was called a crossover and allowed the actors to walk from the wing to wing while remaining out of sight of the audience.

Each of the dressing rooms was about the size of a large, narrow office cubicle. They were designed much like cubes, too, roofless and with openings instead of doors. Fortunately, oscillating fans mounted high in the surrounding rigging kept the air circulating. This, combined with the shading canvas above, made the atmosphere backstage bearable despite the high temperature.

We split up, men and women, with each gender claiming one of the rooms. That was, except for Chris. As I headed to the cube we'd established as the women's side, I glanced back and saw the youth looking panicky. I immediately realized the issue. No matter which side he . . . she . . . chose in which to change, the Chris/Christina deception likely would be found out.

"Hey, Chris," I said. "I know it's a bit crowded back here. If you don't want to wait for one of the guys to clear out, maybe you can use one of the wings to change in."

The youth gave me a grateful nod. Since they were curtained off from audience view, if Chris hurried he'd have a relatively private spot in which to change. Satisfied that I'd helped him out, I ducked into the ladies' dressing room to costume up.

Fortunately, the cubicle did have a couple of full-length mirrors, as well as a narrow built-in table that ran the length of the cube's longest side, along with numerous hooks for hanging costumes. I had on my black tights under a pair of cotton pajama-style pants, so I was half-way dressed already.

The tights, combined with the doublet and cape, the former padded with the suggested throw pillow, proved a surprisingly effective yet simple costume. I pinned on my cap at the designated rakish angle and slipped into my black ankle boots. Then, checking myself in the mirror—unfortunately, I didn't need that big of a throw pillow to achieve a flat silhouette—I decided I was ready to go.

Tessa's and Susie's costumes were far more elaborate as befitted their roles, with lots of brocade and overskirts and wide sleeves. Tessa's costume was green and gold, with a standup, ruff-like collar that called to mind Elizabeth I. Her plunging décolletage was covered with strands of faux pearls and emeralds. She'd wrapped her gray braid around her head in a surprisingly elegant style and topped her coiffure with a large gold crown.

"Painted aluminum," she told me, indicating the latter. "That's the only way you could wear something this big for an entire performance. Any other metal would be way too heavy."

Susie's costume was equally elegant yet simpler in its lines, as suited her character's youth—a cream-colored gown with sky-blue, slightly puffed long sleeves and braided gold trim. Instead of the jewelry and crown, she wore chains of flowers around her neck and threaded through her hair, which she'd left partially loose and partially braided.

"You both look great," I told them as they put on the finishing touches. The pair preened a bit at my compliment, but before they could answer I heard the brief blast from a whistle.

"That's your ten-minute warning," came the lilting and slightly Irish-accented tones of Mrs. O'Malley, who'd either absconded with Harry's gym whistle or had one of her own. "Let's start gathering in the wings. From this point on, no talking over a whisper."

We hurried to comply. Based on our first entrance, we each already had our wing assignments. The butterflies in my stomach began to flutter as I, along with Marvin, Radney, and Chris, would be onstage as the curtain opened, waiting for the ghost of Hamlet's father as played by Bill. I already had my marching orders from Harry: look alert, keep my mouth shut, and pretty much do what Chris did while I was on stage.

Chris was standing beside me, costumed as a solder with the additional props of helmet and sword. The youth glanced my way and gave me an encouraging nod.

"Remember to stay back a few paces from everyone whenever we move from one mark to another so you don't trip or run up on anyone's heels," he softly advised. "And look scared when the ghost appears."

I nodded. The looking scared part was going to be easy. Then I felt a hand on my shoulder, and heard Harry's voice in my ear. "Ready for stardom?"

I shook my head, feeling even more nervous if that were possible, yet suddenly grateful for that steadying touch. It was all I could do not to reach up and grip his hand, though I knew if I did someone would have to pry me loose with a crowbar.

I didn't dare look over at Harry, either. I had already caught a glimpse of him in costume, with the black tights and knee-high black leather boots topped by a black velvet doublet with slashed sleeves and just a hint of a ruff. The doublet didn't look like something from a theater's wardrobe, but had the rich yet faintly worn appearance of everyday clothes . . . that was, if the sixteenth century was your everyday. The combination of all black along with the energy I could feel emanating from him now was suddenly and dangerously attractive. Despite my incipient stage fright, I realized I was about two degrees away from going full-blown fangirl on him.

Get a grip, Nina, I told myself. *It's just velvet and leather and eyeliner. Underneath it all he's still the same thorn-in-my-side Harry.*

Fortunately, Mrs. O'Malley the martinet was there to save the day, in a manner of speaking.

"All right, act 1, scene 1 actors," she whispered to us. "Professor Joy is welcoming the festival team and merchants. You have thirty seconds to hit your marks before the curtain opens. And go!"

The next hour and a half went by faster than I thought possible. After the first few dizzying minutes of jitters from being onstage, I found my acting stride and followed along obediently whenever a warm body was needed. As the troupe was small, and Chris the only player taking on a variety of smaller roles, that meant I was in the background of almost every scene. Which gave me the chance to see all the others at work.

I'd been impressed by everyone's acting ability even during the more casual rehearsals, but here on stage I could see just how talented they were. They might be amateurs, but their passion for their subject added yet another layer to their performances. The audience seemed to agree, for enthusiastic applause followed each act. Still, and not surprisingly, the star of the show was Harry.

He smoldered and stalked his way through every act, a character lost between brilliance and madness. Sure, some of it was melodramatic, even campy (it was hard to watch Harry as Hamlet praise the departed Yorick, when I'd previously seen that skull hanging out on my porch swing), but I and the rest of the audience hung on every word of every soliloquy.

And when Harry as Hamlet and Radney as Laertes launched into their sword fight at the end, I along with everyone else felt my heart racing as the pair battled. Of course I knew how it ended, but I found myself hoping against hope that this outcome might be different. And, when Hamlet succumbed to his wound from a poisoned sword, I know I wasn't the only one with tears in my eyes.

But, caught up as I was in Harry's performance, one particular scene midway through had temporarily dragged me out of that fantasy world and given me an idea.

It was during the "play-within-a-play" when the high school students in their roles as the traveling players acted out *The Murder of Gonzago* for the entertainment of the King's court. Renamed by Prince Hamlet as *The Mousetrap,* he becomes playwright and gives the actors new instructions, changing the script so that the pantomime shows the way the ghost of his father claimed that he, the true king, was murdered.

The play's the thing wherein I'll catch the conscience of the king— this is the famous line that Hamlet speaks to himself in the hope that his Uncle Claudius's guilty conscience will kick in as he's watching the play Hamlet has so neatly rewritten. And it works to the extent that the new king, obviously flustered, calls a halt to the performance. Watching that scene, it had occurred to me that maybe Hamlet wasn't the only one who could use a bit of playacting to his advantage.

But, now, the applause from our small audience went beyond enthusiastic as the curtains closed on the tragic scene wherein half the cast had met their stage deaths. And when the curtains opened again, the applause became cheers as we actors gathered in a line downstage to take our bows. Even Mattie from her place in the bleachers woofed a couple of times in approval.

Harry didn't hog all the glory for himself, but generously recognized the rest of the troupe with grand gestures. He waved Mrs. O'Malley onto the stage too, and then the high school players, applauding them all before tossing a salute toward the tech crew at the control booth.

Professor Joy, meanwhile, had clambered up the side steps onto the stage, big hands slapping together in enthusiasm and smile broad. He went down the line with a handshake for each of us, then turned to the audience.

"I've seen many performances of *Hamlet* in my time," he began, "and I must say this is one of the finest ever. Mr. Westcott and his troupe have done a bang-up job."

He paused as the small crowd echoed his sentiment with more applause, and then went on: "Now, folks, remember that we don't charge admission to watch the play, but we do suggest that people make a donation. And all those funds go right back into the festival coffers so we can keep putting on Shakespeare on Cymbeline Square year after year. So if you enjoyed the dress rehearsal"—he paused while the audience gave yet another cheer—"please tell all your friends and all tomorrow's festivalgoers to be right back here again tomorrow evening for opening night."

With that, the curtain closed a final time. Both Mrs. O'Malley and the professor made their way through the front curtain, with the former calling before she left, "We will compare notes tomorrow at noon, Mr. Westcott." Harry nodded, then turned to the rest of us.

"That's a wrap," he said with a smile. "I'll have a few final notes for everyone at breakfast tomorrow, of course, but you all did excellent work here today. Even our newest player"—he paused for a gesture at me—"acquitted herself in respectable fashion. All of which means that I am anticipating a smashing opening tomorrow night. Now, while you're changing, let me arrange for our driver to pick us up."

Harry went backstage to retrieve his phone, while the other players headed for the dressing rooms. I had started for the front curtain when a tug on my doublet stopped me short.

"Where you headed, Number Nine?"

I looked at Marvin, who was clutching my sleeve. "I was going to get Mattie so the Tanakas don't have to wait around," I said, momentarily puzzled.

The man shook his grizzled head. "No can do. This ain't Disney. The rule is, you never appear in public in costume or stage makeup. Right, Rad-man?"

I glanced over to Radney, who nodded.

"He's right, Nina. I mean, no one's going to drag you off to acting jail, but anyone who knows anything about the theater will give you the side-eye if you do it. Plus Harry will slap you upside the head if he catches you."

And with my luck, he probably would.

"Fine, I'll change first," I agreed with a sigh. "But can I at least stick my head out the curtain and tell the Tanakas that I'll be out in a minute?"

Marvin threw up his hands. "Amateurs!"

Radney grinned. "Technically, not even that, but since this is dress and not an actual performance, we'll pretend we didn't see you."

Giving him a thumbs-up, I hurried to the front curtain and peeked out. Sure enough, the Tanakas were there chatting with the Hills. I opened the curtain just wide enough to show my face.

"Gemma!" I called. "Hang onto Mattie. I'll be there as soon as I change."

The woman smiled and nodded, so I flipped the curtain shut again and hurried upstage toward the nearest wing. I was smiling, too, now that I'd actually survived a performance. I could even understand now the lure of being on stage . . . not that I planned on acting as a second career!

As the stage area wasn't exactly soundproof, I could hear the men laughing and joking on their side, and Tessa and Susie chatting on theirs. So buoyant was the mood that I almost forgot not only that we had lost Len but that his killer was among our number.

Almost. As I slipped into the wing, I heard another voice—this one seemingly coming from the other side of the canvas, right outside the stage. And the voice, if I wasn't mistaken, was Chris's. All of which sent me back into full alert.

The words were muffled, but as I didn't hear a second voice I guessed that the youth was on the phone. Though why would Chris suddenly be making a call right after a performance, when all I'd ever seen him do was text? As I was hidden in the wing, with no one nearby to see me, I succumbed to curiosity and put my ear to the canvas, unabashedly trying to make out his words.

There was a long pause, long enough that I wondered if he had hung up. And then I heard the youth say, "I don't know what to do. I think she knows what I did . . . and pretty soon everyone else will, too."

Chapter
Twenty-Four

"I have to say that I'm feeling a little whiplash here," Harry proclaimed, and put a dramatic hand to the back of his neck by way of illustration. "This morning, Chris supposedly almost succumbed to a poisoned burrito. Now, he's your number-one suspect in Len's death."

It was well after ten PM, and I was once again up in the tower room with Harry, having informed him that we needed to talk. It had occurred to me before I'd made the climb that I could have asked him to come down to my room. Just as quickly, I had decided there was too great a chance that he'd take my request the wrong way. Especially if he had any inkling of my brief but intense lapse into schoolgirl crush at the start of dress rehearsal. Besides, letting him into my private quarters meant allowing him to cross a line that I couldn't afford to let him cross . . . not with the currently unspoken yet still unresolved threat of lawsuits hanging between us.

And so, once again we were sitting in shadow, Harry in the comfy chair and me perched on the ladderback. I made a mental note to check the house in the morning for another upholstered armchair that could be hoisted up there.

"Fine," I conceded, "I'm probably jumping the gun. But you have to agree that the phone call I overheard puts the spotlight back on Chris. Here I was sure that Chris was the one being targeted by someone, but now Chris thinks that I think he . . . she . . . killed Len. And why else would that even be something on Chris's radar unless she . . . he . . . actually did it?"

Harry sighed.

"First off, you don't know that the *she* in the phone call meant you. And second, you don't know that the *thing* Chris thinks that this unknown person knows has to do with murder. And, third,"— he clutched the sides of his head in dramatic fashion—"for the love of all that's holy, would you quit that *he/she* routine and just say *they*?"

I leaped to my feet and did my own dramatic bit of hand-flinging.

"Harry, quit focusing on pronouns. We're talking about murder. And if you'd let me finish, I've got an idea that might pry a confession out of Chris. But I'm going to need your help."

He sank back into his chair, crossed his arms over his chest, and gave me a long-suffering look. "Fine," he echoed my earlier response. "If I promise to listen, do you promise never to badger me about this again if I think your plan is insane?"

I hesitated—*never* being a long time—and then nodded. Because I knew Harry well enough by now to be certain my idea was right up his devious alley.

"Let's just say that the play's the thing, and we're about to prick the conscience of a killer."

*   *   *

"All right, people," Harry announced at breakfast the next morning while the troupe milled around the buffet table. "To save time, I'm going to give you your final notes while we eat. Please sit."

Plates and coffee in hand, everyone obediently sought out their usual chairs. I hadn't bothered with the animal dishware this time out. Instead, my plan was to keep a covert eye on Chris this morning, as well as on my own food; and Mattie's too, because all I had was Chris's word that Mattie had swiped the tainted burrito the other day. If Chris suspected me of . . . something . . . maybe my food wasn't safe either.

Once everyone had taken their places, Harry opened his ever-present binder and commenced with the rundown from his observation of the dress rehearsal.

"Radney, excellent work yesterday, especially the sword fight. But I want you to work on your physical interactions with Ophelia. You're her big brother, but you're too tentative in dealing with her. A little clutching at her shoulders, giving her a bit of a shake. As long as Susie's okay with that."

"Oh, I'm fine," the woman replied, batting her eyelashes in exaggerated fashion. Deepening her Georgia drawl, she went on, "I just love it when a man takes charge."

Then, as we all chuckled, Harry went on: "Speaking of that, Susie, your Ophelia is way too cozy with Hamlet. By the time we get to the play scene, she should be looking at him like he's a real creep. So lay off on the mooning expressions."

She pouted a bit, but nodded.

Satisfied, he continued: "And that brings us to Hamlet's famous "Mousetrap." The scene went well enough, but I'm not sure our high school players hit quite the right note. Nina, since there's no dialogue, I want you to join their little troupe and be a part of the pantomime. We'll discuss this offline with Mrs. O'Malley at noon."

I nodded, trying to look surprised, though Harry and I had gone over our revision to *The Murder of Gonzago* in quite a bit of detail the night before. Now, while he continued giving notes to the others, I recalled how I'd presented my idea to him.

As I'd suspected, the showman in him was intrigued by the notion of presenting *The Murder of Len Marsh* to see if someone's conscience would be pricked in real life. And the devious part of him knew just how to go about it.

He'd hastily rewritten the pantomime and Hamlet's dialogue to fit those events that I suspected had gone on behind the scenes. But as this would be a pantomime, we'd cast about for ways to create a better visual impact. We agreed that the obvious solution was to take advantage of the projected backdrops, and so we had scoured online for just the right images. That done, we were satisfied that the festival audience wouldn't pick up on the nuances, whereas any one of the troupe who had been responsible for what happened to Len would recognize their handiwork being enacted onstage. And hopefully, as with King Claudius, their reaction would be swift and obvious.

By now, Harry was winding down with the notes. Closing his binder, he said: "The day is yours until five PM, at which time we will load up with our costumes on the bus and drive over to the square. We have a parking spot there for the duration of the festival, courtesy of Professor Joy. We will use the bus for costume and prop storage between performances, and also as a secondary dressing room, if needed. I will expect everyone to be in makeup and costume no later than six so that Mrs. O'Malley can give notes prior to curtain at seven sharp. Any questions?"

Bill raised a hand. "Since it's a free day, can we go to the Shakespeare festival?"

"Absolutely," was Harry's magnanimous reply, drawing murmurs of approval from the others. "In fact, I was about to suggest that very thing. Feel free to wear a cap or a cloak to draw attention to yourself, and talk up the play to everyone you see. But I strongly urge that you wear sunscreen. Believe me, there's nothing worse than trying to apply full stage makeup over a sunburn."

And on that cautionary note, he raised his cup of rooibos. "To Mr. Shakespeare."

"Mr. Shakespeare," we echoed with smiles, raising our own coffee or orange juice or water.

The breakfast lasted a bit longer than usual, as there was no rush to rehearsal. And while I wouldn't normally have begrudged the troupe the time, I was impatient to get started on my chores. Not only did I have the usual B&B work before me, but I also had something of a scavenger hunt to complete before Harry's and my meeting with Mrs. O'Malley at noon. But finally the actors dispersed, with all of them making plans to head over to the square as soon as the event opened at ten.

"That went well," Harry observed once everyone else had quit the room. "Though I must say that I didn't see anyone quivering in their boots at the mention of the play."

"Just wait until tonight," I assured him. "Do you have the new script written out?"

"A few more tweaks and it'll be ready to go. I'll need to connect to your printer if you don't mind."

I'd recently set up a little business center on a small table in one corner of the parlor, complete with a printer/scanner combo and an old desktop computer I didn't use anymore. While it wasn't high-tech at its finest, the setup was sufficient for those guests who needed emergency office equipment on their vacation.

Leaving Harry to haul out his laptop and review his documents, I started on my chores. By the time I finished and was ready to begin my scavenger hunt, the troupe had long since departed for the festival, which meant I didn't have to sneak around in my quest. Fortunately, I found everything on Harry's list. It was a little after eleven when I packed the last item securely into a lidded box and then went in search of the actor.

He was still at work in the parlor. I stuck my head past the door and told him: "We should leave pretty soon. I know it's only a three-block walk, but it's going to be crowded, plus I have a feeling Mrs. O'Malley doesn't suffer latecomers gladly. Are you about done?"

"Finished," he corrected my grammar, clicking his laptop's mouse and causing my printer to whirr to life. He stuck the printed pages into his binder and shutdown his laptop, carrying it back upstairs lest inquisitive eyes decide to take a look at his files.

A few minutes later, he was downstairs again, having changed from black sweats and a rock-band T-shirt into a more directorial pair of white jeans and a subdued-pattern Hawaiian shirt that looked both vintage and expensive. He was wearing his movie-star wraparound sunglasses that effectively hid the baby blues.

I retrieved my box o' props, grabbed keys and sunglasses, and left Mattie behind to hold down the fort. Feeling a bit conspicuous beside him in a pink-and-purple-striped oversized linen top and matching pink cropped pants, I started off with Harry on foot in the direction of the town square.

The sidewalks between the B&B and the square already were seeing a significant amount of foot traffic compared to usual. We passed probably twenty people walking in the same direction as we were headed. Some were neighbors; others were tourists staying in other B&Bs or guest houses. But all seemed equally eager to take part in the annual festival.

This also meant that Harry and I didn't have much chance to talk with each other during the short trek. It became particularly problematic when, despite the shades, a few people recognized him as *the* Harry Westcott, either as star of the recent performance on my front lawn, or as a character on some random cable show or other. In fact, we stopped more than once for him to sign an autograph, which meant that I ended up carting both my box and his binder.

We finally reached the square, and I saw that three of the four streets leading into the quadrangle were now blocked with concrete traffic barriers. This allowed only pedestrian traffic into the festival area save for the designated spot near the stage. That street was apparently where the fair vehicles were allowed to drive in, for it was blocked with moveable steel-rail panels and hung with signs proclaiming "Not an Entrance." Doubtless this was where Harry would be parking his bus later in the day.

We made our way to one of the designated entries only to find a line already formed there. For beyond each of those short concrete walls was a secondary line of those same portable steel-rail panels. This funneled the festivalgoers down to a single access point at each corner, which was manned by one of Sheriff Lamb's deputies and a couple of members of the festival crew. An unfortunate but necessary precaution in this day and age, I realized with a shake of my head.

Harry's only comment was, "I hope you left all your contraband at home."

Deputy Mullins had been assigned to our entrance, supervising the festival staff members stationed behind a table who were checking purses and bags. As we reached the front of the line, Mullins gave us a friendly nod and waved Harry in, only to catch sight of my box.

He raised a warning hand at me. "Sorry, Ms. Fleet, but we have to take a look inside that carton."

I smiled and handed it over, even as I wondered what the security team was going to make of its contents. "Not a problem, Deputy. But I warn you, it's nothing exciting, just a few last-minute props for tonight's show."

The burly young man behind the table gave the box a quick look-through, eyebrows raising a bit, and then handed it back. "Enjoy the festival, ma'am."

"I will," I replied, already feeling a bit of childlike anticipation despite the seriousness of my and Harry's mission.

More than one festivalgoer was dressed in Shakespearean garb—this not to mention the wandering entertainment. I could hear baroque-style melodies coming from a nearby quartet of costumed musicians, while a jester on stilts was breathing fire not far from us. I gazed longingly from the craft booths down one side of the square to the food vendors down the other. Much of the festival did live up to the Shakespearean theme, though a few of the vendors and performers leaned more toward fantasy and pirates than Renaissance. I even spotted my yoga instructor, Wendy Tucker, leading a collection of tourists in a sun salutation there at the bandstand. Then I spied Daniel at a grill set up across from Peaches and Java and made up my mind what my first stop would be.

"We've got almost half an hour before we have to meet up with Mrs. O'Malley and the crew," I told Harry and showed him my watch as proof. "Since it's almost lunchtime, how about we stop by the Tanakas' booth, and I'll split a grilled peaches and peanut butter sandwich with you."

The actor shot me a look of faint horror. "Please tell me you're joking."

"Not a bit. Come on. I promise you, it's fabulous."

I led the way with Harry following after me and muttering dire predictions about my future gastronomic well-being. Not that I'd be the only one sliding down that slippery unhealthy food slope. Already, seven or eight people were lined up in front of Daniel's grill.

"Hey, Nina," Daniel called as he saw us approaching. "Harry, good to see you again, bro. It's been awhile. You two here to try one of my world famous Shakespeare's Peachy PB&J sandwiches?"

"Absolutely," I told him.

He was wearing yesterday's yellow logo T-shirt again, though today he'd added one of those black velvet slouchy Renaissance caps with a curly yellow feather in it. Jasmine stood a few yards away wearing a matching tee and a similar cap atop her golden ringlets and carrying a tray filled with sample cubes of the special PB&J.

I dragged Harry over to her. "Come on, take a bite and see what I'm talking about. I promise you won't be disappointed."

With an exaggerated shudder, Harry took one of the cubes and stuck it in his mouth. I watched his face, waiting for the reaction. Sure enough, after cautiously chewing for a moment, he began to smile. "Not bad."

Still, when we reached the front of the line, I was the one who ended up paying for our snack. Each with half a sandwich in hand, we munched away as we headed off to meet Mrs. O'Malley and the tech crew.

Fortunately for us, the festival volunteers had not yet removed the panels that surrounded the stage, which meant we would be able to do a run-through with the lighting guy using our revised visuals for the play-within-the-play. First, however, we had to clear everything with our martinet of a stage manager, who did not approve.

"I must tell you, Mr. Westcott, that I do not approve," Mrs. O'Malley declared in her lilting Irish accent.

Today, she wore a crisp, blue-striped seersucker jacket—short sleeved—and a matching short skirt, the latter showing off legs that looked darned good for a woman of any age. Her high-heeled pumps were blue as well. In deference to the heat, she was sporting an oversized and flower-strewn straw sunhat more suitable for Derby Day than a Shakespeare festival perched atop her red curls. Her expression was implacable as she sat in the bleachers reviewing the updated script pages that Harry had given her.

"Let me be blunt, Mr. Westcott," she went on. "To make such a change mere hours before opening night, when the scene played just fine at dress . . . well, I simply cannot countenance it."

"I know, and I'm sorry," Harry told her, putting on a contrite expression. "And I assure you, this is no reflection on your high school troupe. They did excellent work yesterday. But it's important that we make this change."

He paused and sighed. Then, with a subtle catch in his voice, he went on: "You see, this new version of *Gonzago* is a tribute to our deceased troupe member, Mr. Marsh. We lost him just a few days ago, and we're all still rather bereft. The new play would be just for tonight, a little salute to a fine actor who is no longer with us."

Mrs. O'Malley's stern mien thawed slightly. "Very well. I still do not approve, but under the circumstances I will not attempt to override you. But I must have your assurance that we'll go back to the original script for all subsequent performances."

Harry put an elegant hand over his heart and favored the woman with his patented Harry Westcott "This is just for you" smile.

"I promise, the revision is for opening night only. And thank you. You have the undying gratitude of our entire troupe for allowing this homage to a talented actor. Your professional generosity will not be forgotten . . . right, Nina?"

"Right!" I declared through my final bite of PPB&J sandwich.

Mrs. O'Malley's pale cheeks had gone faintly pink at Harry's praise. However, she swiftly recovered herself with a *tsk* and a brusque "If that is all, Mr. Westcott, I must be off to contact my troupe concerning this wardrobe change. I hope they will be able to accommodate."

She stuck the pages in her binder and stalked off, flowers on her sunhat quivering in disapproval. Harry called after her, "Mrs. O'Malley, your notes for me?"

The woman paused without looking back and reached into her binder. Pulling out a sheet of paper, she crumpled it in one hand and then dramatically tossed it over her shoulder as she resumed her exit walk.

Harry glanced my way and winked.

"All right, now that's settled, let's see what kind of magic our tech crew can do with this," he declared, and pulled a thumb drive from his shirt pocket.

Fortunately, the lighting technician—a tattooed, long-haired blond guy who looked like an ex-roadie—was up for the challenge.

"Nope, don't even want to know," he said, waving off Harry as the actor began a convoluted explanation as to why the changes. "Just tell me what you want, and I'll make it happen."

This session was a bit more extensive, perhaps an hour long, and included practice with my props. But with both me and Harry onstage standing in for the various players, we finally had the brief scene blocked out with the new backdrops and lighting.

"We owe you," Harry told him as the man—Matt, I'd learned was his name—finished writing up the new cues. "If you need a favor while you're here . . .?"

"Nah, it's all part of the job," Matt replied with a shrug. Then, as we left the control booth and headed back to the festival, he called after us, "Maybe send me over one of those grilled peach and peanut butter sandwiches I've been hearing about?"

Chapter
Twenty-Five

"All right, people, we're here," Harry announced unnecessarily as the Wild Hare bus rolled into our designated spot at the festival grounds. "It is exactly five PM. Since everyone is already in makeup, all you need to do is get costumed and double-check your personal props."

The drive over had taken far less time than getting the bus out of my driveway, as we'd had to reverse the maneuvering that had gotten the vehicle parked in the first place. Fortunately, Harry had taken my suggestion that we retrieve the bus earlier in the afternoon rather than waiting until the last minute. With Mattie assisting by riding shotgun, and me standing in the driveway pointing right and left, we'd finally managed to get the beast out past the gate and on the street until it was time for us to head to the festival.

"A little free advertising for my tour company," Harry had observed in satisfaction, since I now had a virtual billboard parked in front of my house. The fact that it effectively blocked my discreet metal sign on the fence that proclaimed *Fleet House Bed and Breakfast* apparently hadn't occurred to him.

Since things would be hectic on opening night—particularly if our mousetrap ended up sprung!—I'd left Mattie to watch the house for the evening. She'd hear all about it from me in the morning.

Now, just as with an arriving plane rolling to the gate, we were already up and moving before Harry put the bus into park. While we gathered our costumes and props, he gestured to the small air-conditioning unit that was mounted in one of the bus's windows.

"I'll plug in the AC so we can use the tour bus as a greenroom, as our outdoor stage isn't equipped with anything other than fans. Feel free to relax here before the performance and enjoy the cold air. Once the curtain rises, you'll be stuck in the wings or backstage."

He paused and made shooing motions. "What's everyone waiting for? Go get dressed. And don't forget that we have a meeting onstage with Mrs. O'Malley at exactly six to receive a few final technical notes."

While the rest of the troupe headed out the bus's bifold doors, and Harry left to find the electrical outlet, I hung back a moment. I hadn't been inside the small beast of a bus since Harry's last stay in town, so I was curious to see what he might have done with the vehicle since then.

It was mostly unchanged, except that any personal belongings were stored in suitcases or trunks strapped onto overhead racks or stowed beneath the seats, giving it a much more open feel than before. In fact, the bus looked more like an airport shuttle, with the original face-forward rows resituated so that they ran the length of the bus on either side. Certainly, the arrangement made the vehicle more convenient for tiny house living, though for Harry's sake I hoped he was done with that.

"Still here?" Harry asked as he climbed back inside and turned a couple of knobs on the air conditioner. The unit began blasting air that started out warm but quickly cooled. "You're not changing your mind about our surprise performance, are you?'

I smiled a bit nervously and shook my head. "Still on board. And when it's over, I'll be ready for those three little words that every woman loves to hear."

"You mean, *You were right*?"

He flashed a grin, looking surprisingly boyish despite his gothic stage makeup, and then sobered. "But what if you aren't?"

"As you said before, we'll just tell everyone it was a tribute to Len. And then I'll drop the subject forever. I Secret Squirrel promise."

While I was busy swiping hand over heart and zipping lips, Harry had begun drawing the curtains on the bus windows. I hurried to help, and once he'd pulled shut the fabric divider behind the driver's seat, the vehicle had become a cozy and private room. With a few of those batik throws draped over the seats, I told myself, it actually wouldn't be a half-bad place to hang out. Maybe Mattie could have come, after all.

"Well, I'd better get going," I told him, and retrieved my garment bag containing my costume. "Fingers crossed this all works out."

"Fingers crossed you hit all your marks, you mean. Your box of props is hidden behind a couple of small flats in the stage-left wing. That's where you'll make your entrance for that scene. You've got that black cloak I gave you, right?"

I nodded and indicated the garment bag. "Safe in here."

"Good. Stow it with the box so you can swap your costuming there in the wings just before you go on. Anyone says anything, tell them it's been cleared with me and Mrs. O'Malley."

"Got it," I replied. With any luck, the rest of the cast would have the same opening-night jitters I was beginning to feel, so they wouldn't even notice anything out of the ordinary.

Moving from bus to stage involved a good fifteen-degree temperature change, but fortunately the stage's high canvas roof let in a bit of breeze along with the oscillating fans. The audience would be fine too, as the sun was now low enough in the sky that, between canvas and rigging, any direct rays were pretty well blocked.

All the privacy fencing that had kept the stage a relative secret these past days was gone now, though the main curtain was drawn until showtime. I mounted the short series of steps near the rear of the stage and cut through the stage-right wing, heading for the dressing room. I passed Chris in the crossover. The youth had already changed into costume and so merely gave me the quickest nod before heading, I presumed, back to our makeshift greenroom.

I hadn't seen anything in Chris's expression since that overheard phone conversation that indicated any suspicion of me. Still,

I had to remind myself that all of these people were actors and, thus, practiced at pretending. With luck, this whole situation concerning Len would be resolved by the time the curtain rang down on our opening night. But in the meantime I was keeping my guard up.

Not that I had much chance to worry. Once I had located the box where Harry had left it and draped my black cloak over it, I headed for the dressing room. Inside, there was a sudden flurry of action, with the three of us women hurrying to change into our costumes and seeming to bump into each other at every turn.

As my wardrobe was the simplest, I hurriedly dressed and then helped Tessa with her more elaborate gown. Susie was seated before one of the mirrors muttering over her garland of posies, which had managed to tangle itself since the previous day.

"Stupid flowers," she said to no one in particular. "And you know, I really hate that speech I have to make about rosemary being for remembrance, and pansies, and fennel. I mean, what woman wants pansies? Len always brought me roses . . . big old red ones, and not the kind you buy at the grocery store."

Tessa and I exchanged glances. It was on the tip of my tongue to say that I actually rather liked pansies myself. But before I could, Susie looked at both of us via the mirror and asked, "Do you think Len will be watching us tonight from somewhere?"

You bet . . . or, at least, his stand-in will.

Of course, I didn't say that either. And while I was pretty sure there was a *somewhere* from which folks who'd passed on could watch us, I felt a bit uncomfortable getting into a discussion about that likelihood.

Fortunately, Tessa was willing to wax philosophical on the matter, and so replied, "Of course, my dear."

"Good. Because I want him to see that I'm doing okay."

Once costumed, we all made it back to the bus just long enough to cool down for a bit before it was time to meet with Mrs. O'Malley. The stage manager was minus her earlier sunhat now but still wearing her seersucker suit, though she'd exchanged the heels for a pair of practical running shoes. Her high school troupe—three of them with actual roles, and the rest background players to fill the stage— was gathered around her while she gave them final instructions.

"Ah, yes, Ms. Fleet," she called as she spotted me. "Over here, if you don't mind."

I obediently "here'd," and she introduced me to the three students who would be part of the Mousetrap play with me. They were all wearing long cloaks, but I caught a glimpse of modern street clothes underneath, which hopefully meant they had managed to re-create the wardrobe we'd requested.

"You have your notes," she told the players, "and we've already rehearsed these changes. You will have seen from the script that Mr. Westcott, as Hamlet, will be narrating events in the pantomime as they unfold, while Ms. Fleet will serve as the leader of Hamlet's players. So follow their lead, and if it goes badly it is on their heads."

The three nodded and cast glances at me as Mrs. O'Malley headed over to meet with the GASPers.

"I played Annie in summer stock," the female of the trio told me. "And Dorothy in a revival of *The Wiz* last winter. What have you been in?"

Obviously, I wasn't going to get any respect from these kids—or, at least, from Annie—if I didn't have a decent acting resume. And so, thinking quickly, I leaned a little closer and confided, "I played the title role in an all-female version of *Hamilton* in Atlanta a few months ago. And before that, I played Nala in a country-western version of *The Lion King*."

Her eyes momentarily widened, then narrowed in suspicion. Before she could call me out on my fabrications, I brightly told the three, "Sorry, gotta go join the rest of my troupe."

We spent a few minutes with Mrs. O'Malley listening to her notes, which were mostly technical and having to do with pacing. At Harry's previous request, she did not mention the change to *Gonzago* to the rest of the troupe.

Their characters are supposed to be confused and put off balance by the pantomime and Hamlet's commentary, he had told her. *So their reactions will be quite appropriate to the scene. And as soon as Claudius exits, we'll pick right back up with the script.*

Afterward, we deposited our valuables, including cell phones (turned off, not just set to vibrate) into an oversized lockbox that the stage manager would stand guard over for the duration of the performance. Then we were dismissed back to our greenroom, where we remained until our call ten minutes before the curtain was to rise

"Get moving, folks," Marvin urged at the knock on the bus door. "It's showtime."

"Break a leg, everyone," Bill added. "And remember, there are no small parts—"

"—only small actors," the rest of the troupe chorused with varying degrees of enthusiasm. I smothered a smile. Given their reaction, I guessed that Bill habitually pulled out the old Stanislavski quote as a pep talk prior to every performance.

"It's standing room only," Mrs. O'Malley whispered as I joined my fellow act 1, scene 1 players in one wing while the rest of the cast gathered at the opposite. "Let us look sharp, ladies and gentlemen. The curtain will be rising shortly."

And so it did, a few minutes later to great applause. As the stage manager had indicated, the bleachers were packed, and numerous people had gathered on the grass in front of the stage. Assuming everyone attending kicked in the suggested donation, it looked like the festival fund was off to a healthy start.

That was, as long as no one demanded a refund once they saw Harry's slightly modified version of the play.

From the opening scene, Harry was again the star of the show. Not that the other players didn't get their fair share of appreciation. Maybe it was the outdoor venue—or perhaps the abundance of grog and mead available for sale—but the audience behaved much as an Elizabethan audience might have, applauding every soliloquy and cheering each act. By the time the scene with the traveling players being taken aside by Hamlet arrived, everyone was well invested in the outcome.

Harry and I most of all.

While I had managed to contain the worst of my stage fright during the first couple of acts, knowing what was to come brought it back with a vengeance. As the second scene of act 3 commenced, I watched the projected backdrop switch to that of the castle's inner hall. The entire troupe entered from both wings, forming a semicircles at either side of the stage: Bill and Tessa—King

Claudius and Queen Gertrude—seated side by side on their thrones, along with Radney and Chris on one side, and Susie, Marvin, and Harry on the other. The high school drama students who were the extras scattered themselves behind the main cast, serving as other ladies and courtiers to add a bit of living background.

I was the only member of the main cast still waiting in the wing. By now, I'd exchanged my cloak for the hooded black robe Harry had given me. I'd tied it tightly about my padded waist so that I was enveloped inside it and, hopefully, unrecognizable with the hood drawn up. Clutching my props, I watched the onstage action and waited for my cue.

Harry, as Hamlet, rushed onto the stage from the side steps, his movements erratic, as by this point in the play he had descended into madness—or, at least, pretended to do so. And so his eyes were staring widely, his hair and costume disheveled.

"The entertainment begins," he exclaimed to his court. "The play is called *The Murder of Gonzago*. But if my lords and ladies will indulge me, I shall present a version of this famous drama far different than you may have seen before. First, I beg you, we must have music!"

At that, the costumed Renaissance quartet that I'd seen playing around the festival grounds earlier in the day made an entrance up the same short set of steps located downstage. They settled there, stage left, and began softly playing their instruments.

I saw Bill and Tess exchange quick puzzled glances at this obvious deviation from script. They'd soon find out that for this particular performance, the "play" portion of *Gonzago* had been cut, leaving only the pantomime—which also cut Queen Gertrude's line about ladies protesting too much.

Harry, meanwhile, dramatically pointed to his stage relatives. "Wait, not a word from you, my dear uncle king. Nor from you, Madam, my mother queen."

Swinging around with pointed finger, he encompassed the rest of the cast with his gesture. "Nor the rest of the court. Be silent, all, and watch in wonder. As I said, this play is well-named *The Murder of Gonzago* . . . but I prefer to call it *The Death of A Man of Business.*"

The backdrop behind the cast abruptly changed to one that Harry had selected, a quite ordinary dining room. I heard a murmur from the audience. Then, with Mrs. O'Malley's cue, the first of the student players took the stage.

The murmur became faint laughter, for the young man had a modern and distinctly hipster vibe about him. He was dressed in tight black jeans and an oversized black-checked flannel shirt. A knit cap was pulled low on his ears, and black-framed glasses perched on his nose. Even Chris couldn't fail to notice the resemblance, I told myself.

"See this callow youth, how he pays no mind to what is around him," Harry narrated as the young actor slouched his way to center stage, gaze ostentatiously fixed upon a cell phone. "An arrow could go flying past, and he would not notice. But let us see another."

At that, the second drama student made his entrance, his appearance drawing more chuckles. He was taller than his classmate by a good head, and dressed in khaki pants and a polo shirt.

Len's personal uniform, I thought with a nod. The Len character made his way to where the other player waited, continually glanced about him with a self-important air, his phone held to his ear.

Harry rushed to center stage. "This"—he pointed at the taller of the pair—"is our man of business. As the name implies, the man is busyness personified. Even at his leisure, he is quite like a bee."

Harry spun around, hands tucked in his armpits to simulate wings, and drawing outright laughter from the audience. As for the troupe, they had begun to break character just a bit, glancing from Harry to each other, as if not sure whether to play along with him or intervene in what was seemingly a play going off the rails.

Then Harry rushed downstage, only to stop and turn again. "Both of these fair gentlemen, unalike as they are, soon find themselves in a most interesting predicament together. Behold, the toast!"

Which was my cue. Drawing my hood down lower and pulling the cloak closer, I slunk my way onstage toward where the two mime players stood playing with their phones. My back to the audience, I raised both arms high, displaying an empty champagne bottle in one hand, and an oversized saucer-style champagne glass in the other. Then I turned so that I was at right angles to the audience and dramatically pantomimed pouring from bottle to glass.

Bending to set down the champagne bottle, I turned again so that I now faced the bleachers. I reached into the belt tied about my waist and plucked out a plastic medicine bottle. I gave an exaggerated look over each shoulder, as if fearing I might be being watched, and then shook the bottle over the glass.

I heard a sharp gasp from one of the cast—who, I couldn't tell. But it seemed I'd struck a nerve with someone.

"What is this?" Harry as Hamlet demanded, rushing over to where the king and queen sat, leaning forward to get a better view. "Is a villain coolly plotting some dreadful mischief? Let us see what happens next."

At that, I tucked away the pill bottle again. Looking once more to either side, I carried my glass of champagne over to the pair still busy with their phones. I tapped the hipster on the shoulder and with a magnanimous gesture handed him the glass. My job done, I slipped away to one side to watch.

The player representing Chris raised the glass to take a pretend sip from the tainted drink, when another player rushed in. It was my new friend Annie aka Dorothy. Like the other two players, she was dressed in modern garb, bright cropped pants and a flowered top, her dark hair pulled up in a messy ponytail. She only vaguely resembled me, but anyone in the know would recognize who she represented.

Faux Nina snatched the glass from the hipster youth's hand and wagged an admonishing finger at him.

"Aha!" Harry exclaimed, nodding. "Fate in the form of a lovely young woman has stepped in. She tells our young man that he is not of an age to indulge in strong drink and so has saved him from the poison. All is well now. Or is it?"

At that, Faux Nina looked from the Len character back to the glass she held, and then gave an exaggerated shrug. She walked over to him and tapped him on the shoulder. He looked up, and she offered him the glass.

"No, no!" Harry cried as the Len character accepted the champagne with a smile. "Our lady thinks not to waste a fine drink and so gives it to another, not knowing it is tainted. Will our man of business realize the error in time?"

The stage abruptly darkened, and while the student players rushed off to the wings, the projected backdrop changed. Now, it was a scene of tall green hedges.

"What the—" I heard Radney softly say, out of character, while Bill and Tessa had both half-risen from their seats. As for the audience, they'd fallen silent, seemingly sensing that something beyond the scope of the play was about to happen.

Now, the only sound was the quartet's lute playing a doleful solo. As the lights rose again, Harry moved with sober purpose downstage before turning back toward the hedges. As we all watched, the Len character wandered in front of the hedge backdrop. He stood there smiling, champagne in hand. Slowly raising the glass, he pantomimed drinking it down.

"'Tis done," Harry intoned in a voice that sent a shiver through me. "And now we can but wait for the end."

"This ain't right," Marvin muttered, loud enough for me to hear as he put an arm around Susie's shoulder and glanced at the rest of the cast for support.

I was watching too, clutching nervous hands together as I waited to see who else of the troupe reacted to the scene. It was then that the Len character clutched his throat and began staggering in front of the hedges. Finally, with a silent cry, he dropped to the stage and lay quite still.

The backdrop flashed and changed again. This time, an image I recognized as Len's headshot appeared, almost filling the screen. The image began to waver, and then swirl, until it splintered into dozens of virtual pieces and vanished, leaving behind a backdrop of sky and clouds.

And at that, a scream shattered the silence.

Chapter
Twenty-Six

"It wasn't supposed to happen like that!" Susie shrieked, breaking away from Marvin and rushing downstage. "And if Nina hadn't interfered, it wouldn't have!"

Tearing the flower garland from around her neck, she glared my way and then swung about to stab a finger in Chris's direction.

"You were supposed to drink that glass of champagne, you stupid girl, not Len. It only would have made you sick . . . sick enough to get you out of the way until I could decide what to do about you. Because I knew who you were from the start. And I knew what your crazy mother was up to, too. I even told the police she had to be the one who'd tried to kill Len that night while he was riding his bike, but they wouldn't believe me. And when running him over with her car didn't work . . . well, I knew you'd try to finish the job for her."

Chris stood there opened-mouth during the woman's tirade, pretty much like the rest of the cast. Even the audience sat in stunned silence, while the lute player, with a sudden discordant flourish of strings, abruptly halted his playing.

And supposedly Chris's mother was the crazy one?

Susie's voice had been steadily rising. "You thought you could fool us, but I was smarter. I had the perfect plan to get rid of you, to keep you away from my Len, and no one would have suspected a thing. They'd all think it was just one of those silly tricks, like all the others I'd been playing on the troupe."

With a final screech, she abruptly charged in Chris's direction, crying, "And then you made Len drink from the wrong glass, and that ruined everything!"

"I–I swear I don't know what you're talking about," Chris managed to choke out as she turned and sprinted toward the nearest wing.

What would have happened next had Susie caught her, I wasn't sure. But the drama ended almost as soon as it began, when Harry rushed across stage to block Susie's progress. She sidestepped him with greater agility than he expected, however, which left it up to me. And as I wasn't sure that I could hold onto her even if I did catch her, wrapped as I was in my bulky cloak, I did the next best thing. I stuck out my booted toe and caught her ankle, sending her tumbling to the stage.

For a moment, there was dead silence, so complete that I could hear passing traffic a block away. And then a man's enthusiastic, "Bravo, bravo!" rang out from the audience, followed by a slow clap.

I gazed out into the bleachers to spot none other than the Reverend Dr. Thaddeus Bishop, who had risen from his seat and was applauding. A few others stood, and then more, until the whole audience had leaped to their collective feet in a standing ovation.

Harry, being Harry, responded to the adulation with a sweeping bow. Then, with a gesture first to the audience, and then to Susie, still huddled where she'd fallen, he called, "Sheriff Lamb, can we prevail upon you to send a few of your finest up onstage?"

Looking again toward the bleachers I saw Sheriff Lamb, along with at least three of her deputies. Presumably, they'd been sitting there the entire time. As the officers made their way onto the stage amid still more applause, Harry turned back to the wings.

"Mrs. O'Malley," he called, "would you be kind enough to ring down the curtain on this tragedy?"

* * *

"I tell you what, Number Nine, I'm sure going to miss these fine breakfasts. You think that Tanaka fellow would ship to Atlanta?"

It was the Monday morning after the Georgia Amateur Shakespeare Players' final performance at Shakespeare on Cymbeline Square. Despite being down two players after opening night— Len, who was temporarily lying at the Heavenly Path Funeral Home and Crematorium, and Susie, who was still in the county lockup waiting to make bail—the subsequent performances of *Hamlet* had gone off pretty much flawlessly. Chris had been bumped into the role of Ophelia, and another of Mrs. O'Malley's students had filled the parts left open in the wake of Chris's moving up in the ranks, leaving me to sit happily in the audience.

But more importantly—at least, for the festival coffers—was the fact that the crowds for Saturday and Sunday had been even larger than that for opening night. *Probably because they're hoping we'll unmask another real-life criminal onstage,* had been Harry's cynical explanation.

Now, I grinned at Marvin over my cup of coffee and replied: "I don't think Peaches and Java has a mail-order business yet, but I'll be glad to pack up some of the leftovers for you and Radney. You two are going to stay long enough for the service this morning before you drive back, aren't you?"

Because more than the cast of *Hamlet* had changed since Friday night.

Following Susie's onstage confession, both she and Chris had been taken into custody. The younger woman—she had revealed her gender deception once the cuffs were on—had been released a few hours later, however, once Sheriff Lamb agreed that nothing tied her to Len's death.

Apparently, the sheriff had accepted Chris's claim that her infiltration of the GASP troupe had been a sincere if perhaps misguided attempt to get to know her estranged father before she revealed her true identity to him. As for the Pazaxa, her doctor had confirmed that the antidepressant was a legitimate prescription, to be taken as needed. And as the bottle held the exact number of pills as the refill was for, that meant the benzos in Len's mimosa had not come from Chris's stash.

Radney, however, had done a count of his meds and decided he was a couple of pills short. And given that none of the troupe had bothered locking doors during their stay, Susie would have had easy access to Radney's shaving kit, which also would have given her the opportunity to loosen the cap on his body wash as one of her "tricks."

Chris's mother, Amanda Boyd, had not been so lucky when it came to her dealings with the law. After Sheriff Lamb had contacted the Atlanta officials citing Susie's claims, they'd agreed to take a second look at the hit-and-run. Fortunately, the paint-transfer evidence results had finally come back from the Atlanta lab, and the data showed that Len's road bike had been hit by the same make and model car as Amanda owned. With that, Amanda Boyd had confessed to the attempted homicide by vehicle of her ex-husband and was waiting to be bailed out of an Atlanta jail cell.

As expected, Chris had been devastated by twin losses. First, of the father she'd barely known but had hoped to establish a relationship with, and, second, of the mother who had raised her but had turned out to be deeply flawed. I suspected she also was dealing with guilt over the fact that Len might still be alive had she not unknowingly handed him the tainted mimosa that had been meant for her. For it now was common knowledge among the troupe that Len probably had died, not from just the Pazaxa, but from a drug interaction made more deadly by the alcohol.

As for me, I was definitely rethinking the whole peach mimosa toast thing. In fact, I'd about decided that my next guests would be lucky even to get orange juice with their breakfast!

Unexpected, however, was the way Tessa and Bill had swooped in as surrogate parents. The pair had taken Chris under their collective wing as soon as Deputy Mullins had dropped her off at the B&B late that Friday night. They had been the ones to encourage her to go on with the play, reminding her that it was the best way to keep her mind occupied. They would take their surrogacy even further, as I'd learned the next evening from Bill.

"Tessa and I told Chris we'd look out for her when we all get back to Atlanta," he had explained as he accompanied me through my ritual lockdown of the house. "It's probably too late for her to get a dorm for the school year, but we have a spare room at the house she can stay in until she figures things out."

They also had coordinated with Dr. Bishop, whose appearance at our opening night had not been coincidental. He'd been intending to let Susie know that the autopsy was complete and that Len's body would be released. Instead, the Benedicts ended up arranging for the pastor to conduct a private service and cremation in Cymbeline so that Chris could take her father's ashes home with her.

"That Dr. Bishop is quite the persuasive man," Tessa had confided to me after speaking with him on Sunday. "Do you know he actually drove over to the county jail and got Susie to sign a letter allowing Chris to approve all the arrangements? So after the service on Monday, we'll drive the rental car to Savannah to sprinkle some of Len's ashes on his parents' graves. And then Chris will take the urn with the remaining ashes back to Atlanta."

Which was the reason for the separate travel arrangements with Radney and Marvin.

There ain't no point in just the two of us rattling around in that bus with Harry, Marvin had told me when Tessa had announced their plans. *I'd rather rent us a Lincoln and drive home in comfort.*

Now, however, Radney was nodding in response to my question about Len's memorial.

"Yeah, we'll be there. Len and I might not have been bros, but I worked with him for a good while. And Marvin was the guy's partner for years, so I guess it's only right he's there too. Mostly, though, we're doing it for Chris . . . er, Christina."

"Chris is fine," a familiar voice spoke up behind us. "Christina sounds, I don't know, kind of prissy."

Chris came strolling into the room, trailed by Mattie. Since her masquerade had been revealed, she'd pretty much abandoned her hipster wardrobe for clothes that, if not more stylish, were a bit more feminine. The jeans were the same tight black ones, but she'd topped them with a tailored pink blouse that showed off a figure no one had known she had. As for the dyed black hair, while nothing could be done about the color for the moment, instead of scraping it back off her forehead and covering it with the knit cap, she'd let it dry to its natural wavy state.

She poured herself some orange juice and grabbed a slice of quiche, then sat down at the table. "I really appreciate everything all y'all have done. Right now, I don't have anyone else. As far as I'm concerned, my mother's dead to me, too. I mean, she tried to kill my real father . . . and for money."

Abandoning the quiche, Chris grabbed a paper napkin and abruptly swiped at her nose and eyes, while Mattie laid a consoling muzzle on her knee.

"She called me from jail last night and admitted everything," the young woman went on. "She acted like she'd done it all for me. She said that my father still had a life-insurance policy in my name that was worth a lot, but if Susie found out about it, she'd make him switch it to her. So Mom told me she had to . . . you know, take care of him so I could get the money. She said it was to make up for the back child support he owed."

She paused and snuffled into her napkin again. "I mean, I could have used the money for school and stuff. But no way would I have gone along with something like that. Besides, even if her stupid plan had worked, she probably would have kept all the money for herself."

Talk about ironic, I thought. Chris probably was going to get that insurance policy settlement, after all . . . and maybe a lot more, depending on what Len's will said.

Then the young woman straightened. "But that's not the weirdest part. I still haven't figured out how Susie knew who I really was."

"Actually, my dear, I'm afraid I may be somewhat responsible for that."

This came from Tessa, who had just walked into the dining room along with Bill. While the latter went to the sideboard to fetch coffee for both of them, she took a seat alongside Chris.

"Oh, I didn't do anything on purpose," she hastened to clarify when Chris shot her a disbelieving look. "But you know that, as secretary of the Georgia Amateur Shakespeare Players, it is my job to do the preliminary screening of all prospective troupe members. And it just so happened that Susie was volunteering in the GASP office the day your application came in. I remember that she was looking at your headshot and said it reminded her of photos she'd seen of Len when he was a teenager. Except your hair was black, and his used to be blond."

"My real hair color is blond too," Chris said in a small voice.

Tessa gave her a comforting pat on the hand.

"Anyhow, we laughed about it—well, at least I did—and then Susie offered to do the research on you. I was swamped with work that day so was glad of the help. She must have found out something on the Internet that allowed her to put two and two together. Not that she said anything to me about what she'd learned. In fact, she even recommended you for membership."

All the better to keep an eye on her unwanted stepdaughter, I told myself. Obviously, Susie had connected some of the same dots I'd linked together to figure out Chris's true identity. Though, as Wife Number Two, she would have had the advantage in already knowing about Wife Number One.

Chris sat silent another moment. "And what about my father?" she finally asked Tessa. "Do you think that Susie told him about me . . . or that maybe he guessed on his own?"

"I'm not sure, my dear. But if he did know, I think he probably was pleased that his estranged daughter had gone to that sort of effort to get to know him again."

It was the smallest of straws that Tessa offered, but Chris seemed happy to grasp it. She snuffled again for a moment, and then excused herself from the table, leaving the rest of us to a silent meal.

Well, almost the rest of us.

"Anyone seen Harry this morning?" I asked. For the actor's usual spot at the table was empty, without even Yorick there to serve as placeholder. And while everyone else's suitcases and hanging bags were already lined up at the front door ready to be loaded into respective vehicles, I didn't recall seeing Harry's luggage.

"Spielberg? He's probably upstairs still packing," Marvin opined. "Don't worry, Number Nine. I'm sure he'll be down in two shakes."

But when we'd all finished our respective breakfasts and Harry had still not made an appearance, I did begin to worry. Excusing myself, I headed for the tower room.

"Harry?" I called as I knocked on the panel then opened it. I could see light from the landing, and so I called up the ladder, "Harry, are you up there? You're late for breakfast."

"I guess I wasn't hungry this morning," he called back down.

I frowned. Sure, maybe not hungry, but he'd not yet missed a morning drinking his appalling cup of tea.

"Harry," I called yet again. "I'm coming up. You've got about five seconds to get decent if you aren't already."

I didn't wait for him to agree or protest but hurried up the ladder to the landing. I found him decent, modesty-wise, in jeans and the familiar nubby-textured brown shirt. But rather than packing, as I might have guessed he would be, he was sprawled in the comfy chair and contemplating Yorick, who was balanced on one knee.

"I wondered when you'd come up here," was his careless greeting as he briefly glanced my way. "Because I forgot to say them, didn't I?"

I frowned again. "Them?"

"Those three little words. *You were right.*" He picked up the skull and turned it so it was facing me. "What was that, Yorick? Ah, yes. *Brava*, Nina Fleet. All the Secret Squirrels are proud of you."

What was going on? A frisson of alarm swept me, and I gave him a wary look. Because unless Harry was deliberately reinterpreting one of Hamlet's mad scenes for his own amusement, something definitely was rotten here in Cymbeline.

"I might have been right," I agreed, "but the only reason my plan worked was because of your acting. Without you, Susie never would have broken down and confessed."

"I suppose that's true. I am quite the brilliant thespian, am I not?"

Now the alarm bells were going full blast. I edged a bit closer. "Harry, I don't know how to break it to you, but you're acting kind of strangely. Is something wrong?"

"Wrong?"

He and Yorick exchanged quizzical looks. "What could be wrong? Oh, wait, of course. She must mean that phone call I received from my agent this morning. You know, the one where I found out my new series was axed before it ever aired."

"Oh, Harry." I sagged in sympathetic disappointment. "I'm so sorry. Did they tell you why it was canceled?"

"It seems that our director has been accused of sexually harassing some of the female crew during our shoot. Not that anyone spoke up about it at the time . . . at least, not that I ever heard. But that doesn't mean it didn't happen."

He shrugged. "Anyhow, my agent said that the women are lawyered up and going public as of today, so it's about to make headlines on all the news outlets. And the fact that my character isn't the most woke guy out there is being mentioned as some sort of contributory factor. So the network is doing damage control by firing the guy and burying the show."

"But you did get paid for all those episodes, right?"

"Sure. And after my agent got his cut, and I caught up on the loans I'd taken out to keep afloat, and sunk a little money into the bus . . . well, let's just say I can probably scrounge enough to buy gas for the drive back to Atlanta. Of course, I won't be able to pay the rent on my apartment anymore, but I can live in the bus again until another job comes along."

He lapsed into silence. I did too, not knowing what to say.

And then, suddenly, I did.

"Look, Harry, you don't have to go back to Atlanta and live in your bus . . . at least, not today," I said before I had too much time to think about it. "Tessa and Bill and Chris are taking Len's ashes on tour around Georgia after the service, which means they've arranged for their own car. Marvin already told me that he and Radney are renting a land yacht for the drive back to Atlanta. So unless you've got somewhere to be, you might as well stick around for a bit."

Harry slowly straightened in his chair. "Let me get this straight. You're offering to let me stay here in the tower room. For how long?"

"Not permanently, of course. But maybe a couple of weeks, even a month. Just until you have a chance to regroup."

"And what about when your next paying guests arrive?"

"Well, it's not like I normally rent out this room to anyone, so I'm not losing any revenue there. And it'll be a few more weeks before we start up the yoga class again."

"And how much would I be paying for the privilege of being a guest here?"

I considered that for a moment. When Harry had first shown up the week before, I'd been concerned about his using some sort of dirty trick to bolster the legal case he thought he had against me. But maybe we could resolve that situation here and now.

"How about we make a deal? You can stay here in the tower room for thirty days, rent free. But in return, you'll sign a letter stating that you'll cease pursuing any sort of legal action against me as far as ownership of this house."

Something flickered in his baby blues. What it was I couldn't read, and for a moment I thought he was going to refuse my offer outright. Then he got to his feet and plopped Yorick on the stacked suitcase table.

"I assume breakfast is included?"

I shrugged. "As long as the paying guests fill up first, you're welcome to the leftovers. Oh, and you wash your own linens and make your own bed."

"Done," he said and stuck out his hand. "You have a deal, Nina Fleet."

Then, as we shook, he added, "But I'm going to need a place to park the bus while I'm here. Now that the festival is over, I don't think Connie and her deputies are going to keep looking the other way."

"Maybe the Reverend Dr. Bishop will let you park it in his lot if you let him borrow it to haul around his congregation," I suggested with a smile, pretending I wasn't feeling just the slightest revival of that schoolgirl crush as he held my hand in his.

Slipping my fingers free, I swiftly regrouped and added, "Speaking of which, we've got a memorial service to attend in just over an hour. I need to get breakfast cleaned up, and both of us need to change before—what?"

For a sudden expression halfway between amusement and horror had flashed over his too-good-looking-to-be-safe-for-me features.

"Sorry. I just remembered what I did to get on Dr. Bishop's bad side all those years ago."

"So what was it? Drawing mustaches on the dearly departed?"

He grinned. "Even worse. Don't worry, I'll tell you all about it on the drive over. But for now, let's just say that Sister Malthea never climbed into that big old Caddy of hers again without checking the back seat first."

I was sure my face now reflected the same expression of mingled amusement and horror that I'd seen on his, as several Harry-in-a-Caddy scenarios had just flashed through my mind. And, to be truthful, a couple of those scenes had been of the not-safe-for-work variety.

"Maybe we can save your story for a more appropriate time," I hastily told him. "Like, when we're not on our way to eulogize a dead man. So how about I meet you at the front door in forty-five minutes?"

Leaving him and Yorick to decide on a proper outfit for the service, I hurried down the ladder stairs. Mattie was waiting for me in the hallway, blue-and-brown gaze fixed on me with what appeared to be disapproval. Doubtless, her supersonic doggie hearing had made her privy to the deal I'd just struck with Harry.

I sighed and gave her a quick scratch behind the ears.

"You're right, I should have asked you first," I wryly told her as we started down the corridor together. "But the guy just lost his job, and he was going to have to live in his bus again. Besides, it's only for thirty days. On day thirty-one, Harold A. Wescott III and his Wild Hare Tours bus will be gone from here for good. In the meantime, what could possibly go wrong while he's here?"

Before I could answer my own rhetorical question, Mattie halted midway down the hall. Plopping herself onto her fuzzy haunches, she raised her muzzle and let out a howl.

Acknowledgments

Thanks as always to everyone at Crooked Lane Books, as well as my team at Hannigan Getzler Literary . . . all of whom work hard to keep me on track. And a special thank you to author Maggie Toussaint for her assistance with life in small-town Georgia. Her color commentary was invaluable in bringing my fictional town of Cymbeline to life.